BOLT

(A NOVEL)

from K[...]

BOLT

(A NOVEL)

DOUGLAS W. ROSE

Three Towers Press

MILWAUKEE, WISCONSIN

Published by
Three Towers Press
An imprint of HenschelHAUS Publishing, Inc.
2625 S. Greeley St. Suite 201
Milwaukee, WI 53207
www.henschelhausbooks.com

ISBN: 978159598-228-5
E-ISBN: 978159598-229-2
LCCN: 2013935573

Cover photograph by Niki Rose
Author photograph by Zachary Swearingen

Printed in the United States of America.

For

Meghan Rose, rock star

Dr. Nancy Kiger

Dr. Steven Rose

My three ex-wives,
all of whom contributed in their own ways

Niki / Sascha / Ruby

PROLOGUE

The four-inch-wide bolt stared out that day, that day in 1968, and it stared in the only direction that it could stare—straight out and down the river. And there were yellow birds and green fish. And on the banks of the river were trees—big willow trees and small oaks, scrub trees, and even one tall pine, and gray squirrels and sorrel deer and possum, and lizards and a cauldron of bugs.

It was 2:33 in the afternoon.

The four-inch-wide bolt was shiny steel, flinty, solid and secure. It was threaded tightly into a steel girder. Impenetrable. Immovable. And it stared its stare down the river, to the south.

It was a usual day. An average day. A few clouds. Not too hot for summer. The great and mighty Mississippi River was at its normal depth, ten feet from flood stage. Some cars, not too many, crossed the bridge as people went to and from various parts and places. Plymouths and Chryslers, Chevrolets and Fords. There was even a Honda, from Japan, small and boxy, with a manual gearbox and no air conditioning, and the driver's window was cranked down. Her hand stuck out to catch the breeze.

The massive bridge was named after the city's disgusting, bigoted mayor, Henry Loeb. The bridge spanned more than just the impressive width of the river itself. At the east end of the suspension wires, the end where the city of Memphis was, the bridge came to an abrupt halt on a high bluff. But on the other end, to the west, to Arkansas, the bridge rose up and over not just the river itself but also the marshes and inlets, the swampy

1

recesses and lowlands, the untillable, unbuildable muck. And there, to the west, though at some point the bridge itself stopped, the road was still raised so that it traveled a causeway, ten feet or so high, for another mile.

And then, finally, the land underneath became sturdy enough that the causeway ended and alongside the road there were a few scattered, decrepit homes and then some sordid businesses—a Firestone tire dealership, an Esso station—this wasteland was where they had somehow found their resting places. And there was, of course, a liquor store and a bar. And the Ranch Motel.

At 2:33 p.m.—and a few seconds, actually—on a Wednesday in August, on the Loeb Bridge, in Memphis, Tennessee, in 1968, for the first time since it had been wrenched into place almost nineteen years earlier, an object passed in front of the four-inch-wide bolt as it stared out to the south. And the bolt saw the object fly past, or at least it would have seen the object if a steel bolt could see. Which of course it cannot. But if it could, it would have seen the object, for it flew so close to the bolt. Inches from it, maybe less. Startling, actually, as it would have been so unexpected to the bolt, never before having had anything like that cross in front of its hypnotic, fixed stare straight down the river.

An object. Not a bird or a bug. An object.

It was the severed hand of a human being, the whole hand intact but the wrist mangled and bloody, as if torn from the arm, which it actually had been. The hand had been ripped off upon the car's first impact with the girder. It flew in front of the four-inch-wide bolt first, a forewarning. It spun around slowly as it flew by right in front of that particular four-inch-wide bolt.

Then, after the hand, came an orange cone. A traffic cone.

After the traffic cone came the arm. The whole arm, without the hand. The arm had been severed from the woman's torso. And it, too, passed right in front of the bolt.

2

The woman was spinning clockwise, left to right, as she flew off and away from the bridge. Her head was spinning away, and her legs were oddly spinning back towards the bolt. And as she spun clockwise along her vertical axis, head to feet, down to up, she was also spinning on her horizontal axis, so that her body was becoming contorted. As if she were a gymnast performing a dismount. But a dead gymnast, or one soon to be dead, for the water was over a hundred feet below.

It was a wedding ring that actually hit the bolt, that made actual, physical contact. Everything else—the hand, the arm, the body—just came close. There was a small ping when the ring hit the bolt, and then the ring fluttered down to the river, spinning end over end, making a tiny splash when it hit the water. It landed before the woman did. The tiny diamond was still embedded in its setting.

The four-inch-wide bolt continued to stare straight ahead, for it could only stare straight ahead, and the body and the parts and the wedding ring fell, out of its myopic line of sight.

But if the bolt could have looked down, tilted its eye downward, it could have watched the woman as she fell. It could have had time to notice more about her. It could have seen the look on her face, not of horror or fear, but of despair. It could have seen the tears swelling up in her eyes. It could have seen that she was handsome, with long lashes and fine features. And if the film were reduced to slow motion, it could have even seen that she was also gaunt and tired, disheveled and unclean.

And if the bolt could have looked down even further, tilted its eye almost straight down, it could have watched the woman hit the water, her body almost perfectly parallel to the river itself when she hit. The impact would crush her lungs and break her neck, sink her eye sockets, fracture her pelvic bone. The black water would envelop her, creep into her cavities and muscle its way through her thick hair.

And if the bolt could have continued to look down, it could have seen, in the woman's unsevered hand, that she was holding something. Clutching something. Strangling it. A wristwatch. A man's wristwatch.

And if the four-inch-wide bolt saw all of that, which of course it could not, for it could only stare straight ahead, but if it could have seen all of that, at that moment, it would have been too much to bear. The bolt would have had to look away from it. For it would have been too grisly, too sad, too upsetting, even for a strong steel bolt. And it would be too much to watch the woman take what seemed to be a desperate gasp of air just before she hit the water. And it would be too much to watch the severed hand float down the river. And it would be too much to watch the wedding ring sink to the bottom of the river and be forever lost in the dark depths.

But of course the severed hand and the arm and the body would not float all the way to New Orleans. They would bloat and drift, get caught in flotsam and natural debris, branches and twigs, the detritus of a living river. The hand would never be found, the arm only months later and very far downriver.

The next day the police would recover the body of the handsome woman, what was left of the body anyway, and discover her lone remaining hand still clutching that watch. And they would put the evidence into a locker, and they would investigate, and they would take statements and they would keep notes.

"The watch has an inscription," the detective would say, as if that were a difficult discovery that only he, a detective, could have uncovered. "It must be her husband's; they were married for thirteen years," he blurted out. And he would write that in his little notebook, a notebook with a pencil attached to it with a graying string, a notebook with pages with squares and not lines. And on the graph paper, in heavy pencil, he would sketch notes and circle things, draw connection lines between the names of people.

And the bolts on the bridge, thousands of them, would watch the officers as they investigated the scene, measured the distance from the bridge to the water, ran calculations and talked among themselves.

Individually, for the bolts could only see straight out, individually each bolt would have only a snippet of knowledge about what happened that day in August, 1968. What happened to the woman. How she went off the bridge. Why she went off the bridge. At 2:33 that afternoon.

But collectively, if all of the bolts could combine their snippets of knowledge, and if they could have had the eyes of hawks, and if they could have listened with the ears of elephants, then perhaps they would know what happened. Know how it happened. Why it happened.

Some of the bolts would have seen that the woman was crying. Other bolts would have heard her calling out his name. Some may have heard her whispering to herself that she still loved him and that she could not stand the pain any more.

One of those bolts, since there were so many, each with different angles and viewpoints, one of them may have seen her turn the wheel. When there was no reason to turn the wheel. Turning the wheel, as sharply as she did, would have consequences.

And so it was. That day.

The tragedy was printed in the newspaper. At the time it was published, the investigation was not yet complete. So the cause of death was reported as unknown. But there were enough details so that the reader could understand. The cause was, oddly enough, love. That much was clear.

And the bolt, the bolt that had seen the hand, that had seen the arm, that had felt the ping of the wedding ring—that bolt—

continued to stare. Straight ahead. A sentinel standing watch over the river below.

So that was the woman. The woman who went off that bridge. The woman whose name we don't know. The woman whom the bolt saw fall to her death.

There was also a boy. A boy who read everything he could find, including the newspaper. And that boy, Charlie, several days after the day, that boy read the story about the woman. About the bridge and the river and the hand and the arm and the death. And for some unknown reason, since he did not know the woman, Charlie, still just a boy, became sad and cried. It affected him. He would remember it.

There was also a girl. A girl who did not read newspapers. And she did not read about the bridge or the river or the hand or the arm or the death. And so she was blissfully ignorant of it all. Even though it happened. Even though it happened so close to her. And her name was Ruby. Ruby Clarisse.

The bolt on the bridge looked out over the river, and as it was looking out, the bolt started to think.

Of course, a bolt can't think.

But if it could, this would be the time—right after the woman—that it would take some time to think. Later that day, that day in August, in 1968.

The bolt would think about the hand and the arm and the woman and the death.

And it would think about things like love. And perhaps, after thinking about those things, and after having years after that to observe and stare out, and collectively having other inanimate objects observe and stare, and having them tell the bolt what they knew. Well, then that bolt might be able to tell quite the story. An intimate, intricate story about, in the end, beautiful things like love. And horrific things like death.

It could tell a story about a boy named Charlie. And a story about a girl named Ruby.

CHAPTER 1

CHARLIE. 1971. 15 YEARS OLD. RUSHFORD, TENNESSEE.

The man was dressed in overalls and a green plaid, button down shirt. A dirty ball cap covered his thinning, combed over hair. He looked older than he was, which was just under forty. He had wrinkles in places most people don't. He was spitting and screaming.

He was clenching a slimy green garden hose with both hands. He was waving the hose up and down from his waist, haphazardly, so it began to look like a wriggly snake. He was spraying dust off his trailer home. He was ridding himself of boiling anger. He was coping with untreatable mental illness.

The water pinged and echoed against the metal. The soprano tics echoed across the valley in stark contrast to the off-key baritone groan of his voice. He stammered and swore; at nothing, really, at no one.

His wife, Mary, was inside making dinner. She heard him, but she didn't acknowledge him. She cocked her head, gritted her teeth, and fought back tears. She went back to slicing celery stalks; tried to focus on the sharp knife. It was better to stay quiet, better to let it pass, better not to fight back. Don't fight back. Never fight back.

His son, Charlie, had just finished chores. He heard his father, too, but like his mother he didn't acknowledge him, either. He was about to take a shower, so he stripped out of his work clothes and let them pile on the floor; thick, heavy boots, Levi's blue jeans, white jockey briefs, white socks, a gray t-shirt with "LSU" in gold letters across the front. He had a

7

farmer's tan, dark arms and face and neck, pale white everywhere else. He was thin, like most boys his age, and his stomach was tight as a drum; ripply. He ate everything in sight, but it was never enough. He would often get up in the middle of the night and first find something to read; an old magazine, the back of the cereal box. Then he would pour the sugar-coated cereal into a mixing bowl, and bring the cereal and the milk to the table with him so that he wouldn't have to get up to pour another bowl.

Charlie squeezed into the tiny fiberglass shower stall and let the warm water run over him, let it slowly seep into his dirt-encrusted forearms. He bowed his head down and watched as the water and dirt swirled down the drain, sucking everything into an eddy, a little hurricane right there in the shower. He reached for the shampoo, started to lather his thick, dark hair with his fingers. He started thinking about his father, then consciously tried not to. Lori Anderson; he would think of Lori Anderson instead. He would think of her long, thin, straight blond hair, her tight jeans. He was just about to touch himself.

Then he heard it. It was a scream. It was his mother's scream. But it was more than that. It was shrill, eerie. Charlie slipped on the tile when he heard it, banged his head on the hot water faucet. It hurt, bled a little.

Charlie quickly turned off the water, grabbed the towel hanging over the glass door. He threw it around his waist, tried to tie it up. He ran toward the front of the trailer. He saw his mother. She was on her knees, her hands to her face, her eyes darting out from between her outstretched fingers. She was gasping for breath, keening, making sounds Charlie had never heard before. The towel slipped off Charlie, so he grabbed it and pulled it around himself again as best he could. His wet, bare feet slid on the linoleum.

Then he saw his father, in the fetal position, with his face awkwardly straight down on the worn linoleum. A small stream of blood was coming out of his ear, gooey and wet and not red. Charlie thought, *No, not really red, more of a bluish brown.* He thought about how his science teacher had taught him blood was blue when it wasn't exposed to oxygen. He thought about the quiz in class, the fire drill where they all walked single file out the exits, the bus ride; random thoughts that did not make sense, not at that moment.

Then he looked away from the blood, and looked at his mother. His mother who was kneeling next to his father. His mother who was pulling and tugging at his father's body. His mother who was crying and bobbing up and down. His mother whose hands then covered her eyes and started to sob uncontrollably.

And he knew, right then, it was over. His father was dead.

* * * * *

At the funeral, Charlie thought back on that moment. Why had he been so mesmerized by the color of the blood? How long had he hesitated? Why had he just stood there, staring at his mother—why hadn't he gone to her, hugged her, tried to comfort her—something, anything. If he had, perhaps her later episodes of sporadic, intense insanity wouldn't have happened. Instead he watched, silently, as his mother shook him and shook his father, then so clearly and undeniably, well, dead.

"Wake up, wake up," she sobbed as she struggled with the heavy man, pulling and pushing, trying to get a response.

"Mom," Charlie finally said to her.

Then louder, still from a safe distance.

"Mom. Stop. Dammit. Mom. Just... Just stop."

He didn't remember calling 911, but apparently he had. The recording was his voice.

"My father. He's, he just collapsed. He's on the floor. He's got blood coming from his ears. He isn't moving. You just...."

The operator, her voice calm and monotone, interrupted.

"Your address, young man, what is your address?"

They were there within fifteen minutes. Pretty fast, really, not that it mattered.

* * * * *

Chuck McGurn was 39 years old at the time of his death. The doctors said it was unusual to have a heart attack that young, such a massive one, but no autopsy was done. There had been a lot of drugs. There had been more alcohol than drugs, daily even. The doctor knew that, the townsfolk knew that, his son knew that, his wife knew that. It still didn't make sense. Life never really does. Death never really does, either.

Apparently the heart attack occurred just as he walked into the trailer; hit him so hard he lost consciousness and fell face first to the floor, hard enough to knock out two of his teeth. But it wasn't the fall that killed him. It was the heart attack. His heart gave out. *His little, cold, bitter heart*, Charlie thought, as the doctor was talking. For the first time, Charlie let himself think it, then softly, Charlie said it.

"Bastard," Charlie whispered.

"What, son?" The doctor turned his way, startled at what he had just heard.

"Nothing," Charlie said quickly. Then again, this time in a whisper. "Nothing." Those thoughts, he vowed then and there, he must keep to himself. That vow would eventually be broken, but not until many, many years later Only then, and even then only hesitatingly, in a moment of intimacy with a pretty woman, did he ever call his father a bastard again. And even then, when he did, he was shocked by his own words. But they were true.

Little Charlie—the best term of endearment his father could ever muster to call him was "little Charlie"—didn't cry at the funeral. He didn't cry after his mom broke down six months later and sobbed uncontrollably in front of him, for hours, her now skinny frame boney against him when he tried to hold and console her. And he didn't cry when he sat with her and the life insurance man when he told her that the paltry $10,000 would be paid out "within just a couple weeks, Mrs. McGurn." He didn't cry either of those times, and he certainly never cried in public.

Charlie never showed any emotion in public. But one night, when he couldn't sleep, still a boy, not yet a man, he snuck out and walked the edge of the rural, little-used highway. He walked for miles. And there he cried. It was just a little at first, and then a little more. But even then it wasn't much. And after that bit of crying it just turned into a dull, blank stare, and the tears that had fallen from his face dried up.

He stood by the side of the road. He stood there on the gravelly shoulder. It was dusk. A big pine tree cast a long shadow. A squirrel rustled leaves in the woods. Two birds chattered to each other. And Charlie contemplated life, and his future. Life would get worse before it got better. He didn't know that then. He couldn't imagine that possibility.

A blue sedan drove by, the driver surprised to see the boy standing by the side of the lonesome road. The car slowed down as it passed. Its lights were on hi-beam, its windows open. Music was playing on the car radio. The Beatles, *Let It Be*. Then, as the car went around the bend, the music just faded out. The squirrel ran down the ravine. The leaves rustled again, this time from a soft wind. Charlie stopped crying. Everything got quiet, and then went silent.

RUBY. 1975. 13 YEARS OLD. MEMPHIS, TENNESSEE.

I n the middle of the subdivision was a one-story ranch, pretty much just like all the others. Its dark green vinyl siding was melting in the midday sun. And in the back yard, surrounded by a stained wood fence, was a glittery little pool. And in the very middle of the glittery pool, lying on her big, yellow, inflatable raft, wearing her white string bikini, was Ruby Clarisse Kale.

Ruby was lying on her back, with one arm behind her head. Her other arm was lazily stroking the water, twirling her and the raft around and around in circles. Big sunglasses covered her pretty blue eyes. Half a summer lying in the pool, combined with a little Cherokee Indian heritage, gave her a deep, golden brown tan. She looked like a movie starlet, but she was barely thirteen.

The raft twirled and twirled, around and again, until it randomly made its way to the shallow end and got stuck on the stairs. Ruby's foot scraped the cement. It startled her from her lazy, sun-stroked haze. She slowly rolled over and the raft—all blown up and billowy—popped out from under her. Ruby deftly reached out, and in one smooth movement, lifted the raft out of the water and flipped it onto the lawn. It floated cleanly through the air, landing gently on the fresh cut grass.

She tossed her head back, and as she did her long, wet, dark brown hair flew up and spewed water over the pool, sprinkling little bubbles in tight, concentric circles. Then she dropped back into the water and swam a slow breast stroke, head up, arms and legs stroking rhythmically, towards the edge, to the spot on the west end where the depth was marked 5 FEET, the very spot she had been so many times before.

When she got there, she put both hands on the cement overhang, enough to keep her head and shoulder above the water, and she let her legs and feet sink down. Then she let her whole body drift to the left, just a tiny bit, to where the water jetted out from the heat pump. She positioned herself just right. She shut her eyes, tilted her head back to face the full sun, and held a little tighter onto the rail edge. When she felt the jet's pressure on her thighs she dropped a little further into the water, until the jet pushed up against her bikini bottom, pushed up against her. She opened her eyes for a second, looked around the yard to make sure no one was looking. Then she closed her eyes again, repositioned herself, let the water pressure build.

Ruby finally let go of the pool edge, reached down, adjusted her bikini bottom, pushed off the wall, and did a cool, smooth backstroke back to the shallow end and got out of the pool.

She dried herself off with a big, white, beach towel, then went inside. For the rest of the afternoon, she just sat on the long, green, vinyl sofa, the beach towel wrapped around her slender body so the sofa didn't get wet. She stared at the TV; half an hour of a *Gilligan's Island* rerun—something about the Professor and a UFO—then a half hour listening to Gene Rayburn hosting the *Match Game*. When the Watergate hearings interrupted the regular shows, she got up and turned it off. She picked up the phone, its long, spirally cord stretching from the kitchen wall and kinking up on the shaggy carpet. She tried calling her friend Stephanie—but the line was busy, so she stretched out on the sofa again, curled herself up, and fell asleep with her face resting in the palm of her hand. About an hour later, the serenity was broken by her sister banging open the screen door.

"Hey." She entered with a rush, her voice loud.

"Hey," Ruby replied softly, sleepily.

Tanya stared at her little sister for a minute, laughed at the sight of her sprawled out on the sofa, then went to the kitchen, took out a Jungle Juice, seemed to be looking for something else.

"Nothin' good to eat. I looked," Ruby mumbled.

"We got cheese," Tanya said.

"No bread."

"I don't care." Tanya took out two pieces of processed cheese, molded each one into a little ball, ate each with a big bite, her mouth bulging at the cheeks. Then Tanya pushed her sister's feet to the side and forced her way onto the single couch in the small living room.

"Move over, bitch."

"Fuck you, bitch."

"You go to school today?" Tanya had noticed the beach towel covering up most of her sister.

"Don't tell."

"Whatever. Like I care."

Tanya turned the TV back on. Then they both kind of watched an episode of the *Brady Bunch*, and kind of slept, until they heard a car pull up the side drive.

"Mom's home."

Maxine Kale-Vinson walked in carrying a paper grocery bag, not too full.

"You got bread?" Tanya asked her mother, not bothering with pleasantries.

"I got bread. Y'all better get off that couch; he'll be home pretty soon."

"He better bring us more fuckin' food than you did," Ruby complained to her mother.

"You better straighten up, missy, and be thankful for what ya got. No more potty mouth."

Ruby didn't move from the couch, and didn't respond to her mother. Maxine walked away, too tired from the day to fight about things.

An hour later a black, Ford F-150 pickup truck pulled into the drive. A Winchester lever-action rifle was bolted to the back window of the cab, a "Memphis Office Equipment" magnetic advertising sign stuck to the drivers' side door. Jimmy Vinson, Ruby's stepfather, sold copy machines. He was good at it. He also liked to go on hunting and fishing trips with his buddies; truth was, though, they didn't do much actual hunting or fishing.

Jimmy dutifully kissed his wife on the cheek as she made dinner. The little family ate on TV trays, hardly saying a word to one another. The girls helped with the dishes, but not much. As the night wore on, they all watched more TV, now not talking at all. Neither girl did any homework; neither Jimmy or Maxine asked them about school. Tanya thought about telling them her sister had cut class, but then her favorite commercial came and she forgot. Maxine, as usual, went to bed first, well before Jimmy and her daughters.

"Night, girls. I'm going to bed. Honey, do you want me to wake you up?"

"Naw, I'm all right. I'll be to bed in a bit."

The girls said nothing, just continued staring at the TV. Half an hour later, Jimmy was snoring gently in the easy chair, his breathing labored, heavy. Half an hour after that, Tanya and Ruby quietly got up, and tiptoed past him to Ruby's room.

Tanya and Ruby each had their own room, and each had their own closet. After moving in three years earlier, and especially after he married Maxine just two months later on a trip to Vegas, Jimmy had spoiled his new stepdaughters with more clothes than they could have ever imagined before, so their closets were now practically overflowing. There were swimsuits and sun dresses, blouses and jumpers, gauchos and formals and hats and, of course, shoes. There were heels and flats, sandals and pumps, jelly shoes, and flip-flops. There were

15

lace-up boots and soft leather loafers. "Jimmy daddy" bought a lot of things, just for them.

Tanya, the older sister, had a queen bed with four pineapple pillars, white lace stretched in a canopy. There was a white down comforter with matching feather pillows. Stuffed animals with beady eyes stared at the beige carpet and the bare walls.

Ruby had her own bedroom, but it still had the old bunk beds from before the move to Jimmy's. Her daddy—her real daddy—had bought the bunk beds. She hadn't seen her real daddy in two years. She missed him, but she had trouble remembering what he looked like. Sometimes she would close her eyes, squint, and concentrate real hard, trying to remember his long thin face, the mop of coarse hair. But the image most often didn't come.

Lately, Tanya had been sleeping in Ruby's room. For the past several months, Tanya's bigger, queen-sized bed stayed perfectly made up, and the stuffed animals all sat alone. Nothing changed, nothing moved. Ruby's room was messier; hair pins and knick-knacks on the dresser, dirty socks on the floor, posters on the walls. Tanya slept on the top bunk. It felt safe to her, safer than her own room down the hall. She didn't tell her mother why.

So that hot night in early July, in the big subdivision just outside of Memphis, with the air conditioning on full and noisy, Tanya stretched out on the top bunk in Ruby's room.

Tendrils of Tanya's feathered, long, wispy, dyed-blonde hair fell down from the top bunk as she leaned over the rail and whispered to her little sister. "You awake?"

"Yup, uh-huh," Ruby whispered back. Tanya didn't say anything. Ruby replied again, just a little louder. "Hmmmm? What?"

Tanya hesitated. For months, she had been debating whether she should tell her sister. For months, it had eaten her up inside. This night, this particular night, it was not a conscious decision; sometimes you just can't help yourself.

She chose her words carefully, like a lawyer questioning a witness. She was trying to flesh out information. Though she was only 15, she was very bright, and she was growing up—suddenly—very fast.

"Has Jimmy-Daddy...?" Again she hesitated

"What?" Ruby asked. She was irritated; this wasn't the first night Tanya had started talking to her, then stopped, claiming she "forgot," or that it "didn't matter."

"Forget it. Let's just go to sleep." Tanya said, then hesitated yet again.

This time Ruby wasn't going to forget it. She didn't want to just let it go. She knew her sister had something to say. And just like Tanya, Ruby had things she wanted to say, too. Difficult things, thoughts she had been struggling with for a long time. So she opened the door a little to the dark places.

"How long has he been doing that?" Ruby asked her older sister.

The words hit Tanya like a small, hard bullet.

"What? Doing what? What do you mean?" Tanya's response was instinctual, a vague denial.

It wasn't the response Ruby wanted, or expected, from her older sister. She had hoped the floodgates would open, tears would come, they would both let it all out and talk through the night and hug and think and plan a strategy. That by the morning, it would all be better because they would solve it together and not alone, that together they could conquer the beast. Ruby thought her older sister would know what to do, that she would have the answers.

"A long time. I don't know...I just....," Tanya was leaning farther over the bunk rail now, leaning down towards her sister, her arm holding onto the side rail for support. Her hand was shaking in the dark. Her voice sounded a little more scared, but she still chose her words carefully.

"I'm not saying...anything...you know, just, some-times...." There was a pause. And then that was it. And then it was out. It wasn't said, never really was said, not in words. Tanya started to tear up, stifled her sobs as well as she could, tried to keep quiet. She rubbed her face on the big pillow, got it all wet.

Then another, longer pause before Tanya, her voice a little choked, asked her sister.

"Does he ever do it to you, Ruby?"

Both Ruby and Tanya knew exactly what the other was talking about. They were both living the same nightmare. Both girls knew the stakes were high, the consequences severe and severing. Real life smashed into their childhoods; it crushed their fantasies, it killed their teddy bears and Barbie dolls, it scared them more than any imaginary demon in the closet ever could.

This time it, was Ruby who hesitated. But just like her sister, Ruby couldn't hold it in either. The monster had to come out.

"Yes."

And thus, at that moment, in the little house in the subdivision, the stars out and the wind calm, the night warm and muggy, there it was; the insidious monster was out. It had been there all along, actually. The air conditioner kicked in again, just then, whirring and grinding through its machinations.

Both girls lay on their backs, their eyes wide open, hands at their sides. Ruby stared at the bottom of her sister's bunk. Tanya stared at the ceiling. The air conditioner kicked out again, tired of fighting the stifling night air. Three minutes of almost total silence passed. It seemed like an eternity.

They softly said good-night to each other, the two little girls, their voices crackling with emotion, empathy for the other and for their own selves.

And then they never talked about it again. Ever. Not to each other, anyway.

* * * * *

The next morning, the sun came up, just like it had the day before. Tanya was in the kitchen eating cereal. Ruby could hear the metal of the spoon each time it hit the ceramic bowl. The TV wasn't on like it normally was. Instead there was only the clink, clink of the silver spoon on the cereal bowl.

Ruby woke up slowly. She stretched her legs, rolled her arms. She shook her head a little. Then she leaned over to the little night stand, and turned on the pink, plastic clock radio by her bed. There was a little static, then some music started playing. It was *I'll Take You There*, by the Staple Singers. The music was nice. It helped her forget.

CHAPTER 2

Every part of the shoes was white. The soles were white rubber with a gritty feel. The uppers were made of a shiny white plastic called Coraform, slick to the touch. The white nylon laces had little white tassels.

Perfectly tailored white pants broke just slightly, as they should, at the top of the white shoes. A white belt with a polished brass buckle was centered on the gig line, where the zipper of the pants met the brass buttons of the white Nehru jacket.

Military creases ran parallel to each other, down each breast line in the front and each shoulder blade in the back. The high, tight collar had a cheap metallic clasp that chafed against the neck. Black epaulets on each shoulder were emblazoned with two gold lines, one thick line and then one thin one, signifying rank; U.S. Navy Lieutenant, Junior Grade. The head cover billowed out in the front, centered by an oversized brassy emblem that featured crossed anchors and a golden eagle, the emblem pinned to a band of stretch elastic that wrapped around the brim. A glossy black visor jutted prominently to shield the eyes. Brass buttons stood guard at the temples.

Lieutenant Junior Grade Charles Michael McGurn— Charlie—stood at attention in this military-issue, white dress uniform, his arms hanging straight at his sides, his fingers curled up slightly, eyes forward. He stood alone in the freshly cut grassy field, sprinkled with sporadic, patchy tufts of noxious weeds that had been sprayed to noticability with chalky chemicals. The field had no shrubs, no ornamental trees, no statues or sidewalks; the military didn't spend much money on aesthetics, but it did spend money on maintenance. Once a week, every week, May first through November fifteenth, regardless of weather, regardless of whether spring was late or winter early; once a week the Toro riding mower—with a rickety back platform where the maintenance crewmen hung on —once a week the nasty machine sliced and diced and threw fan-shaped green swaths to the sides.

At least twenty acres of field and grass undulated down-slope from the square concrete and red brick buildings that made up the Naval Training Center, Newport, Rhode Island. Closer to the icy ocean, the field gave way to stubbly rocks, a few boulders, and a narrow, gravelly beach. The tides of the Atlantic lifted brackish water and seaweed-trapped debris up and down on the swells near the shore; further out, little sailing ships anchored and gulls squawked and drifted. Off in the far distance, past the soaring steel towers of the suspension bridge, way off on the other side of Newport Bay, lumbering orange cranes bellied up to the navy's frigates and suppliers and destroyers. The ships' hulking masses were silhouetted subtly against the misty sky, a sky colored just slightly darker than the ships' military gray.

The photo of the young lieutenant taken that day, carefully and slowly lined up and focused and adjusted for the right light, didn't turn out as his mother had hoped. Her son was too far away, the white mass tiny compared with the huge expanses of the green field and the gray water and the overcast sky and the metal ships. And though the uniform looked sharp at first glance, it seemed out of place when stared at; painfully missing, of course, were the shiny metal flashes and the bright colors of the ribbony medals and awards, the successes and accomplishments of the veteran Navy man. Emblazoned across LTJG McGurn's left chest were nothing but the military crease and the uninterrupted fabric of the white uniform. It was graduation day, Officer Candidate School, May 22, 1982, and anticipated and hoped-for medals and ribbons were yet to come.

"Great, that's great, honey, oh Charlie, I got some good ones," McGurn's mother shouted to her son after snapping half a dozen pictures.

McGurn let out some air, let his chest exhale and settle, then he reached up with his long right arm and whisked off the cover. The cover was too tight, and it left a straight, red, stretch mark that circled the front of his forehead. His hair was wavy and dark, cut military short, and this day, it glistened with little beads of sweat. His jaw was chiseled square, his complexion dark, his beard shaved close but still noticeable. His eyes were big, widely set, brown, with long eyelashes and bushy eyebrows. He cast the handsome look of a young naval officer.

"Mom, that's enough already. Okay?" It was a plea, really, a plea for her to stop embarrassing him.

"I know, I know," she replied. "I just...I am just so proud of you, you know."

"Thanks, Mom. Really. I just....Well, thanks."

His stepfather was just coming up the hill. Charlie saw him, thought about turning away.

"There he is. All spit and polish. Graduation day. Who would have thought?"

Peter Hopkins had married Mary McGurn only three months after they met, and she willingly took his last name as her own. She was, in fact, so terribly taken with the businessman that she could hardly control herself. Wedding plans were made, but quickly abandoned in favor of an elopement in Las Vegas more appropriate to a couple decades younger. But Mary was all for it, and loved everything about it, and loved Peter. Never before, really, had any man been nice to her, and Peter was that. For Peter had found a woman far more beautiful than he had ever imagined, and a woman who needed him, if only to help her forget the past.

The lonely widow never much compared Peter, her new husband, and Chuck, her old one, now almost ten years dead. There were similarities, sure, but certainly differences as well. Chuck, despite his obvious faults, drinking and carousing, and nasty temper, had certainly changed over time. But when she first met him he was undeniably handsome; then a tall, strong, well-built man with a full head of thick hair and a striking jaw line. But he had bullied his way through life, narcissistic and cruel to most all others, including his own family. And, of course, he was a belligerent drunk, a sometime drug addict, and a habitual liar. And his good looks had deteriorated quickly.

Peter, on the other hand, was quiet, tight, an accountant by education, later a businessman who was successful through tedious hours and sheer will only. He had thinning brown hair, thin lips, a pale complexion, and tiny features; his feet were a size 6, sweaters and gloves and hats were always a small, and even then often looked too big for him. He was passably tall enough at five-foot-six, but seemed shorter, and as thin and frail as his arms and legs were, there was at least an extra ten to fifteen pounds that stretched his waistline.

Yet, in spite of his appearance, Peter could be horribly arrogant. To Mary, whom he adored, he was always incredibly sweet. But to many others, his screechy voice grated and spit venomous epithets and harsh criticism. He was known to kiss up to clients and those more fortunate, but to kick and backstab those below him. His stepson had always fallen definitively into the latter category; but the gap was closing, and Peter didn't like that.

"A Navy man," Peter practically shouted across the lawn. "A goddamn Navy man." The word "Navy" was long and drawn out, the "a" stretched out interminably.

"Sittin' on a fairy boat while the real action is far, far away."

Peter had a knack for belittling all accomplishments, and for finding the frailties others believed they had in themselves. Until that moment, Charlie had never thought of the Navy as anything more or less than any other branch of the military. He needed to get away, he needed to prove himself, and the recruiter had wisely talked of foreign, exotic places and honorable Naval traditions. Yet with that short, crisp sentence, Charlie's stepfather stripped away the months of effort the Navy had just spent trying to instill pride and confidence into this young officer.

"No, really, you did good," Peter continued, too late to repair the damage. "I know your mother's proud of you."

"Thanks," Charlie managed to respond, quietly. Peter held out his hand, Charlie shook it weakly. Peter moved forward a little, as if to engage in an embrace, but Charlie instinctively reeled back, and the two awkwardly separated.

They all walked back up the hill together, but Peter kept a good ways to the side and back, a rare moment of deference. Mary's petite frame was all the more fragile next to her son as they walked side by side.

Charlie held his cover in his left hand, and as he walked next to his mother, he jokingly put it on her head. Her permed red hair was puffed up enough to keep it balanced momentarily, but as she walked, it bounced back and forth comically until it eventually slipped to the side and started to fall off. Charlie reached out, grabbed it just before it hit the ground. Military regulations required Naval Officers to keep the cover on at all times when outside, and even though the drill sergeants had long since gone home, their voices could still be heard, their bellowing orders still echoing. Charlie felt uncomfortable without it on. So he flicked the cap back on his head as they continued to walk up the hill to the base.

At the top of the hill, just outside the barracks-style officer candidate's quarters, sitting on the concrete stoop with his arms crossed and his eyes closed, was LTJG Victor Booth. Booth was also wearing his formal dress white uniform, and no medals or ribbons adorned his chest either. Booth was thinner, but just as tall as Charlie. Booth's pale complexion still showed signs of adolescent acne, little pock marks interlaced with new red bumps. Booth had beady greenish eyes and his teeth were crooked, but he managed an incredibly bright, engaging smile. People felt comfortable with Victor Booth; he was like a soft-pressure car salesman, with low-key style and natural charisma. His voice was anchorman Midwest, which contrasted nicely with Charlie's southern drawl when they whispered half-true, enticing stories to the local girls in the wee hours of the mornings.

"Hey, Vic," Charlie called out, his casual tone implicitly acknowledging a trusted friend. "Hey, you've met my ma, right?" They shook hands, exchanged pleasantries, nothing more. Then Mary McGurn drifted down the hall, aware that the two young men wanted to be alone.

Charlie and Vic laughed and talked a while longer, and then they walked away from each other with seemingly purposeful strides, the stresses of their future lives not yet having weighed down upon them. They each made one last pass through their little dorm rooms, with the beds made tight, the sheets tucked in and the blankets tucked more, with the old, now-bare wooden desks pushed up to the lone small windows, heavy metal lamps shining up at the glossy white ceilings. Two canvas bags were packed and waiting in foot of each of their beds, and on top of the canvas bags was one thin blue garment bag with three dress uniforms folded inside; one more white one and two dress blues.

The two young men's morning routine had been exactly the same every weekday morning for the past nine months.

Reveille at 5:30 a.m., in sweats and in the old gym by 6:00, physical training and four laps around the cinder track, showered and shaved and at the mess hall by 7:00, wolf down the meal and catch a nap for an hour. Then classes and marching and lunch and drills and dinner, some studying and then either early to bed or horseplay until late.

Although the countdown had begun months earlier, scratching the days off the calendar one by one, it was only now, the afternoon after the graduation ceremony, that Charlie and Vic—LTJG McGurn and LTJG Booth—began to realize that their mornings from now on would no longer be routine. Time moved forward, candidates enrolled, drilled, graduated, moved on; to duty stations and cruisers and training bases, to mundane little northern coastal towns, to lush tropical forests, to sweaty industrial ports.

The time when Booth and McGurn finished Officer Candidate School and left Newport, Rhode Island, was neither a time of peace nor a time of war. As was all too often the case, it was a time of tense anxiety where the world teetered on the brink of one or the other. Politicians debated, mothers feared, veteran soldiers looked away, never-tested warriors rattled their sabers and spoke mightily of honor and the necessity of battle. There were intermissions, some long and some short, needed and required respites, but always leading to another act in the great play of man's history. Neither officer knew the plot or the script, neither would produce or direct. March in step, eyes forward, left, right, left, follow the drumbeats and lead others to do the same.

Proud parents packed up their cars and drove back to their little hometowns and farms and big cities. Drill sergeants and senior officers in charge looked out on yet another graduating class, waited for the next. Flags were neatly folded and put away and the bleachers were taken down, board by board, and stacked behind the machine shed. Quiet enveloped Newport like a blanket, like the fog that so often drifted in under the big suspension bridge. It crawled and stretched and stealthily reached up the grassy knoll, snaky tendrils wafting almost to the road, where Charlie—Lieutenant Junior Grade McGurn—stood alone, waiting.

Charlie was one of the last to leave the training base, his flight schedule a later red-eye. The sun had set by the time the driver rolled down the hand crank on his window and yelled out.

"Hey. Wake up. Airport, right?"

"Yeah, sorry." Charlie dragged himself up from the curb, looked around. No one else was there, the buildings had all gone dark some time ago, and only the hum of a generator far away and the cab's engine could be heard.

"Hey. Thanks. Yeah, the airport. Thanks."

"Sure." The cabbie turned off the engine, got out of the cab, used the key to open the spacious trunk. Charlie almost slipped and fell on the wet pavement as he tried to lug the heavy, canvas bag up over the trailer hitch. The cabbie had already gone back for the two other, smaller bags. It might have been the late hour, it might have been the fog rolling in. But it seemed just like a movie scene, right then, as a single streetlight shone upon that very spot, just right, and the young, handsome Navy lieutenant slowly got into the cab. It seemed the camera should pan out, slowly, and then the credits should start to roll across the screen. Even Charlie sensed it, one chapter closing and another about to begin, the orchestra playing a finishing song.

The cabbie had the radio on, and as they drove off, the cinematic moment passed. A popular song started to play. It was Elton John, *Little Jeannie*. The song was comforting, and within minutes, Charlie was sound asleep. He did not wake up until they were on the outskirts of New York City, a panorama of light floating in front of them. LaGuardia was just minutes away, and they were on time for him to catch his flight out.

RUBY. 1981. 19 YEARS OLD. MEMPHIS, TENNESSEE.

A spider web of electrical wires criss-crossed the intersection. They were stretched taut but were weighed down in the middle by heavy, hooded stop lights that dangled like Christmas ornaments. It was late fall. It had been dry. A gust of wind swirled sun burnt leaves, dust, and litter around and about, up into the stop light's glare: green-orange-red, green-orange-red. Up and down in both directions, on each side of the road, intermittent street lights stood like soldiers, evenly spaced, like a narrow airport landing strip.

Winchester Road stretched a full twenty miles north to south, almost all of it through sprawling suburbs with cookie-cutter houses in new subdivisions, little strip malls, Piggly Wiggly groceries and Fred's pharmacies. From a distance, it was just twinkling lights, the lights of middle-class America in the mid-South. For those who happened to live there, the lights and buildings created a cocoon of comfort with a false sense of civilized security.

Ruby drove across the intersection in a blur. The light was orange, had been for some time; it turned red before she fully crossed. It didn't matter, as the minimal cross traffic was blocks away, stopped at their own red lights.

She drove further south, past Getwell Road, then Airport Road, then Hack's Crossing. Then further on, Winchester Road became State Highway 101, and fading away in her rear view mirror were the bank towers and churches and factories, the trains and planes and wood-grained station wagons speeding randomly to places unknown. She drove past the parks, the red brick schools, the coves at the end of tree-lined streets with perfect grids of sidewalk and manicured sod.

Ahead of her, the homes became sparse, and the highway began to serpentine through open prairie and cotton fields, dusty swells and valleys stretching to the black horizon. A lone brick smokestack broke the symmetry, its tall spire of industrial majesty belching tendrils of man-made clouds.

She sped up in a cadence as the highway rolled out of the city: 30, 40, 50, 55, 60, 65 miles an hour. She would have kept going faster, oblivious to speed limits and safety, her mind dulled by the day and by the boredom of the road. But then the car coughed, choked, as if there were congestion in its metal lungs. It lurched forward, then back, like a bucking bronco at the rodeo. She never let her foot off the gas pedal, but her speed slowed right back down: 65, 60, 55, 50, 40, 30. There was a loud metal crack from the front of the engine, probably the radiator, and a sudden stop. The power steering went out, and she muscled the wheel to bring it to the shoulder.

Scalding white steam snaked through the cracks and crevices of the 1967 Buick Riviera's front hood, then billowed into the gray night sky and melted into the city-lit horizon. The big brown sedan, velvety bench seats, 430 cubic inch, V-8 engine, sat by the side of the road, its hood up, exposed. Ruby stood next to the car, debating what to do next. She had just turned nineteen. Her adult life was about to begin, but she didn't know that yet.

Off on the empty horizon, the one away from the city, toward the scary, remote places few people yet lived, Ruby saw the flash of the neon sign. It pierced through the darkness, through the street lights, through the radiator steam. It spoke to her. It told her to go away. Stay away.

The car was dead—not sick or disabled, dead. Its wires were frayed and crackled, its oily parts gummed and stuck together.

The once-soft landau top was now a tattered mesh that whistled songs to Ruby when she drove her normal routes, lefts and rights from here to there, one way then the next again, to work to home, to the store, to home to work to her sister Tanya's house, to the store, then home, then work. The whistle changed over time as the fabric twisted and tore; the muffler continued to rust and the engine kept getting louder. But the numbing pattern in its limited permutations did not end. Rather, somehow, it remained resolutely the same day after day after day. And now, thanks to God or something else powerful, the car was dead and the pattern had come to a merciful end. Things were about to change.

She waited a while after the car had died, moments of silence out of respect for what had once been. Not that what had once been was good, something to honor; sure, the old, dead car had once been a source of pride and joy, but that time had been fleeting at best. The car gave her a false sense of freedom, one that was never truly there. The stark, cold reality was undeniable, and it hardly amounted to freedom.

Hers was a dim life at 19; no high school diploma, an old car, two part-time jobs—one seating families of five at Corky's restaurant, and another one at the arcade at the Hickory Ridge mall, where her young friends loitered and her minimum wage paid for their sodas. Eventually, inevitably, it would all collapse into the void and crush all feeling, and hopes and dreams of interior design or even long runways with popping flash bulbs. Those would be erased and nailed into a box so tight it would never open, never see the light of day.

Get out. Get out. What the hell is going on in my head? Ruby thought to herself. She tried to catch her breath, her hand grasping at the door handle for some balance. She was not scared, for the moment was not a scary one. Rather, it was a foreboding of the future. It was not a flash back, like in the movies, but a flash forward, where she could see the future and its mixed blessings and curses. Get out. Get in. Go there. Don't.

It's cold out here. I really should get inside, she thought. But the car was dead, and dead things do not generate heat. The metal bittered, the vinyl hardened, even the steam now just spattered a few droplets that were damp and moist but hardly warm. The last vestiges of heat were in the bowels of the engine, and Ruby buried her face deep beneath the hood, breathing in the reek of worn-out rubber hoses, oily belts, and melted plastic parts. She let the last gasp of its internal combustion magnificence redden her cheeks and water her eyes, her tears a combination of both her own emotions and the stinging of the engine's spit.

Then Ruby reached both of her thin arms up, curled her long fingers around the front of the hood, tapped her finger ring—a narrow, less-than-14-karat simple band—against the now-cold metal and then, "Shit," she said, jumped up slightly and slammed it shut. It would never open again, and her life would never be the same.

It would never be the same because of the damned, incessant neon light, the light that, in her time of silent, lonely despair, at the crossroads of her young life, shone like a soft beacon beckoning her to go to it, but at the same time humming. Get out. Get out.

When she turned her back to the car, the street light lit up Ruby Kale just right, as if it were a spotlight and Ruby were the lone actor on a small stage. Ruby was pretty, there was no doubt about that. She was too young to be considered beautiful, and she was not sexy—perhaps that would come with time, but it hadn't yet. Still, although part of her looked like she should be hugging a teddy bear, Ruby had fine features and wide-set eyes, smoky eyes, if there were such a thing, eyes that could tell a story. The night was crisp and summer long gone, but Ruby was still wearing her jean shorts. They were cut off high, tight around her thighs, loose and baggy in the middle, drawn in around her waist with an oversized belt she had gotten at the Salvation Army thrift shop, old and worn, a belt both too wide and too long, a belt held together by a big buckle of metal.

She wore a cutoff tank top, a small part of her belly showing beneath, belying her innocence and naiveté. Brown suede kicker boots, not cowboy but close, stretched up to just below her still-smooth knees. Her brown hair cascaded in loose, natural curls; she wore no makeup, no perfume, and no earrings or necklaces, just the one juvenile ring on her right index finger. Her nose was pierced on the side of the nostril, a tiny—very tiny—diamond stud embedded into it. She had flawless skin and a dark tan; countless days floating in the pool, twirling the air mattress around and around, worked her color to perfection.

She liked to think of herself as a young rebel, and she showed off her nose piercing whenever she could. The truth was, though, that Ruby was little more than a fairly normal teenager, maybe not prim or proper, but hardly a rebel. And in spite of the nose piercing and the boots, Ruby had no real understanding of the world beyond where she had just come of age, the world of the manicured lawns and the family-owned drug stores back down the highway, back where it was still Winchester Road. But the world beyond—literally and figuratively—was the world she was about to enter. If she ignored the voices in her head, repeating like a drumbeat: "Get out, get out, get out."

She turned, did not look back—not ever—and slowly started walking the gravelly edge of Winchester—no, now it was 101—out toward the distant places where people did not yet live, but probably soon would. She kept her head down, watching her step and marveling at the roadside debris; plastic Wonder bags, cigarette butts, broken bottles, crumpled Kleenex, a t-shirt. How did these things end up, travel their journeys to their end, only to end here, on the gravel strip of shoulder on the side of the road? Had someone thrown a Kleenex out a car window? Perhaps. But a Wonder bag? Do you throw the bag out of your car after you eat a loaf of bread?

The mind games helped. Time passed. She moved forward. She pushed her hands into her pockets, felt the $12 in bills and some loose change, thought about the $150 in her bank account; not nearly enough to fix a car.

"Shit," she mumbled.

She scraped the gravel with her boots, little dust balls popping left, then right, then left again, then through a puddle and a splash of mud. Not a single car passed, not yet. *Odd*, she thought. Her mind cleared a little, her head lifted up some and her eyes scanned further ahead.

She knew what the neon sign was, though her mind did not want to admit it. She had known all along, really. It wasn't some dream or apparition. Her friends had told her about it, she had seen the ads in the paper, inside the sports section on the lower left hand corner. She knew about the amateur nights, about the prizes, about the money. She had heard the stories about the money, incredible amounts of money that Ruby did not believe could be true. The neon sign lit up the entrance to Tiffany's Cabaret, and now she was determined to go there.

"Get out, my ass," she said to herself, cursing the voices in her head from before. She was thirsty, literally and figuratively. She needed, wanted, her life to change.

The entrance to Tiffany's seemed oversized; huge white columns cornered a big, square, cement portico, and a topless mermaid sculpture stood in the center of it. There was a valet station, with a guy wearing a cheap, wrinkled, unkempt tuxedo, but a tuxedo nonetheless. A frayed red carpet was glued onto the cement, and it led up to big, carved, wooden double doors.

On each door were huge brass handles, and the doors were so heavy they were hard to open. *It was kind of like a weird castle*, Ruby thought to herself, but it was all lit up with neon. There were probably thirty to forty cars in the big lot, most of them parked in the back, away from the street; lots of pick-up trucks, a minivan Ruby couldn't help but notice, even a BMW and a few Cadillacs. Surveillance cameras scanned the lot like hawks on the prowl, streaming video to a little booth inside where the bouncer was supposed to be watching, but was instead talking to some girl. And, of course, there was the big neon sign that Ruby had seen from so far down the road... "TIFFANY'S CABARET," right in the middle of the parking lot, towards the highway.

One of the big, wooden, double doors with the big, brass handles was slightly ajar. Ruby spit her gum into a garbage can as she walked in. The lobby was lit up and she heard muffled music from further inside. Ruby coughed, tried to suppress the tickle in her throat, and got a little dizzy. She took a deep breath to get rid of the dizziness and nerves, summoned all her confidence.

Behind a long counter was a young girl. A small glass jar was next to her, a piece of note paper taped to it and in black magic marker the word "TIPS" was spelled out. The girl was reading a magazine, and didn't look up when Ruby came in. She spoke, though, still without ever making eye contact.

"Girls get in free. Ya can tip me, though." The door girl slurred her words, and had a little lisp. She still didn't look up from the magazine. How she knew Ruby was a girl without ever once looking her direction or hearing her voice Ruby couldn't tell.

"Amateur night. How does that work?" Ruby asked, as she walked right up to the door girl.

"Ya' gotta see Barbie"—it almost sounded like "Bowbby," some sort of odd speech impediment, but Ruby had already made the mental adjustment to compensate so Ruby understood. The door girl looked up now; she really wasn't any older than Ruby, at least not much anyway, but she looked different; makeup, eyeliner, big hoop earrings. Her eyes were sad looking, they kind of drooped, and she had a bad complexion that was covered with makeup. Her lips were full and red on their own, without any need for lipstick.

Door Girl swung around and picked up a microphone on a stand, whispered into it. The whisper was picked up by some sound system, quite well actually, and the whisper turned into a blare which echoed into the big room behind them. "Barbie to the front door. Barbie, front door." A little feedback from the microphone faded into a riff from a Def Leppard album, which was vibrating through gargantuan speakers spread throughout the entire room, twelve in all.

Through a small window with "DJ" above it, a bust of low-slung cleavage and a head of huge, teased hair popped out. It was obviously Barbie, later determined to be the "club manager," a.k.a "house Mom." She looked to be 40ish, but she was the type of 40 that had seen every minute of all four decades. The hair was overwhelming; strawberry blonde, teased to the extreme with big curls and totally split ends, bangs just above the eyes. The breasts were just as unreal; huge, really, more than double D, they hung low and the blouse let them. Barbie no longer had a pretty face—perhaps it once was, but not anymore—and her voice was husky; not just deep, but husky. The whole package was almost, but not quite, scary and masculine.

"What is it?" Barbie looked directly at Door Girl. It wasn't really a question, but a statement.

"Amateur," Door Girl replied.

"What?" Barbie asked.

"Whatcha really lookin' for, huh?" Door Girl turned to Ruby, and for the first time, made eye contact. Door Girl thought this was strange. The amateur girls never came early, never asked about it, they just, well, they just did it. They all came in about half an hour before, they all just went back to the changing room, they all seemed to know what they were doing. This girl didn't. Really.

"Amateur. Dancer." Ruby said nothing else. She paused. It seemed to Ruby like a long silence, but it probably wasn't.

There was a little laugh, hoarse, condescending. "We don't need no amateurs, we need full-time dancers." Barbie blurted back, her curt response not really making sense to Ruby.

"Oh," Ruby said, lowering her head. "Well..." She didn't know what else to say.

Barbie apparently did not hear her, as Ruby's voice had turned soft.

"So?" Barbie said. It was hard to tell whether she was addressing the question to Ruby or to Door Girl. Then, without waiting for a response, Barbie summarily pulled her big hair and big breasts out of the window, and rejoined what sounded like a party inside.

Door Girl didn't know what to do. She stared at Ruby a minute longer. Then she reached under the counter, looking for something. There it was, in a box, black marker scribbled on it: 'Amateurs Night. Forms." *Huh?* Door Girl thought to herself, *Never seen those before.*

"Here. Here's an application form. Fill it out, what the hell. It's not tonight, you know. I'll give it to her. She can call you. Barbie can call ya." Door Girl reached over the counter and gave Ruby the form. "Might as well fill it out." For some reason, Door Girl was being nice, but the reasons were unclear. Maybe Ruby looked a little desperate, maybe Door Girl was just bored. "Here, you can sit back here with me on this other stool and use the counter. Amateur nights are Fridays. You just have to fill out the form. She'll call ya. You're cute enough."

Door Girl pushed over the little light used to check IDs, and it lit up the form just right. It said simply "Employment" on the top. It did not specify amateur, waitress, dancer, bartender, bouncer, or door girl. "Proof of Age" was highlighted with yellow marker. Ruby filled it out. She put her mother's address and phone number as her own; she still lived with her mother, most of the time anyway. She took extra time with her penmanship, and tried to spell everything right.

"Thanks," Ruby said, and handed the form over to Door Girl.

Door Girl took the form. "A thousand bucks. Thousand bucks." Door Girl's sad eyes stared at Ruby for a second, then went back to her magazine.

Ruby walked out the door. She shivered a little, tiny goose bumps rose in odd places, her hair flew back with a wind gust. She rubbed her nose, pushed her hair back into place. She hardly got three steps out the door when she realized she had nowhere to go, not on foot anyway.

Damn, she thought to herself. Then she turned around, walked back into the club, and asked Door Girl if she could use the phone to call a cab. Door Girl did it for her.

* * * * *

Two nights later, Barbie called, a Thursday. Ruby was to be there the next day. "Be here at 7:00," Barbie said.

"So I bring my own outfit?" Ruby asked.

"Yeah, an outfit," Barbie replied, chuckled a little. "You know. Sexy. Show some skin. Ok, hon. We'll see ya," and she hung up.

Ruby was grateful she was there when the call came in, and more grateful that her mother was not. She did not say one word to her mother, but more to her surprise, she said not one word to anyone else, either; not even her best friend Dawn.

But the next day came, time passed, and Ruby found herself there in the parking lot of Tiffany's Cabaret at 6:45 the next evening. Had it been a conscious choice? she thought years later.

Yes, but not really. It was more something that just happened; she needed the money, there was no other way to get it, and Ruby just let it happen, let events unfold.

It had just turned dusk, and the few lights in the parking lot, set on automatic, were just turning on, still dim, humming to speed. The cabbie didn't say much, not anything she could hear, as Ruby hopped out of the back seat. He rolled down his window, she gave him $10, he gave her $2 in change. She didn't tip him, just forgot.

She had on black, old-fashioned, womanly high heels she had borrowed from her mother's closet, and she almost tripped as she walked away from the taxi. She had never really worn high heels, and even though she had spent several hours trying to walk in them the night before (just after the phone call from Barbie), it was still tricky. Ruby was wearing a white buttony blouse, cut low from the shoulders. It was tight around her chest, and it puckered up a little as Ruby breathed in and out. She also had a duffel bag over her shoulder, stuffed with slivers of cloth, bottles of perfume, colored dresses, white stilettos, and two packs of cigarettes.

It was always rock 'n roll at the club, always. That particular night, extra bass cranked up through tinny outdoor speakers mounted to the side wall. Van Halen, *Runnin' With the Devil*.

CHAPTER 3

The commercial jetliner landed at Haneda Airport ten minutes ahead of its estimated arrival time. The three-hour layover was welcomed after the ten-hour flight from Seattle, but the terminal was crowded and Charlie had to sit on the terrazzo floor and rest his head against the wall, his long, muscular legs stretched out in front of him, aching from the cramped quarters of the plane. He stared out the huge windows of the terminal complex, and watched as the sun set over Tokyo Bay.

Odd cargo transport vehicles, with cabs far forward and bubbly glass windshields, skittered about the tarmacs like bugs on water. Short, thin Japanese workmen, their hair dark, straight, and thick, bustled about energetically. The Tokyo Monorail, sleek and modern, elevated on pylons, slithered its way south, first with "S" curves and then in a straight bullet. The sun set, the light faded, the ocean went dark.

The soothing female voice on the loudspeaker kept repeating boarding calls, first in Japanese followed by good English. "Flight 407, Manila, Gate 42A, first boarding." Charlie's body twitched, his mind nimbly picking up the 407 and Manila just as it was supposed to. He jolted up a little, shook his head, yawned, and kicked his legs. He pulled his knees forward, rested his head between them for a second, then palms down on the floor, he pushed himself upright. His knees creaked from being prone too long, but standing felt good. He picked up his canvas carry-on and walked across the aisle to his gate.

The airplane for the flight from Tokyo to Manila was a 747, just like the one from Seattle to Tokyo. This time, though, the cloth seats were a different, exotic-looking fabric. And this time, it wasn't the older, haggard-looking American stewardesses on board. This time the flight attendants were, each and every one of them, young Filipino women; small, thin, and very friendly, or so Charlie thought. Yet the instructions about the exit rows, and everything else about a flight on a commercial airliner, were pretty much the same: the choice of beverages, the little snack of rice crackers in the shape of flowers, the fasten seat belt signs and the pilots talking about the weather.

Charlie settled into the routine again, reading another magazine and trying to sleep as best he could. His legs were restless; as they often were, especially after hard exercise. He was thrilled to be in the aisle seat, where he stuck his legs out when the carts weren't coming through.

It was full morning light when the plane finally landed in Manila. From his aisle seat, he tried, but couldn't quite catch, a good view out the windows. What little he did see was simply ocean and flats, then a sprawling city with no visible tall structures; quite covered with trees. There was some extra bustle of the passengers, more than he was used to, when the captain announced they were at the gate. Only they weren't really at a gate; rather, the plane taxied to a spot near the terminal and a stairway on wheels was brought over. The pilots and crew all stood and said their thank-yous, and the passengers all said thanks back, as they walked off the plane.

"Thank you."

"Thank you."

"Have a nice day. Thank you for flying with us today."

"Thank you."

On and on it went, the endless pattern of polite civility and routine small talk. Occasional bad English, odd sentence structure, crept in from the Filipinos.

"Thank. Good."

"Thank you. Have a nice day." The Japanese crew was friendly but stoic, their English almost perfect.

"Good. Good plane. Good air." The Filipinos bowed, subservient, smiling to the uniformed Japanese.

One by one, the passengers all shuffled up the aisle, ducked through the door hatch, struggled with their bags and tried to hang onto the metal rail as they descended the steep, grated stairs. Charlie did the same.

Right about then it hit him—a wave of heat, like opening the dryer mid-cycle. It rose from the black asphalt and up onto the metal platform stairs. It rolled over each passenger and enveloped them; a blanket of muggy, tropical air, dripping with humidity and thick with particulates from the planes' grease and jet fuel. Charlie felt a little faint, closed his eyes. The moment passed, and he regained his senses; but the wet heat did not go away. It sank into his clothes and his skin, and when he got further into the sun, it steamed off him. The few other white passengers looked miserable; the Filipinos didn't appear to notice; seemed to welcome the voluptuous heat.

He made his way to the concrete block building, into a little passageway, and down a long, windowless hall. He followed the others, slowly making their way, still lined up one by one, several couples managing to be somewhat side by side through the narrow space. Then up another flight of stairs, still no windows. Finally they all came to a big, open area, with a beat-up floor of badly cracked ornamental tile. At the end of the room were three lines, each already four to five people deep, green duct tape glued to the floor stretching out to delineate where to go and where to line up. There were even green duct tape "arrows" pointing in the obvious direction, to the little booths set up at the end of the lines.

Customs.

A rather typical process, Charlie noticed. Passports were pulled out, forms scratched in and declarations made. Middle-aged, portly Filipino bureaucrats—customs agents—sat on extra-high, old metal stools, and they rarely looked up. Heavy metal stamps flew back and forth over the paperwork and passports, then back to the ink pads. Every so often, someone in line would be asked to step aside, to the right, to a little booth where more questions were asked and more paperwork put into place. Beyond the booth was another room, this one with no windows, a heavy wooden door, and makeshift walls. There, Charlie guessed, was where nasty interrogations and strip searches, confiscation of drugs or weapons, took place. He tried not to think about the horrific stories of foreign prisons, which Charlie did not find true, but still caused him consternation, for he did not know, really know, if they were true or not.

He tried to act calm as he stood at the double duct-taped green line, some ten feet behind the agent, waiting his turn.

"Next."

Charlie had his military-issue carry-on bag in his right hand, and his passport, military I.D., and customs papers tightly clutched in his left hand. He put the passport and papers up on the table. The agent never looked up, not once. Rather, he pulled out the heavy metal stamper, freshened it on the ink pad, stamped the passport, and scribbled something with a pen on the custom's form.

"Next."

Charlie took that to mean he was free to go, and he picked up his passport and walked forward. To his surprise, a thick metal bar at waist height and a large green button blocked his way. A squat Filipino woman wearing some sort of garish uniform confronted him.

"Push button," she said, in stunted English, pointing a surprisingly well- manicured finger. "Push button."

He set down his bag, pushed the button with his right index finger.

A large light off to his left, one he had not seen before, turned from red to green.

"Go on," the Filipino woman said.

Random luck, perhaps, or fate, had prevailed. *Incredible*, Charlie thought to himself, as he had nothing to worry about; his bags were as free and pure of any contraband as possible. Nonetheless, he was relieved to pass out of the room, only to enter another, eerily similar one. But instead of lines and booths, this room held carousels for baggage, all currently empty.

Most everything in the baggage area seemed familiar. There were the big carousels with their flashing lights, and the moving conveyer belts that crept out from somewhere deep in the ground. But when the lights all started to flash and sirens blared, warning everyone the conveyer belt was about to move, and when things started bubbling up from underground, it wasn't the usual assortment of suitcases and luggage coming up. Instead of suitcases, the baggage area had mostly boxes; tightly packed, duct tape and twine and bold letters written all over. Most often, the twine had been wrapped to create a sort of handle to carry the box. The Filipinos seemed excited as they milled about, reaching for their handmade box luggage; the Americans more complacent as they waited for the relatively few, but now distinct, Samsonites and leather bags.

Charlie's bags had not made their way before the carousel stopped, went dead. There were no benches or chairs so Charlie sat on the floor, his back against a wall, his long legs stretched out in front of him. He was in civvies—jeans and a t-shirt—so he didn't care that the floor was sticky and dirty. His clean and pressed uniforms were all neatly packed away.

Finally the light on the metal pole lit up again and the horns began to squawk. The creaky carousel came back to life, and more bags and boxes—boxes and more boxes—spewed up from underground and bounced onto the conveyer belt, round and round. The locals grew more animated, each box seeming more precious to them than the next. Finally he saw his own big, green, military-issue canvas duffel, and then the blue garment bag with his dress uniforms. The garment bag was smeared with what looked to Charlie like grease and tire tracks. The uniforms inside would be disheveled, but at least intact.

Charlie grabbed the bags, almost too much for him to carry alone. He walked out of the baggage area, one last check by guard dogs, and then into the terminal. He was relieved to have gotten this far, very relieved that his bags had shown up. His step livened, rising; he was excited to be in Southeast Asia for the first time. He had reservations at the Hilton. Probably not so bad, he thought. Air conditioning would feel good.

Then, just beyond some ropes, were the hordes. Literally hundreds of Filipinos, most with little signs, yelling and begging, really, for him. He didn't quite understand the din until he cleared himself from the daze and listened.

"Taxi, taxi. Taxi, sir. Here, here."

Or it was "Hotel, hotel."

It was, to Charlie, an absolutely incredible sight. There were so few passengers, at least so few who weren't locals, and yet so many Filipinos screaming and reaching over the ropes, begging for cab fare money. Before leaving the Naval base in Seattle, he had been told to ignore the begging, how to deal with this. But now that he was actually there, and when it was happening before he even got out of the airport, and when it was happening for a cab ride—something he actually needed—he didn't know what to do. At first he kept saying no, no thank you, and tried to stare straight ahead and avoid the throngs behind the ropes.

Then he realized he was going to need one of them; he did need a cab ride to his hotel. He thought about the small amount of money in his left pants pocket, about $12, and the $40 carefully hidden in his left shoe. He had more but only in travelers cheques, buried deep in the duffel, to be cashed "only when he got to the base," as he had been instructed. How much could cab fare be, and how much is that in Filipino pesos? He ran the calculations, then tried to compare it with what was being screamed out by the taxi drivers. He was pretty sure it was less than $1; Hotel, 40 pesos, 40 pesos.

So he picked a cabbie at random, a local who looked nice enough. The man kept calling him "Sir." The cabbie kept clawing at his bags. Charlie was reluctant to let them go, but had no choice, really.

"I carry, I carry," the cabbie repeated over and over.

"No, it's OK, it's OK," Charlie repeated back. But the cabbie won the little battle, taking the bags and putting them neatly in the trunk.

The taxicab seemed normal. The traffic and the driving did not. It was outrageous, out of control, constant honking and downright bedlam. Charlie sat back and tried to soak it all in. Somehow they got through it, as if this chaos were normal. Perhaps it was.

After about 20 minutes, there was the Hilton, set back from the street quite a ways. It looked just like a Hilton should, a 10-story, high-rise glass tower, all polished and American in appearance. After his bags were safely on the curb, he gave the cab driver one American dollar. Incredible thanks followed, with Charlie nodding and genuflecting and saying again and again, "It's OK, it's OK," Charlie backed up the entire time trying to get away. Then off the cab went, back into the horrific traffic, the driver honking the horn before he even left the curb. Charlie turned and looked to the big hotel, started walking towards it.

Charlie walked up the long, smooth marble stairs to the entrance of the hotel, his two bags weighing him down some, local men and boys begging to carry the bags until he got halfway up the stairs until hotel security staff shooed them away. Several Filipinos were being stopped by security as they, too, went up the stairs and seemed to go to the hotel, but before they got very far, security was there, asking for ID, patting them down. Charlie unzipped his bag and started to reach for his passport and military ID, expecting the same scrutiny from security. But security was not paying any attention to him. Rather, a bellman rushed out from the revolving glass doors and grabbed Charlie's bags, waved him to come in;. Waved him right past the security.

"Please, please, you come in."

"OK. That's fine. I'm coming."

He was still wearing just his jeans and white t-shirt. He hadn't shaved for two days. He looked tired.

Nonetheless, he was undeniably getting what could only be called royal treatment. Were they mistaking him for some VIP? It seemed not.

But then he realized the obvious; over 6 feet tall and a muscular 175 pounds, he towered over everyone there. Literally everyone. And he was by far the whitest. And he had by far the tightest military buzz short haircut. They did not need to check his ID. He was—there could be no doubt—a young American military officer. A young American military officer with money. More money in his left shoe than most of the locals would earn in a year. And the American military was putting him up in the nice, fancy, American hotel. Of course it was. And of course they were giving him the royal treatment.

So when he walked into the hotel, and when the bellman pointed and the pretty receptionist encouraged him to come over, he relaxed a little. He had a layover in Manila, with nothing really to do but make sure to catch the bus three days later to get to the base at Olangapo, where he would catch a military flight to the carrier. He checked in, asked for an upper floor, got the keys to his room, found the elevators, reluctantly leaving his larger bag with the bellman to bring up for him.

The elevator smelled humid and stale. There were no overhead fans like in the lobby. The carpeted floor was stained, musty. He pushed the button for the 14th floor. He held his breath. It moved slowly.

The hallway smelled a little better, more open. The lush carpet was a dull green with royal crests running along on the sides. Beige wallpaper and wainscoting of dark, exotic wood, scraped and battered from luggage carts, lined the hall. The door to his room was of the same paneled exotic wood, tall and heavy and ornate.

The room held two double beds with a nightstand in the middle. A beautiful white orchid was on the nightstand. Charlie opened the heavy, chocolate brown curtains, and looked out over the rooftop of the convention center adjoining the hotel. Heavy black tar covered the roof, some stone to the sides where the water drained, four large air conditioning units stationed in each corner. He pulled the curtains shut, waiting for the bellman to bring his bag. It didn't take long. He tipped the bellman, went to the bathroom, lay down on the bed, but only for a moment. He wanted to go out, to see this new foreign, exotic city. He unpacked his bags, hung up his uniforms, then locked up what he could in the little safe in the closet.

When he got back to the lobby, American music was playing through the hotel sound system. The lobby was all marble, quite empty, minimal furnishings, only a few people. The speakers in the lobby were bolted into the cove between wall and ceiling, and angled down. They echoed a little, over the marble, through the open room. Michael Jackson, *Beat It*; more than just an odd choice of song, it was almost spooky. Charlie paused a minute. It was late. He was tired. He should go back to his room, go to sleep. Wait until daylight. But he didn't. He kept walking, through the lobby, out the big glass doors, the security guard holding them open for him.

"Good night, sir. Taxi?" the man in the beige uniform asked.

"No. Thanks. I'm fine." Charlie had no idea where he was going, no need for a taxi.

The music was piped out to the courtyard, again Michael Jackson, but this time *Billie Jean*. It still could be heard, but barely, at the street corner where Charlie waited, watched the wild traffic. By the time he crossed the street, it had faded and was gone, replaced with the raucous sounds of the Manila night. A local boy, no more than twelve years old, his English better than the rest, was badgering him, walking backwards and staying with Charlie step by step.

"I show you. Girls. Beer. Best clubs, I know best clubs. Let me show you."

Charlie fell into the now-standard response. "No. No, thank you. No."

"Come on, it's okay. No problems. I show you. Pretty, pretty girls."

"Okay, okay," Charlie finally let his guard down. "You show me."

And the little boy did. And the clubs were dark, and the beers were cold, and the Asian girls were very pretty. And the little boy followed Charlie everywhere, pulled him from one to the next, until Charlie became entranced with a particular one of the girls. And the little boy smiled, held out his hand for his tip. And Charlie tipped him. And the little boy went away. And the girl stayed. And the girl stayed at his side, every minute, until Charlie had to leave.

And two days and two nights later, Charlie was back in the lobby of the Hilton, where he waited for the bus to take him to Olangapo City. And from Olangapo City, he would fly to the island of Diego Garcia, would look down from the plane at its picture-perfect atoll, the greenish waters of the lagoon in stark contrast to the ocean's blue. And from Diego Garcia, he would fly to the aircraft carrier, at sea, off the coast of the Gulf of Oman.

And as he stood with his bags in the lobby of the Hilton, the hotel speakers played the same song as when he had arrived: Michael Jackson, *Beat It*. It still seemed as odd then as it had when he first got there. And he would remember it. And although he would remember Manila, and what happened there, he would talk only of some of it, and the rest he would keep to himself.

RUBY. 1981. 19 YEARS OLD. MEMPHIS, TENNESSEE.

Of all her senses, smell was undoubtedly the one that created Ruby's first impression of what she would then refer to only as "the club." The entry, where Door Girl was still working, still reading her magazine, had a hint of it. But it was only after going through the second set of doors that it hit, and then it hit hard. The odors that assaulted her nostrils were a combination of many things, but perfume and smoke were predominant. Human sweat, not necessarily body odor but something close to it, was also there, and stale beer, and moldy carpet perhaps—all of those were part of the smell that seeped into everyone's hair and clothes, that didn't go away without some passage of time. After a few minutes, most people didn't really notice the smell, but for Ruby, it was always there.

The next thing that struck her about the club took a while. It took a while because the club was so dark. Her eyes started to adjust, her pupils dilated. As she struggled to see, trying not to trip or fall into anything, she felt it best to just stand still and not move. As she stood there, she first saw bright blurs of color, blurs of glow-in-the-dark hot pink and lime green and white. These iridescent blurs whirled about the room, lit up the stages, sat on the stools. As Ruby's eyes adjusted, the blurs clarified, and she began to notice the chiffon fabric, the flowing capes draping the floor, the billowing of the cover-ups. All the girls wore them, and each cape seemed fundamentally the same; sheer blankets of fabric covering their backs and cascading, flowing, like wedding dress trains, to the floor. In the front, the capes had only a few flimsy, fabric-covered buttons that strained to hold tight against the push of flesh. Silhouetted underneath the cover-ups were padded push-up bras and g-strings covered in sequins and beads, not lingerie but costumes, specifically made for entertainment and enticement. Ruby had never seen anything like them before, and her first, visceral reaction was that she had entered an old-time, Wild West whorehouse; some sort of Petticoat Junction.

No one said hello. In fact, no one seemed to notice Ruby at all. Of course, she hadn't expected a greeting party, or even a welcome, but she had expected something. Instead, Ruby just stood there between the bar and the entry door, looking back and forth for Barbie. But Barbie was nowhere to be found. So Ruby tried to take in everything else—not just the girls and their showy costumes. There was a long bar, just like any other bar, with a bartender behind it and stools in front—20 feet long probably, with a dark Formica top and a brass foot rail.

It took a while to realize in the dim light, but then she noticed everything was purple. Purple chairs, purple counter tops, purple-patterned, commercial-grade carpet. It seemed, incredibly, all purple. A ring of white neon lights circled all the way around a big, raised main stage, in the dead center of the room, and about ten feet away from that, spaced one each towards the sides, were little round stages, tiny ones, just big enough for a girl to walk around holding onto a pole, and on those side stages were little, recessed lights that flipped on from yellow to blue to red. And the lights and the stages and the brass railings, so you didn't slip off, all lit up, the purples melding into different hues and tones, but in the end it was all still, well, it was all some kind of purple.

Several groups of "regular" customers sat or stood around the room. Ruby didn't know any of them yet, but all of the other dancers did.

At one table were two that came up from Mississippi, usually together; Elroy, the skinny black man with the short afro, and his buddy Bubba, a husky farmer. They were there most every day. They sat in the deepest, darkest corner by satellite stage three that was never used except on the very busiest nights. Their table had the free liquor, because they brought in big bottles of their own, and they shared it with the girls. So their table was usually packed full of strippers getting free drinks. But Elroy and Bubba also had a lot of crank, and often twist-tied corner baggies of coke, available to the right people for the right price.

At another table, always right next to the main stage, was a group of long-haired Southern rock n' rollers. It was Jim Dandy and his entourage. You knew he was a rock star because it was obvious. He was full of smiles and was always ready for the stage, with leather chaps, big belt buckles, bare chest, and long blonde hair. He tipped well, was always friendly to everyone. He ignored, or at least didn't seem to mind, the whispers from the newer girls and other customers; "That's Jim Dandy, you know, Black Oak Arkansas ... "

The single businessman next to satellite stage two, came in the later afternoons, probably after work. He always wore white shirts with bold, patterned ties. "Love your tie today," the girls teased him.

Then off to the back, away from the stage and the long bar, off in a relatively well-lit corner, Ruby saw six nervous, young girls. Barbie was back there, too, smoking a cigarette and drinking coffee. Every so often one of the customers wandered back there; Barbie shooed them away.

Ruby made her own way to the group of six girls, the amateurs for that night. With Ruby, there were a total of seven.

Two of the younger ones were chewing gum and talking, chirping, like birds, rat-a-tat, gibberish high and shrill. "Yup." "Betcha." "Wow." Never more than two, three words. Insecurities and complexes covered up by their friendship and banter.

One girl twirled her hair, tried to look bored. Another leaned up against the rail, her long legs apart a little, her arms behind her back, her eyes looking up at the ceiling. The remaining two milled about, anxious, pacing in frenetic circles. Scared looks in their eyes, not pretty. One was bony, with a thin but protruding nose, the other pale white, blotchy skin, a whitehead on her left cheek.

Ruby walked up to the girl leaning against the rail; they made no eye contact, said nothing. Ruby spread her legs apart a little, mimicking the posture. Barbie talked to the air. The girls were listening, intently, but tried not to show it. All but the two ugly ones.

"Fifteen minutes. Decide who goes first. Two songs each. Tops off, bottoms stay on. Dance however ya like, don't matter. Then ya stand at the end of the stage, wait for the applause, then ya get off. Then ya get off the stage before the start of the next song. Don't be nervous. Nothin' to be nervous about. Let 'em holler."

There was a pause. Nobody asked questions. The scared girls looked more scared than before.

"So."

Another long pause.

"Y'all will be fine. Changin' room's back there. Y'all go on in and get pretty. Pauly'll help ya out there." Pauly, feminine and girly, was a woman trapped inside a man's body. It was his job to help the girls with their hair and makeup. For him it was a safe place, it was his escape from a judgmental world.

Behind them was a hallway, then a red door. On the red door was a big sticker, and on the sticker, printed with a blotchy magic marker, the single word "Dancers." Behind the red door was a big room, two rows of lockers with padlocks, two rows of countertops with mirrors, two rows of panel lights above the two rows of countertops, twenty twirly stools with twenty vinyl seats, the purple vinyl torn and ratty. The speckled green linoleum floor was crusted over and sticky, the counter-top contrastingly smooth and shiny, with a marble faux finish.

The scared girls looked for empty lockers. The cool girls sat on the stools, checked their makeup. Ruby sat down, too, looked at herself in the mirror. The light was good, the makeup on just right; she looked at herself objectively, as if it were not her. Young. Pretty. Calm. Surprisingly calm. Then an over-whelming urge to pee. By the time she finished up in the bathroom, it was time.

"OK, let's get out there," Barbie yelled at them, and they obeyed her, and one by one, single file, they slowly marched out.

Black side curtains framed the little stage, the narrow runway promenading out from it, a deck into the ocean. Stage lights focused on tight spots, the mirrored globe glittered around the room. Smoke wafted everywhere, from the floor to the ceiling, around and into the lights, feeling its way through the room ghostlike, creepy.

Barbie tugged at Ruby, half pushed her up the little stairs. A little strut to the center, the music blaring. She just kept going, walking, let it flow. Tried not to think.

Ruby unbuttoned her cover-up, let it fall to the floor. She didn't look into the ocean, walked the deck head up, arms stretched out to her sides. She thought of floating in her pool as a little girl, twirling on the air mattress, the sun burning into her. She twirled her arms, lazily moved to the music around and around, let her wrists drop and her long fingers butterfly across her face and back outstretched again, swayed her hips. It was good, sexy, feminine. It was what they wanted.

It was almost the end of the second song. Thirty seconds at the most. The light caught just right, to the side, the spotlight askew. It shone where it shouldn't, out onto the ocean. And Ruby caught it just right, caught the light, had a moment of disarming clarity. It caught an ugly man, his eyes boring into her, his garish t-shirt untucked, dirty.

She moved past it, back into the glare of the other spotlights, into the haze of the smoke that she followed to its settling places. Her dreamy dance started to wilt, her mind had been snapped out of its dreamlike trance by the ugly man, by the awesome reality of it, of what she was doing, of where she was. Her breath caught, her arms fell to her sides, her fingers—just moments before seductively outstretched—now clenched. She stopped dancing, started walking, walking back, off the deck promenade and back to the stage, quickly now, quicker, get out, get out.

Fate struck a fortunate blow as she stumbled behind the side curtain, clutching her stomach, for just as she did, the second song ended and the crowd erupted, clapping, cheering, whistling, some stomping their feet.

Ruby would not dance again that night, would not dance again for a long, long time. Bartend, waitress, that might be fine for a while, she decided. Then she would go back to school, be a nurse or a secretary, a housewife or a teacher. She would live in a little house in the crossword grid, just like where she grew up. She would marry, she would take care of him, she would be loyal, dutiful. But she would not be sexy. She could not have him stare at her like the ugly man had, just then.

But the pull of the club, the pull of the money, the pull to be the object of desire was like gravity, it was never-ending and constant, its grip like slimy octopus tentacles reaching and writhing and subtly latching onto your soul. The look of the men, staring, and the smoke and the costumes and the liquor and the black light and the strobe lights and—at Tiffany's Cabaret, anyway—all of the purple imprinted on her mind and stuck there like glue. She tried to knock it loose. She spent sunny days in the park. She went to the movies.

When she was away from the club, she listened to her own music, not the blaring rock 'n roll the DJs insisted on. She loved Blondie, Stevie Wonder, Diana Ross. When she stretched out on the back patio with her sister, the afternoon sun blistering through some old shade trees, she made sure the stereo was turned up so they could both hear it. Eric Clapton was singing *Lay Down Sally*. It was sublime, in a way, almost enough for her to let it go, to move on, to get out.

It was almost enough.

But not quite.

CHAPTER 4

CHARLIE. 1985. 29 YEARS OLD. USS NIMITZ, AT SEA, NEAR THE EQUATOR.

Charlie's knees had started to bleed, and the blood was oozing through the heavy khaki fabric of his pants. Charlie was on all fours, crawling on the flight deck of the USS Nimitz, the namesake of the Nimitz class aircraft carriers, the first to use nuclear power. Two reactors were embedded in the depths of the hull way below, churning out huge amounts of nuclear energy that supplied the floating city of over 5,000 men.

Brutal heat enveloped the huge ship as it crossed the equator.

It was the most incredible hazing ritual imaginable. He had heard the stories and he had complied with the requisite responses; "Wow," and "That's hard to believe." But deep down, Charlie truly hadn't believed the tales. The United States Navy, a naval warship, at sea, with admirals and captains and a whole battle group, would not allow it. Some small hazing rituals, sure, but not to the extent the old sailors—the master chiefs and senior chiefs—had described it to him at the base back in Lemoore, California.

But it was as they described. The metal spikes on the flight deck were intended to provide friction for jet wheels at takeoff and landing. Now, though, all of the planes were safely tucked away in the hangar bay, and instead, thousands of men were on the flight deck, half standing and orchestrating and the other half on all fours crawling. Crawling on the metal spikes. Crawling until their knees and hands bled.

The metal spikes on the flight deck kept cutting further into Charlie's knees and elbows and hands. He crawled along now, wincing with each movement, his back starting to ache badly. Whooping and hollering shellbacks whipped cut pieces of fire hose—"shillelaghs"—onto his back, and onto the backs of the two thousand other pollywogs crawling around. Shellbacks were any men on the ship, regardless of rank or age, who had previously crossed the equator on a naval vessel. "Pollywogs," like Charlie, were the rest of the men who had never done that. It was about an equal split on the Nimitz for this particular crossing; two to three thousand men were shellbacks, about the same number pollywogs.

The hazing had started at 4:00 a.m., and just as he had been told, he showed up wearing his underwear outside his pants, and just as he had been told, he didn't walk into his workspace, he crawled in. And as he was then told, he and four other men, two enlisted and two officers, started to lap water from a dog bowl. A bucket full of thrown-away food had been saved from the garbage area of the mess. The shellbacks, laughing and full of energy, ladled the slop over Charlie as he continued to lap up the water. The smell soon became overwhelming.

The worst was three hours later. Still on all fours—never allowed to rise for fear of whippings with the shillelaghs— literally thousands of men shivered on the aircraft elevators, which took the planes from inside the hangar bays up to the flight deck. From the flight deck above them, at least three stories, more than 24 feet higher, stood perhaps a hundred shellbacks holding large fire hoses, spraying salt water sucked up from the sea. The force of the gushing water knocked some down even from their crouch, and turned all of them into a writhing mass. Charlie struggled to breathe, gasped for air.

When the spray passed momentarily, he greedily gulped up the air, knowing another pass of the hose would come soon. The salt seeped through his clothes and caused his developing blisters and scrapes to sting, and it got into his eyes and he tried to sit up a little or kneel, to rub his eyes, but when he did so, another spray of the hose knocked him back to the ground.

Another four hours later, the tortured hazing ended with Charlie's face buried in the bare naked belly of the oldest, ugliest, fattest master chief the ship's crew could find, wearing dirty gym shorts and nothing else, his stomach slathered with oil, his legs spread a little as he pushed the big stomach out for the passing line of pollywogs, who as soon as they buried their faces into that disgusting belly, would officially become shellbacks.

The master chief sat on a little handmade throne and laughed, his head rolling back and forth like a drunken king. After one more harsh spray of seawater from a lone fire hose, intended more as a cleaning effort than further hazing, Charlie stood for a moment at the very stern of the ship. There he watched as the bilge was emptied and a huge, lathery snake of excrement and piss and garbage and debris fouled the ocean behind them. But the ocean was immense, and slowly, most everything just disappeared into the depths, sinking and sinking to the dark, lifeless depths of the Mariana Trench.

Victor, standing next to Charlie, having just survived the same experience, stood looking off the back of the ship also, and he and Charlie just stared at the bilge debris and tried to recover their sanity. They shared glances. Charlie was the first to speak, and he spoke softly. "Damn," was all he said to his old friend.

Victor spoke softly, too. "Holy shit."

That was it. They were too tired and exhausted for further conversation. They walked unsteadily back to their quarters, which consisted of four bunk beds in a space the size of a dorm room, tiny desk spaces, and a communal shower and toilets across the hall shared by twelve others. Charlie squeezed into the narrow, plastic-enclosed shower stall and, for a full hour, soaked up the warmth of the desalinated seawater, his body temperature slowly rising back to normal. Then, still groggy, he made his way to his bunk, crawled up and lay down, his feet hanging over the edge. He turned on the tape player strapped to the bulwark. A song crackled into tune. Dire Straits, *Money for Nothing*. Charlie lay on his back, eyes open, thinking of nothing. Within minutes he was sound asleep. He dreamt of his childhood, of Lori Anderson.

RUBY. 1981. 19 YEARS OLD. MEMPHIS, TENNESSEE.

Six months had passed since Ruby had performed at Tiffany's Cabaret on Amateur Night. Six months of trying to forget, trying to move on. At age 19, six months seemed like a long, long time. And the time went by so slowly, and she just kept thinking about it. All the time. Too much.

Compromise, Ruby rationalized to herself. I'll be a waitress. That's all. Nothing further. Good money, not that hard.

And when she called Barbie, Barbie remembered her, said something nice. Barbie told her to come to Tiffany's at 5:30 Friday. Waitress was fine, always need pretty waitresses, she said, or something like that, but she chuckled when she said it.

At almost exactly 5:30 that Friday, Ruby walked into Tiffany's Cabaret, now for the third time. She looked for Barbie, but Barbie never came. Instead the head waitress met her—Brenda. Brenda was about fifty, not very friendly, short and skinny but big in the middle from age. She had skinny hips, skinny legs, skinny arms; she was just big in the middle, where everything had settled in. Someone—a regular customer it was—later told Ruby that Brenda had been beautiful in her younger days, that Brenda had once been the club's prize dancer. It was hard to fathom.

"You Ruby? Come with me." Brenda didn't bother with introductions.

"Here's a tray," she said. The tray was round plastic, with a little rubber glued to the middle, and clipped to the side of the tray was a little cup called a "tip caddy." The club paid maybe a dollar for each tray and tip caddy, but they charged each waitress $20.00. You had to pay for it (you could pay at the end of the night); the tray held the drinks and the tip caddy held the coins and dollars from the customers.

"We pay for the drinks ourselves, then get the money back from the customer—that's yours to keep. Cigarette machine's here, kitchen window's over there. It's open 'til midnight. Kitchen's open 'til midnight. Empty the ashtrays. We don't have stations. Just walk around and deliver drinks, cigarettes and food, occasionally walk back in the dressing room and see if any of the girls need something."

Ruby kept saying, "Unhuh...unhuh..." Not really a yes or a no, more of a grunt acknowledgment that she had heard something, not necessarily that she understood it. At the end of the instructions—training, you might call it—Brenda looked at Ruby for a moment.

"Well, that's it. Get to work," Brenda said. And then she left, off down the hall and out of sight. And Ruby stood there, with the world spinning around her.

Douglas, the bartender, motioned Ruby over, talked to her for a while. One of the customers called her to his table, called her "Honey," and asked for a drink. "Just a beer, honey. Bud. Get me a Bud."

Within a matter of an hour or so Ruby was more than keeping up. Her tip caddy even had a couple of bucks in it. As she busily changed out the beers and whiskey sevens and whiskey Cokes, she got into a decent rhythm and routine. Once or twice, she glanced at the stages, but only a quick glance. It was a Friday night, and it wasn't hard to keep busy. As the night wore on, she thought it would slow down, but instead more and more men, young and old, all sizes and shapes and clothing, kept coming in. The early crowd was quieter; some businessmen in suits and ties; others were laborers, still showing the dirt from the day.

But after several hours, the crowd grew rougher and louder. There was a group of college boys from Rhodes, dressed very preppy with white Izod shirts and narrow, blue striped ties, with perfect hair short in the back and long in the front, almost a pompadour and a little greasy. They were at the pool table, paying more attention to the girls on the stages than the game. Another group of guys watched football on the big TV, a couple of them were wearing jerseys with the numbers of their favorite players. They were loud and drunk, groaning at the bad plays and screaming at the good ones. There were also the men around the stages, of course, mesmerized, mingling with their seat mates but always looking ahead.... they stayed relatively quiet, didn't seem to drink much. Then the bachelor party boys, two different sets—loud as could be, childlike in their revelry, wide-eyed and raucous.

Suddenly, at the end of the night, all of the lights in the club were turned on, as if the sun had come up all at once, blasted over the horizon to full noon strength. Moments before the music had been blaring, the girls dancing, the drinks flowing. The DJ, his radio voice deep and melodic, had kept telling the crowd it was their last chance, last chance for drinks, last chance for dances, last chance for tips. But the warnings were mainly lost in the din, lost in the whispered conversations of the lonely men and each one's carefully chosen girl, lost amid the hooting and hollering of the two bachelors and their buddies who were loose for the night, who had their hall passes, but who were destined to pay penance the next morning to their wives and girlfriends and fiancées.

Darkness casts spells; light eliminates them. When the lights all splashed on at once at closing time that night, just as they had all the nights before that one, the spells were all broken and the fantasies all ended. The romantic whispers, and each and every one of the hoots and hollers, came to an abrupt, total and complete halt. For several seconds, in fact, everything was silent, and everyone seemed stunned. When the shock wore off, the men and the boys all started shuffling towards the door, zipping up coats, fumbling for keys. Ruby worked her way to a quiet corner to count her cash.

For the first hour or so, she had tried to keep track of her take; the tip jar started to fill, the math worked through her head. But after that, the drink orders kept getting longer, the smoke kept getting thicker, and the math kept getting harder. She thought she had cashed out her tip jar, squished the wads of bills and coins into her purse, at least six times, maybe more. Now she sat sorting the bills one by one, straightening them and putting them into neat stacks. Mostly singles. She brought it all to Barbie, sitting at a table next to the bar, smoking. About two dozen of the dancers and another three or four waitresses were all sitting around her, each one waiting her turn. Anyone who worked at Tiffany's had to pay the house, their rent for being there that night. Ruby waited her turn, asked to "cash out," repeating the phrase she had already heard from the others.

Barbie didn't say anything; she just picked up the money with her surprisingly delicate fingers and started counting it.

"There you go," she said. She handed Ruby back eight twenty-dollar bills, a five, and two ones.

"Cool," Ruby said.

Four cabs were waiting outside when Ruby walked out of the club that night. She picked one, crawled into the back seat, and breathed a little sigh. She told the cabbie where to go. The ride home was short. Her mother was asleep. She lied to her mother the next morning, telling her she had been out with some friends; had a good time, nothing special. Several nights later, Ruby changed to a new lie. This time she told her mother she had picked up a different job, this one working nights, at a Denny's; she liked it and it was okay. There wasn't much discussion about it; Ruby told her she thought it would help bring some money to pay to fix the car again. It all made sense.

She quit the mall job. It took a week to clear $160 there; it had only taken one night at Tiffany's. The job at the Cupboard lasted only a couple days more. She didn't quit that job; rather, she overslept her morning shift and just didn't bother ever going back. The club had its talons in her by then, that quickly, smooth, and sure, it enveloped her psyche and took hold hard. "House Mom"—Barbie—looked after her, in a way. Head waitress Brenda left her alone, told her she was "doin' pretty good." The bartenders and bouncers all flirted.

Then there was Vanilla. Vanilla was a dancer, her name a total irony, for her skin was dark black. Somehow Vanilla became a friend. Ruby never quite understood how that happened. Days turned into weeks, then a month. It was early December, 1981. Blondie's *Call Me* was at the top of the charts.

CHAPTER 5

CHARLIE. 1986. 30 YEARS OLD. PATTAYA BEACH, THAILAND.

The *Nimitz* lay at anchor in the bay, unable to find a berth large enough for it in the harbor. A skeleton crew remained on board, cursing the luck of the watch logs and counting the minutes until they, too, got shore leave. Across the bay, half a mile away, lights shimmered on the waves: Pattaya Beach, Thailand.

Shuttling men back and forth, day and night, were six or seven small, old, wooden boats. A Thai, probably a local fisherman, stood far aft in his longboat, retrofitted with a motor instead of oars, steering it with a long metal rod attached to the awkwardly placed propeller motor—an obvious, modern add-on. Each longboat had bench seats where the oars used to attach, enough for maybe a dozen men to sit. This group clutched the benches tightly as the three-foot ocean swells crisscrossed wind-driven waves, creating a nasty and nauseating yaw and pitch. The massive carrier, juxtaposed, lay perfectly still; to it, the bay was a dead calm.

The ocean, the sky, even the carrier, were eerily dark as the longboats embarked from it for the half hour trip to shore. As the sailors got closer, though, they could almost hear the hum of the Asian port city and the night sky lit up.

Several blocks from the dock, through sandy streets and a cacophony of smells and sounds, hawkers peddling t-shirts and women, was a two-story, thatched-roof bar. Inside, a group of men, sitting together, all faced the long, wooden, raised stage:

two young, junior-grade staff lieutenants, Victor and Charlie; two staff officers, one a doctor from South Carolina, commander rank, and the other a lawyer from Florida, a JAG full lieutenant. An older man, his face weathered and his skin chalky, was also with the group. He was a Naval Investigative Service agent, supposedly undercover. He was, however, well known to many on board the Nimitz as he routinely ate in the officers' mess.

Victor sat close, with his elbows on the rail of the stage, his neck craned up and his eyes wide. He was yelling, loudly...

"Go, go, go." A Gregorian chant. A rally cry at a college football game. A political demonstration. Fans at a rock concert. Or, in this case, drunken American Navy men—all in civilian clothes, rank and status no longer evident—grunting at the Thai dancing girls up on stage.

"Go, go, go..."

Charlie sat next to Victor, and although he watched, intensely interested in the spectacle, he did not partake in the ribald yelling or stomping of the feet. Charlie was leaning back in his chair, the front two chair legs literally up off the ground as a result. Charlie's feet were propped up on a little table, and his legs were nonchalantly crossed. He was nursing a Sing Tao beer. Charlie felt he was watching from afar, watching events unfold as if he were dreaming—and that at any moment, he would wake up.

Her skin was soft, young, and exotic caramel. She had Asian eyes, like a Siamese cat, adorned with liner and shadow, with theatrical, fake curled eyelashes that blinked intrigue. Her lithe body was adorned with only a shiny g-string and sparkles, and she danced languorously, as if she were bored. When she smiled, which was rare, her large teeth sparkled white and were perfectly straight, an unusual genetic gift.

Long fingers with pretty, fake nails painted iridescent pink reached down and calmly pulled the g-string down and over black high heels. She then contorted herself, her back to the floor, her feet flat, her arms inverted, so that her belly rose up in a bridge. She began to sway, and her pelvis, with its thin, black pubic hair, swung up and down, and her small buttocks touched the floorboards. The raucous men were subdued, mesmerized, and hushed.

Later, they would all tell the stories, the stories of her, of her and of others like her, and of the snakes, of the blow darts and the enlisted men holding having balloons popped above their heads, of sex on stages. Embellishments were not needed; the truth was better, unbelievable anyway.

Charlie, almost writhing inside with sexual energy, tried to remain calm, even aloof. He kept his cool even when, after the show was almost over, she crawled toward him. Victor and the others in his group, all stared in bewilderment as she made her way right to Charlie, strangely ignoring the others in the room. Charlie kept his feet propped upon the table and his arms and hands lazily at his sides, almost unknowingly exuding an air of confidence. His face, though, turned towards hers.

As she crept up to him, he kept his posture, and he kept remarkably calm.

She reached out, touched his face. Her long hair, dark brown, a sliver of it dyed blonde, swept over him; resulting shivers went up his spine. Her hands moved down the sides of his face, cupping it carefully. Still naked but her legs now tight together, she sat on her knees, her long, thin body arcing up like a cobra for a snake charmer. She continued to caress him, first his face, then his shoulders, back to his face; over his eyes, his mouth, a single finger touching his lips. Charlie stayed still, only his eyes connecting with hers. She was in total control.

Very, very softly, she whispered to him, her voice as sensual as everything else about her.

"Okay? You like? Handsome man...you are handsome man." Broken English, but elegant.

The moment lingered. Eventually he responded, so quiet no one but she could hear. "Yes. I like." His voice was deep, gravelly, more so than usual.

She caressed him more, and her face came closer to his, so close he could feel her eyelashes, feel her breath. She smelled wildly of oils and flowers, of feminine lotions and hair gels, smells so wonderful he lost his breath. She kissed his cheek, stayed there, then gently pulled away, carefully moved back to the middle of the stage. She danced to the end of the song, then disappeared to the back, a dark area hard to see.

Another girl, just as pretty as the first until she smiled, took her place on the stage.

The music played on, American rock music. Starship, *We Built This City.* Charlie did not really hear it, would never remember the music, would not associate any particular song with that particular night.

But the girl. Her stage name was—Charlie paused—Tia. He would not forget her. Tia.

RUBY. 1983. 21 YEARS OLD. MEMPHIS, TENNESSEE.

The cab dropped Ruby off at the club just as it had so many times before, and she said hi to the valet guy the same as she always did. The mermaid statue stared at her this time. She had never noticed it had eyes. The red carpet was frayed more than usual. The sky was dark, people seemed weary. Winter was setting in. The heavy wood doors were extra hard to open. Ruby was tired, almost constantly tired lately. But tonight was going to be different. Tonight she wasn't going to be just a waitress.

Instead of her waitress outfit—black pants and buttoned white blouse—tonight Ruby wore her old Levi jeans and a tank top, the same boots she had on the night her car broke down what seemed so long ago. She had a big duffel bag with her costumes neatly folded inside. She walked back to the dressing room. The girls were walking around, half naked, some dressed, some not, all talking shit. One of the dancers was helping another with her hair. Finally, after sitting for what seemed an eternity, Vanilla came bolting through the door, all smiles and full of energy.

"You look sooooo cool. Good for you, ya know. This is gonna be so good, and you know this is the smart thing, ya know? You're just gonna make so much damned money, girl."

Ruby drank too much. It was something she rarely did; but that Wednesday night—who could blame her?—she kept drinking wine coolers, right from the bottle. Vanilla was always there, it seemed, whispering in her ear, taking her by the hand, sitting next to her, talking her up to the guys. The bartenders and bouncers were in her ear, too, but it didn't take long for her mind to tune them out. She needed to touch something tangible, to break the spell, the spell of the dark. She tried putting her face up close against the porcelain sink in the bathroom; it felt cold and wet, and that helped calm her. But only for a moment. When she walked back out to the floor, the room began to spin again.

She needed the lights to come on, but they didn't.

Then somehow, oddly, she got into the game. She blocked the voices, moved the hips. The darkness and the smoke and the drinks were all like a blanket, covering up the insecurities and blemishes at the same time. Vanilla slipped her a little white pill, said it would help, gave her a glass of water. It helped. The voices shut up, the dark crept closer, the blanket drew tighter.

Inside Tiffany's Cabaret that Wednesday night in early December, 1980, the DJ introduced Ruby Kale as "Sascha." The previous dancer was picking up all her dollar bills from the stage, putting them into a wad. She then came down the stairs, waited for Sascha, then helped her up the stairs as if it were a formal prom. That was the dance etiquette, always had been. Sascha walked up to the "main stage" for the first time.

Outside Tiffany's Cabaret that same Wednesday night, about three of the hanging stop lights towards the city down Highway 101, driving his black Toyota Corolla with out-of-state plates, Lewis Foster was on his way to see Missy Perkins, his ex-girlfriend. She went by the name Vanilla at the club.

"Fuck the restraining order, fuck it," Lewis mumbled to himself as the Corolla slid over the dividing line into oncoming traffic, then back onto its own side, then touched on the gravel shoulder before straightening out. "Gonna deal with this shit, gonna deal with it now," Lewis Foster said to himself, alone in the car.

* * * * *

Ruby always thought it would have helped to know what Lewis had been so mad about. What could Vanilla have done to make someone that angry? It never made sense, what with Vanilla never really having boyfriends and never causing people trouble. God, she had been such a nice person, cool. Who, what... it just never made sense.

* * * * *

Lewis didn't use the valet; nobody ever did, really, he was more a bouncer than a valet. Lewis parked, strode past the mermaid statue, pulled open the heavy wood doors, and walked in. He didn't acknowledge the door girl. He didn't pay the cover.

Lewis was barely five foot seven, no more than 150 pounds. He had a moustache, at least kind of a moustache; his facial hair was sparse and blonde, ash blonde anyway. But the wispy hairs covered up the cleft pretty well; you couldn't see it at all in dim light. He was only 31, but his hair was already receding. Scrawny, ugly, bad clothes and bad teeth, narrow-set beady eyes; there wasn't much to like about Lewis Foster, certainly not at first sight. Tonight was worse than usual, his beady eyes squinted and angry, his thin lips pursed tight. Yet the valet, the door girl, the bouncer.... "We didn't notice anything unusual," they all later told the police. "Nothin' out of the ordinary, really."

Ruby left the stage, her first set of dances over, that in itself a success. Vanilla was there, her long, feminine arm reaching out for Ruby to help her down the little stairs. The girls almost fell when they tried to "high five" each other, both speedy and drunk. "Miss Sascha, you are hot," Vanilla shouted, her whisper voice as loud as it could go. "You go, girl!"

"Miss Sascha, huh?" Ruby replied. "Yup, that's me."

"Let me get you another one of those coolers," Vanilla offered.

"Got one right over here." Sascha strode to the bar, surprisingly confident in her high heels. She tucked her cover-up under her knees and sat down. She thought Vanilla was right behind her; but she wasn't. Vanilla had turned towards the front door, having heard a familiar voice that Sascha had not.

It was loud, the gunshot, there was no doubt about that. It should have silenced the club just as the bright lights did at closing time; but it didn't. Lewis had pulled a small-caliber pistol from the front of his pants, an old one, shot just once. It hit her just below the stomach, a lucky shot to be sure, if what he wanted was to kill her.

Vanilla crumpled, bending at the waist, her head falling between her legs. She stayed standing, somehow, her hands open palmed, spread-eagled on the floor for balance and support. Yet her head bounced between her legs and arms, back and forth, three, maybe four times. Then, finally, her legs gave out and she fell forward, her face hitting first. The blood pooled under her, thick and heavy, unable to leak out.

Ruby lost her breath, as if someone had punched her in the stomach; hard. She did not scream; in fact, she did not say one single word for over fifteen minutes after the gunshot. And she did not cry, not once, not ever. Instead she stared. She stared at the body, she stared at the rush of dancers and bouncers and middle-aged men who feared potential publicity. She stared as the lights went on and later as the sirens wailed. Her back against the bar, still standing, she stared as Vanilla was lifted onto the gurney and the bloody floor revealed itself beneath where Vanilla had lain.

* * * * *

The club was closed for two days. Two short, short days. On the third day, Ruby and the other girls were back at work, 11:00 a.m., the same routine. Everything had been cleaned up, there was no sign of Vanilla, or Lewis, or the blood, or the matted carpet, or the spilled drinks or the forensic tape.

"Hey."

"Hey."

"Ya OK?"

"Guess. Ruby, when's the funeral? You goin'? You two were close, huh?"

"Sure. Sure we were."

"Hey."

Barbie was putting together the cash register, counting in singles, fives, tens, twenties; adding change—same as she always did at the start of each shift—and didn't say anything until she saw Ruby. Ruby walked right up to her, stopped at the entry table, stared at Barbie. They stared at each other for twenty, thirty seconds.

"Sorry, Ruby. Sorry about Vanilla."

Barbie looked down for a minute. Then she met Ruby's stare again. Ruby said nothing, let the silence build, debated what, whether to respond. She didn't. She walked away. She walked away and went back to the dressing room. She put on her makeup and eyeliner more slowly than usual; she teased her hair more than usual.

She waited for the music to start, waited and waited. And then, finally, a blast mid-song and too loud, shut down for a second, and then a proper start of a slow song intro. She let the music float in, work its way around her, let it sink through her and take hold. It was southern rock and roll, played so loud that under the big speakers you could feel it in your chest. Lynyrd Skynyrd, *Sweet Home Alabama*. It was good music, music that helped people forget.

CHAPTER 6

H e did not remember finding the hotel, how he got the room or how he paid for it. He just remembered waking up hot and sweating, lying in a single bed with a mushy mattress and noisy box springs. There was a small window looking out from the second floor, and noise of the day crept into it. His clothes lay in a heap next to the bed. He hastily put them on, and habitually reached back to check for his wallet in his jeans pocket. When it wasn't there, he panicked and frantically started searching the room.

"Shit," he muttered to himself. "Oh, my God. I can't...."

Then there it was, sticking out from under the bed, one of the tossed bed sheets partially covering it. A wave of relief crept over him. He opened the black leather wallet; everything was still there—bills, credit cards, his ID.

"Shit," he muttered again. "Wow."

An almost overpowering urge to pee swept over him. He searched the hallway for a bathroom, but found nothing. He made his way down the stairs.

"Good morning, morning," an older Thai woman spoke from behind a small desk. "Sunny day. Beach day. You enjoy. Beach day."

"Morning," he replied. "Bathroom?"

"Here, here. I show you." She led him through a hanging bead door, through a private kitchen area, and outside. She kept walking, he kept following.

73

"There." Down a little dirt path was a wooded area. She pointed for him to go that direction. At the end of the path was a hut—just four big sticks and a thatched roof, no walls, and a bench with a hole in the middle. It stank of human waste. Flies buzzed. An ugly, scarred dog—a mix of maybe Labrador and pit bull—panted in the heat about ten yards away, never bothered to even look as Charlie peed into the hole, the stream forceful and thick.

"Thank you," he told the older woman as he made his way back through the building. "Thank you," he said again.

"Again," she asked him, "Stay again?"

He did not understand. "Again? What again?"

"You stay. You stay again. Stay."

"Oh, no, not again. Thank you. Not again." He bowed, smiled at her. "Thank you, but not again." She looked disappointed.

"Again," she said.

"No." He backed out, bowed to her, smiled. "No, thank you."

A modern-looking ceiling fan whirled above, creating a nice breeze. He wiped some sweat from his brow. "Bye. Thank you. Bye."

She said nothing further as he turned and walked out the door. The harsh, almost midday sun momentarily blinded him. His pupils dilated quickly.

Pattaya's streets were bustling that morning, with snarly traffic of rusty little cars and dusty pickup trucks, mopeds and scooters and Thai on bikes pedaling madly.

Just feet from the dirt and stone streets, off to each side, were tumbled slabs of attempted sidewalks, all askew, sinking into the mud. Food vendor carts, steam rising, little piles of garbage spilling rotten fruits, old toothy dogs—barricades for the wide-eyed sailors weaving and laughing along Silahong Road.

And suddenly, unexpectedly, there was Victor.

"Hey."

"Charlie. Man. We didn't know where you were. Could you believe that last night? I mean, holy shit! She loved you, man, could you believe it? You are a god, huh? Did you find her after? Did you fuck her? You had to have fucked her. God, she was incredible. You son-of-a-bitch."

Charlie didn't like it; Victor was too loud, it was embarrassing. He didn't like the profanity, didn't like others looking at them. Loud obnoxious Americans.

"Shut up, Vic. Shut up. I don't know what happened to her. I didn't see her again. Really."

"Yeah, right," his friend chided him. "That was fucking incredible, I saw it. She was all over you, man. Fuck. Absolutely incredible."

Charlie didn't respond, hoped the conversation would end, wanted to change the subject.

"Where did you sleep?"

Victor wouldn't let it go, ignored the question.

"She had the hots for you, man. No doubt."

Charlie didn't respond, just kept walking. Victor finally shut up, looked at his friend, looked away. "Okay, let's find something to eat," he suggested. "There should be something as we get closer to the beach."

"Sure."

Charlie walked a little slower, moved a little heavier, shuffling his way. There were times when Victor was just too much for Charlie—too loud, too American. Victor, now three to four feet ahead, his gait livelier, glanced back every half block or so, his eyes darting over the heads of the four or five native Thai jostling between him and his Navy buddy. Each time Vic checked on his friend, it seemed Charlie was lagging a little further behind. The fifth time he turned around to look, Victor just stopped, waited for Charlie to catch up. But this time, when he looked back, Charlie was not there. Victor cupped his hand over his eyes, scanned the street, the sidewalk, the street traffic.

Feral cats snarled from the alleys; little children, their bare feet calloused and their dark, black hair greasy, cackled in animated, broken English, their sad brown eyes staring up with dark hunger for pockets of loose change from the tall, white, strange foreign men.

As Charlie knelt forward and down, his eyes locking in on the child beggar he simply could not ignore, he was bumped from behind. It was someone's knee, or maybe a shove. He fell forward and caught himself by pushing his hands forward, leaving him balancing on all four limbs. The child beggar ran away quickly, as if his mission had been accomplished. Yet Charlie had given him nothing.

Just then, with brutal force, a weathered boot swung into Charlie's rib cage. It stole the wind from him; his eyes rolled back a little. Just as he coughed out a breath, another kick hit him on the opposite side, just as hard. A white handkerchief was thrust into his face, slimy, wet. Small but strong hands compressing the cloth over his nose and mouth. A wicked smell of astringent, something unfamiliar to him, reeked through the cloth and quickly burned into Charlie's airway, singeing his nasal passages and throat lining.

At that same moment, the door to the street, green-painted hardwood, heavy iron latches and clumsy iron handle, was pushed open at that same moment. Two more men, angry brown eyes, crinkled crow's feet around them, rotting and missing teeth, helped the other two—those with the weathered boots—lift up the heavy American sailor and throw him, like a sack, into the dark room. The door was shut with a shove, the street left behind with just several onlookers gaping, but too afraid to do anything but move on.

A shaft of light, like a flashlight beam, came through a hole in the thatched ceiling and lit up a five-by-five foot corner of the otherwise pitch-black room. Charlie lay half in and half out of the light, his right side lit up and his left dark. His hands were tied tightly behind his back with thick twine. A long piece of cotton cloth, twisted tightly, gagged him. He struggled to breathe through his nose. He counted backward from ten to try to stay calm, to try to keep from hyperventilating.

They threw his wallet into the lit-up area of the floor. It fell open, money and credit cards already gone. Three or four men were speaking Thai he could not understand, seemingly quarreling with each other, when one walked away from the rest.

Charlie saw him coming towards him, instinctively bowed his head to his chest and looked away. The man stood over him, moments only—to Charlie an eternity. The man bent down, picked up a heavy object. It was difficult to tell exactly, but it appeared to be a square metal pipe of some sort, three or maybe four feet long, straight edges, nuts and bolts protruding. They hit him twice, the first time, a mighty swing, across Charlie's back and shoulder blades. The second time, a shorter, choppier swing, across his head and face. Charlie slumped further over from the blow, then, mercifully, he finally passed out cold.

* * * * *

When Charlie woke up, he was alone. His bound wrists ached. His upper back was numb, his left shoulder blade felt cracked and was opened up and coated with blood, his lower back popped when he moved. The sun had moved further up in the sky, and the little square of light now covered him completely. The heat became overwhelming. He began to sweat profusely. Passed out again.

That was as much as Charlie would remember. From that moment, and for what must have been a full three weeks later, by his own rough calculations, Charlie remembered nothing. Perhaps that was for the better, for perhaps the mind knows what it should—and should not—keep.

Charlie did remember waking up in the military hospital. Not waking up, really, but his eyes opening and staring at the ceiling.

He remembered the horsefly slamming into the overhead light, again and again, a kamikaze mission from which the big pest never seemed to die. Charlie lay on his back, his feet stretching out over the end of the metal hospital bed, and he watched the fly. He wanted it to die, to complete its mission. He begged for it, prayed for it.

"Die. Die already. Please," he spoke, as if to the ceiling, softly at first.

"Die. Die already," this time a little louder. Loud enough that the nurse heard him. It was the first time he had spoken; the first time, in fact, his eyes had even opened since he had arrived three days' earlier. His arms were bandaged, his chest and shoulders in a sort of plaster cast. The sides of his mouth were bruised and still a little bloody. The nurse rushed over, dabbed at his mouth with a wet cloth that had been lying on the metal cart next to his bed.

"Okay, okay. It's okay. You're going to be all right. You were beaten up. Pretty badly."

She kept talking. She had a Midwestern accent, nondescript, wonderful to him at the time; a beautiful voice, he remembered. He didn't respond, his head still staring at the ceiling, but his eyes slowly turned her direction.

"You're lucky you're alive, really. Your spine, well, it was close. Dr. Guenther did a great job. Eight hours of surgery. We didn't expect you to be awake yet." The nurse was American, with red hair and freckles. She was from South Dakota, she said, Pierre. She was gentle. Nice. Kind. Like a nurse is supposed to be.

Charlie started to comprehend, just a little. But when he tried to speak, his mouth was too blistered, or too dry, or both. She sensed him trying to respond, saw the little movements of his tongue.

"No, don't talk. You need to rest." The voice, crystal clear, perfect enunciation, so feminine and beautiful.

The nurse dabbed at the sides of his mouth again, the white cloth now streaked crimson. Charlie decided he liked her. But even though he thought that at the time, he would not remember her later, and he would never see her again.

The morphine from the IV kicked in again. His eyes turned back to the ceiling, then rolled up into his eyelids. She stroked his arm, grasped his hand, and folded it into hers. She leaned forward toward him, her face inappropriately close to his neck. Her words grew even softer, the voice more beautiful than ever, accentuated by the morphine.

"There. There. It's going to be okay. You're a good boy."

She looked around the hospital ward. No one else was there. She moved even closer.

"You're my good boy. You are not alone. I am here. You are fine. You are going to be fine." She wanted to let him know he wasn't dying.

He was no longer conscious. He wouldn't be for another six days. He would stay in that hospital bed for another thirty-one days. He never saw her, the nurse, or maybe he did but by the time he was conscious enough to know it, she was gone. Or maybe, he thought to himself years later, she was still there and he did see her, but without the morphine, she just wasn't the same. Maybe without the morphine, she wasn't special, the voice more a hallucination than reality. He didn't know, never would.

Charlie stayed at a rehabilitation center in Honolulu for six more months. It would be almost one full year to the day before he would be back on the mainland: North Island, San Diego. Then a flight to Seattle, then a bus to Whidbey Air Station for three weeks of training, and finally to Bremerton, Washington. There he would board the *USS AO-51 Ashtabula*, the "Pachyderm of the Pacific," a behemoth of a supply ship in service for over forty years, due to be moth-balled after its final Westpac, or Western Pacific, tour that summer.

* * * * *

It was a relief to walk on board, to salute the officer of the deck, to find his bunk, to unpack his gear and put his books on a little shelf. His muscles ached, his walk not so fluid, his back curved the wrong way and his left shoulder too far front. But he was alive. Just keep breathing, the doctors told him so many times. He took in a deep breath, and when he did, stale air from the bowels of the old ship rushed in, then back out. *I'm okay*, he thought to himself.

The *Ashtabula* would be his duty station for the next two years. During that time, Charlie would follow orders well, and give orders sparingly, but clearly. Those above him in the chain of command respected his ability, tenacity, and leadership skills. Those below him respected his intelligence, calm, and unwavering competence. He didn't make many friends while on board; he wanted to work, and he worked hard. He stayed on board during port calls. He worked out religiously in the tiny space below deck, often alone, his body still recovering but becoming muscular and even tighter than before. His neck, shoulders, chest and biceps grew wider and stronger; his legs, from inactivity, a little skinnier.

His job was to coordinate underway replenishments. The *Ashtabula* would steam as close as possible to a carrier, both enormous vessels traveling at roughly 15 knots in all types of seas, often no more than two hundred yards apart. A seaman, under his command, would fire a gun rigged with rope towards the carrier. If he did it wrong, the supply ship's officers and crew would hoot and holler, berate him; the metal ball at the end of the string falling into the ocean. If he did it right, it would "catch," and the men on board the carrier would begin pulling and pulling, first string, then heavier string, then twine, eventually either thick hoses to couple up to the carrier or metal wires to carry buckets of food and supplies over the open ocean. It was a complicated process, difficult always and especially so in heavy seas. It required teamwork, coordination, and planning. And if something went wrong, it was obvious to everyone.

Charlie and his crew did well. Extremely well. Efficient, quick, and without errors.

He made full lieutenant, earlier than expected given his year of sick leave. The executive officer, XO, awarded him a meritorious service medal.

Charlie wrote to his family, not often but enough. He called his mother whenever he was able, even spoke politely to his stepfather. He kept his uniforms perfect, his quarters spotless. He hadn't smoked since Pattaya; didn't start again after his hospital stay, so really he didn't "quit," he just didn't start up again.

He was proud of his service, that day just one month before he would transfer duty stations. He hoped it would be to another aircraft carrier.

His roommate turned on the tiny television crammed way up between two metal brackets in the corner of their quarters. Casey Kasom was on, people were dancing; black teenagers with afros wearing pastel bell-bottom pants and skinny, fair-skinned white women with freckles and stringy blonde hair. The TV speakers were tinny, and the reception poor. But the music was good; Charlie liked it, even if he didn't understand the words. Glenn Frey, *The Heat Is On*. Charlie crawled into his cot. His watch wouldn't start until they were well underway again the next morning. He had a headache; took two of the aspirin he kept next to his bunk, and shortly fell asleep.

RUBY. 1984. 22 YEARS OLD. MEMPHIS, TENNESSEE.

There were times when Ruby needed to stop thinking, to turn off her mind. Times when real life was just too much. There were times when she wanted to be simple, happy. But she knew she her brain was too strong for that.

Sometimes she liked to cook. It helped her not to think. She could just think about the food. The potatoes. She tried to think about going to the store and looking at them; there were the big Idaho potatoes, the small red potatoes, and there was some other kind, too, maybe russet. Maybe it was the potatoes that had screwed up the potato salad. Maybe she had used the wrong kind of potatoes. But could that really make that much of a difference? She couldn't think of anything else, though. She had followed her Mom's recipe on everything, and there was just nothing else that made sense. It had to be the Idaho potatoes were the wrong ones, and she should have used the small red ones, or one of the other kinds.

And then she just couldn't think of potatoes anymore.

At the club there were no mindless distractions. She was always conscious of what she was doing, conscious that she was standing there naked but for little, sparkly bottoms. Even though the other girls were just as scantily clad, it never felt that way. But that was basically it; dancing was what she now did for a living. It was awful, really, for her, each and every time. And she still felt nervous, scared even. And she felt ashamed. She was a stripper, and she didn't like the idea of it, never would. The only thing that helped her get through it was the money. So she tried to think about the money, rationalized it was a job to make money, and it wouldn't be for that much longer. It was a job, a temporary one, she tried to convince herself.

"What's your real name?" he mumbled, his eyes closed. She didn't care.

"Ruby," she said.

"No, your real name."

Ruby laughed to herself. Nobody ever believed her real name was Ruby, so she just lied instead.

"Stephanie."

"Stephanie," he whispered. "That's a pretty name."

Ruby—"Sascha"—was in the back room of the club. Two old couches, the fabric torn and faded, were pushed up against one wall, and two newer ones were to each side. Practically buried in the deep cushions of one of the old couches was a middle-aged man, his hair combed over, his glasses askew. He had one hand on Ruby's left hip, his other hand at his side. Ruby had her back to him, lap dancing, her hands each on one knee, her head bowed between her legs. Her bra was lying next to them on the couch, thrown there two songs earlier. Her bikini bottoms were still on, and so were her 6-inch- heeled white shoes, but nothing else. She wiggled her hips side to side, and then up and down on her tiptoes, and back.

Ruby deftly reached out and brushed his right hand away from her. She didn't say anything, just brushed it away. He kept trying to inch his hand up the outside of her thigh. She brushed it away again, turned around to face him. She gently took both of his hands into hers, guided them to her waist for just a few moments. As he tried to reach up towards her breasts, she grabbed his hands by the wrists, very gently, and moved them back to the couch. She said nothing. Moments later, the song ended.

"That was four. Two for one again, honey, if you want two more songs." She looked away, played with her hair. He didn't seem interested in another lap dance, acted frustrated.

She knew he was irritated at her for not letting him touch her. She didn't care; she was relieved, knew he had enough.

She turned to face him again. At first he didn't respond.

"Do you want two more?" She asked again, a little more tone to her voice.

"I'm... no, I'm... "

His stammering irritated her.

"$40 then." She reached for her bra as she said it, started putting it on. Then she turned and grabbed her white, lacy cover-up while he dug out his wallet.

He took out two $20 bills and tossed them at her. She laughed a little.

"Thanks. Would you like to tip my garter?"

It's always worth trying for a tip, she thought to herself, although she didn't hold out much hope for this guy. She noticed the shoes. It was usually the shoes that gave them away. Polished dress shoes were a good sign; some attention to detail, cared about what other people thought. Polished dress shoes usually meant a good, solid tip; maybe nothing extraordinary, but certainly decent. Casual shoes were hit or miss; sometimes nothing, sometimes a lot extra. The men with the real money didn't need to wear dress shoes. Then the losers, Ruby had figured out, were the men with ratty wing-tips or, even worse, tasseled loafers. Still working the grind, day after day, but obviously not caring much about what people thought about their appearance. They didn't tip well, if at all. This guy was wearing dress shoes, but they were worn thin and were dirty.

"I'm.. Just a little ..." He started stammering again.

"Next time. Don't worry about it then." She bailed him out.

"Thank you very much," she said, sweet and polite.

She grabbed her bag. A wad of dollar bills, the $40 she had just stuffed in there, and another $100 she had pulled from her regular, an Asian doctor. Or at least that's what he claimed he did for a living.

Ruby walked back toward the main stage. Her friend Bonnie was dancing; "Farrah" was her stage name, which made sense. She was a tall white girl, with long blonde hair feathered back and styled so that she looked a little like Farrah Fawcett. Ruby didn't think it was very creative, but it made some sense. Ruby pulled out a dollar bill as she walked by the main stage, leaned up and held it out for Bonnie. Bonnie danced over, flashed Ruby a big smile.

Ruby whistled at her friend Bonnie, "Whoo-hoo." They both giggled.

Bonnie danced away toward two young men. They looked barely 21 to Ruby when she glanced over. They were hollering. *Nothing but trouble*, Ruby thought to herself. At that age, they never had any money, and they always had to pitch in to buy their buddy one dance. It just wasn't worth it. She ignored them, went up to the bar.

"Vodka cranberry, Topper."

"Sure, Sascha." Topper had been there for years. His white shirts were frayed, his black vest a little gray after years of washing. Ruby always wanted them to buy him some new uniforms. She watched him make her drink, put a five-dollar bill on the bar.

"Hey, thanks. Really." Topper meant it. The $1.50 tip meant a lot to him. Ruby knew his wife had just lost her job, and none of their three kids were yet out of high school. That bastard Steve—the owner—paid the bartenders less than minimum wage, regardless of experience or how long they had worked at the club. Topper didn't do well with the customers when it came to tips; he wasn't into sports, wasn't very good at small talk. The girls liked him, though, because he generally just left them alone—which they liked—but at the same time, he always noticed when they came up to the bar looking for something. Some of the other bartenders just seemed to ignore the girls when they came for drinks, or worse, tried to hit on them. And Topper was good about remembering the drinks the girls liked, and how much alcohol they wanted in the pours.

Topper tapped the highball glass on the bar before he gave it to Ruby.

"Thanks again," he said.

"Sure, Topper. Thank you."

Such little civilities helped them both cope with the club, and they both knew they were among the very few—except for the booze, which was never to great excess—who had somehow managed to stay away from the drugs and the sleaze. They both respected the other, in their own way, they both knew it, neither ever said it. A little nod of the head, a half-wink. *Everyone knew pretty much everything, right*, Ruby thought to herself. "Good guy," she mumbled as she walked away from the bar.

She sensed someone looking at her, from over near satellite stage four, almost twenty feet away. She glanced that direction, found out she was right. When she caught his eye, he looked away a little, trying not to get caught staring. She liked the fact he looked away. That was a good sign; he wouldn't be too bad, probably halfway decent. She hated the true perverts, the arrogant asses who would stare with impunity, feeling entitled because they had some money in their pockets.

"Hi," Ruby said as she approached him. She made a sexy, innocent face and stretched out her southern drawl a little. "Would you like a dance?"

"Hi." He didn't answer the question, just left it at "hi." Ruby put her arm around his shoulder, literally sat right down in his lap, her long legs stretched out and her high heels tapping on the floor. She moved her face close to his, to the side, and whispered in his ear.

"Would you like a dance?"

He didn't say anything further. She didn't say anything further. She stood up, adjusted her costume a little, reached out and helped him out of his chair. She manipulated his arm so he would escort her, but obviously, she was taking the lead. He followed as she led him to the back to the couches. She guided him into one, and he sat down and sank back into the cushions. He let her put his hands to his sides, and he jumped a little— somewhat startled by it—when she reached down and pushed his knees apart. His reaction helped Ruby realize he wasn't local. *Could be a good one*, she thought. She looked around to see if any of the nasty girls were close to them, in the back, within his view. She was pleased none were.

He was practically perfect. He kept his hands at his sides the whole time. She barely had to suggest he buy two more songs and he said yes or just nodded his head. He even had decent cologne and was chewing spearminty gum so his breath didn't stink. And he kept saying yes for a full hour and a half; long enough for her to tally up $280 in her head.

"That's good. I mean, we'd better stop ...," he finally said. Ruby didn't argue with him.

"Sure, darlin'. I understand. Thank you, you're sweet. Sascha, remember. I work days Mondays and Tuesdays, Friday and Sunday nights. Usually." She wanted him to come back, wanted him to become a regular. But she knew the odds were against her, because by then Shawna, an older girl who broke all the rules—gave the nastiest dances possible—was already in the back, and he had noticed the type of dances she was giving her customers.

He slowly counted out $20 bills....twelve, thirteen, fourteen, then he paused, counted out one more for an even $300. She watched him, caressing his neck and face the whole time.

"Is that okay?" he asked, almost embarrassed. She thought about going for more; he'd probably do it. Then her conscience kicked in a little.

"Sure, it's fine. Thank you. You're a doll. What's your name, anyway, so I can remember you?"

"Rob," he said. She knew it wasn't his real name.

"Well, thank you, Rob. Sascha." Ruby kissed him on the cheek. "I had fun. Thank you, Rob." It may have not been fun, but it certainly wasn't bad. He glanced back at her once before heading out the door.

She tried two more guys after that. One talked to her forever but didn't want a private dance. The other went for a two-for-one, but seemed pissed when she wouldn't let him touch her. She really wanted another $40 so she could leave with $400 after her $50 pay out and tipping the DJ, which was a really good night. She could put half of that, like she usually did, on top of the stack of bills in the safety deposit box at Continental Western. Ruby let her mind wander again, trying to ignore her customer. She didn't resist as much, let him touch her hips, and got him to go for the two extra dances.

In the dressing room, she kept thinking about his greasy hair, and the smell of fast food on his breath. It turned her stomach, and she sat for a minute holding her head in her hands, consciously trying to forget. A short wave of nausea hit her, but then it went away. She looked over at her purse; decided to count the money again. That usually helped. A little over $400 after pay out and tips. Not bad.

She gave a little sigh, took off her skimpy dance outfit and slipped into a pair of baggy jeans, a muscle shirt, and a loose gray sweatshirt on top of that. It was a warm night, but she liked the feel of the sweatshirt, liked how it covered her up. She fiddled with her long hair, now reeking of smoke, and twisted it and tied it up into a knot; it was that long.

When she got home, she slid the old key into the lock slowly, trying not to make any noise. Then she unlocked the deadbolt the same way. The door creaked some as she opened it, but not much. She shut it behind her, slowly, locked the deadbolt, walked into the living room and took off her shoes. Barefoot now, she glided across the hardwood floor to the kitchen and put her purse, duffel bag, and the keys on the little table.

Ruby made her way to the old, tiled bathroom, pulled down her jeans and peed. While still on the toilet, she wiggled out of the jeans completely, then she stood up with just the baggy sweatshirt and her panties on. She kicked the jeans to the corner radiator, turned on the makeup mirror. She knew she smelled like the club, she could feel it on her—all sweat and perfume and smoke and liquor; mostly smoke. She badly wanted to take her makeup off and take a bath right then and there, but she was just too tired. She took out her contacts and wandered down the hall.

By the time she got to the bedroom, she couldn't see very well, because it was pitch black and the light from the make-up mirror had blinded her a little. But she knew he was there, because she saw the lump in the covers. She felt relieved; he was home in bed, asleep. She reached out and touched the lump in the covers. He rolled over, but it was clear he was sound asleep. She sat on the edge of the bed for a minute, took off the sweatshirt and gently put it on the floor. After she crawled under the covers, she reached one hand out and touched his shoulder, rubbed it back and forth.

"Goodnight, Wade. Goodnight, honey bun."

She tried to fall asleep, but her mind wandered back to the club, and the last song of the night was stuck in her head.

Madonna, *Like a Virgin*. What the hell, Ruby laughed to herself. What were they playing that song for, in Tiffany's? Like a virgin. There wasn't a single virgin in there, obviously.

She turned onto her side, and consciously tried not to think of anything at all. Ten minutes later, she was asleep, but even so, her breathing was labored, her legs were restless, and her dreams were all nightmares.

CHAPTER 7

A shiny, hardwood floor covered the gymnasium of the armory at Salem, Oregon's Naval Reserve Center. The basketball hoops suspended from the ceiling had been pulled up. Bleachers on the sides were pushed and folded against the tile walls. A curtained stage at the north end was bare; piles of cardboard boxes and stacks of papers crowded the edges within reach, dark empty space behind them.

Heavy electrical cords, duct-taped to the floor, criss-crossed the room. A huge fan pushed the air from one corner. The double doors were propped open in an attempt to force warm air out.

Neatly lined up five to a row, five rows deep, were exactly twenty-five gray metal desks. Each had one aluminum and vinyl swivel desk chair that fit neatly into the slot of the desk, and in front of each desk were two aluminum side chairs which were, over time, gradually scraping the finish off the heavily polished floor.

Arching thirty feet above the floor were cathedral-quality, heavy wooden crossbeams. Bolted to them were metal rods holding four banks of overhead lights covered in wire mesh. One bank of lights was turned on, the rest were dark. It was 0200 hours—two in the morning—on a Thursday night in late October, 1989. The next night would be Halloween.

His military rank was now full commander, so three solid bars ran across the epaulets on his starched and creased white shirt. The left side of his jacket was emblazoned with two full rows of ribbons and medals: a green one with two white stripes, a red one with a solitary white star; perhaps a dozen in all. One, nondescript from the rest, was a bronze star for valor.

Charlie sat alone at his desk in that armory, that night, second from the front, third row in. No one else was in the room. No one else was in the building. He stared again at the thickly bound document in front of him. Then he looked toward the corner of his desk, at the stack of maybe fifteen, twenty more thickly bound documents, all with a similar red cover page.

Just three days earlier, CDR Charles McGurn was still at sea, the XO of the *USS FF-1098 Glover*, a fast frigate steaming from Hawaii back to its home port in Bremerton, Washington. He had been suffering some bad headaches; the CO noticed and had ordered him against his will to the carrier in the battle group, to the medical staff. Arrangements were made for a helicopter flight.

The copter hovered over the frigate, not actually touching down. A rope was lowered, a mesh sling chair at the end of it. The petty officer's muscles strained as he moved a long metal pole, similar to a boat hook or a gaff, with a hook on the end; he moved it around like it was a big magic wand, eventually catching it on the wire dangling from the helicopter overhead to ground the static charge. Charlie climbed into the webbing, was hoisted up to the copter, and it quickly swooped away from the frigate and back to the carrier.

Once on the huge aircraft carrier, Charlie, as ordered, wound his way from the flight deck, through the labyrinthine passageways and narrow stairwells to the medical deck, and eventually to the med tech.

"Just some headaches, it's fine." Charlie started to explain to the tech.

"Sir, I need a history. Bear with me." The medic was no more than 21 years old. Acne covered his chin.

"Headaches. I need you to be more specific, sir. How often? How often would you say you have a headache?"

"Off and on. No more than twice a week, maybe three times."

"Okay, that's a start." The medic wrote it down. Looked up again.

"How bad. Rate the pain, one to ten. Where is it? In the front, the back."

"Oh, no more than a three or four. Really," Charlie lied. "Nowhere in particular."

"Anything else? Blurred vision, loss of appetite, nausea..." The medic was young, but well trained.

"A little nausea, maybe. A little blurry sometimes." The truth, but not the whole truth.

* * * * *

That night, Charlie slept in temporary quarters on the carrier, tossed and turned. He woke up several times, disoriented and sweaty. Only after his eyes adjusted and he scanned the room did he get his senses back and calm down. He was impatient; he wanted to get back to his frigate.

The next morning, after all the tests had been done and after the lab personnel on the night shift had completed their analysis, Charlie was notified that he was to meet with one of them. Instead, when he arrived at sick bay, he was told to wait. It was a full hour before he was escorted into a small office, an office where medical degrees were hung on the metal bulwarks.

"So, what have we found out, sir?" Charlie asked respectfully.

Captain Meyer was about to retire; this would be his last sea duty. His family awaited him in San Diego, where he had already bought a home, up in the hills with a small ocean view far down the valley. His moustache, gray and long, covered part of his lips as he spoke.

"Well, we've got some results that give me pause, young Commander. I've got your medical records here, but they only go back two years. Nothing unusual there; pretty perfect health, actually, for that short time. But I don't have access to the earlier records. We'd have to wire for them, use up some bandwidth. But I want to see them."

He paused, searched Charlie's eyes. The doctor knew there would be something in those records, assumed a previous traumatic injury. Charlie didn't say anything.

"No, I don't, really. I don't need the records; I've made a decision. You're not going to like this, Commander. I know you. But I don't have a choice here. As much as I know you will fight me on it, I have to send you off. Right away." He kept his head down, his balding head shiny from the bright overhead lights.

"Off?" Charlie was incredulous. "Off the ship? Doc, you…?"

The senior officer interrupted him.

"Don't. Don't fight me on this. This isn't a discussion. You're on medical leave. Starting right now, right this minute. I'm sending you to Portland, to see a colleague of mine."

Charlie didn't respond. He looked at the captain, stared for a minute.

"Look, it may be nothing. But your x-rays show trauma to the spine. I presume it's in your medical records, severe enough there's no doubt you felt it at the time. And there's impingement on the nerve. Enough so that we can't take chances. I'm worried about your eyesight, Charlie. I can't take chances on that, and neither can you. I'll put all the paperwork together, and Dr. Simmons—private guy, but Champus will cover it. We went to medical school together. It's serious, Charlie."

"But Doc, I feel fine. I really…" He paused, reflecting for a minute, trying to think of some convincing argument.

"Dismissed." It was an order, sure, but a soft one, an understanding one. It was an order issued for the right reason; to make sure this good naval officer received the proper medical treatment. There could be no further delay. *Time was of the essence, and it might be too late already*, Captain Meyer thought to himself. He stood up slowly.

Charlie stood up, too. He squared himself, as if to salute, then remembered he was on board, with no cover on.

"Thank you. Thank you, sir."

Dr. Meyer responded formally.

"Good luck, Commander." He meant it.

* * * * *

That had been three short days ago. Charlie took a helicopter back to the *USS Glover*, informed the CO, packed his belongings, and flew back to the carrier—all within less than twelve hours. Within the next twelve hours, he was on an A7, his gear and medical records in hand, flying to Diego Garcia, a small island in the middle of the Indian Ocean. Then he took a commercial flight to Portland, where a reservist picked him up and drove him to Salem.

"Medical leave, huh? Lucky bastard. All we've got for ya is a bunch of paperwork. Reservist applications, lots of 'em. It's that time of year. You'll love it. Easy stuff." The CO of the reserve base didn't know Charlie. The last thing Charlie wanted was "easy stuff." The thought of spending all day sorting through reservist applications almost turned his stomach.

"Sir, yes, sir," Charlie responded.

"Yeah, at ease, Commander. You're going to have to take it down a notch around here. Pretty quiet these days. You start salutin' everybody around here and somebody's likely to slap ya. Just make sure you make those medical appointments, will ya? I have strict orders to make sure you do that."

The CO kept a tape player on his desk; judging from the stack of cassettes next to the machine the CO loved jazz, oldies. Charlie paused, took in the scene; the big old Armory, the sleepy CO, all the papers strewn about, the tape playing. It was Louis Armstrong, *Duke's Place*.

RUBY. 1984. 22 YEARS OLD. MEMPHIS, TENNESSEE.

Clouds of smoke billowed through the room as Wade sat on the sofa, laughing with his buddies as his heavy, steel-toed work boots kicked the flamingo-like legs of the old, maple coffee table. Across the top of the table and strewn throughout the living room, was a panoply of bongs, roach clips, buds, seeds, stems and baggies, along with Coke cans, bags of chips and pretzels, stacked cardboard boxes filled with half-eaten pizza crusts. Tangled Nintendo wires wound their way through the chaos. The smell of stale beer and pot permeated the little house.

The heavy, flowery curtains were mostly all drawn, but they didn't come together all the way, so a sliver of bright daylight came in through the middle of the picture window, a smoky laser beam slicing into the room. Jesse, "Hot Rod," had just turned 17; he was a big boy with broad shoulders, shoulder-length, curly brown hair, and a baby face. He was holding a full can of beer that was splattering and foaming as he danced alone in the middle of the light beam, his baggy jeans unbuttoned and falling to his knees. The other boys, Wade, John E., and Matt—"Haystack"—were all sitting on the couch, oblivious to Hot Rod's dancing antics and falling pants. John E. was busy lining up bumps; chopping up a little pile of powder with a razor blade, separating it into four tight lines. Haystack was rolling a joint, making sure the end crinkled together nice and tight. Wade was sitting off by himself in one of the droopy wingbacks, his eyes, red and swollen, were almost closed, and he was humming something.

Wade Santorelli was 22. He was a gorgeous young man. Fine bone structure, symmetrical features, sharp jaw line. He kept his hair long, never wanted to cut it, and it flowed almost to his waist. His eyes were wide set, light blue, thick eyelashes and eyebrows. When Ruby had first met him, Wade was homeless, mostly by choice. She took him in as if he were a lost puppy. She tried to help him get a job, go to school; sometimes he tried, usually he didn't.

Ruby had spent most of the morning visiting her sister. They had lunch together, and then Ruby went grocery shopping. It was 3:00 p.m. when Ruby pulled up in front of her house in her Infiniti sedan. She parked on the street. She pulled a gallon of milk and two paper grocery bags out of the back seat, and struggled a little as she carried them up the front steps.

Cooper Street ran north/south. Young Avenue ran diagonal to the grid, kind of northeast/southwest. Several restaurants and some mom and pop stores, a hair salon and some bars, all nestled around the intersection of Cooper and Young. The little neighborhood there was trying to overcome the blight, but it was a see-saw battle. Every day, it seemed the slums crept closer as it extended north out of the city. But just as often, a young couple would buy another house and work hard to fix it up. Neighborhood watches did battle with teenage gangs. During the day, shop owners swept up litter from the sidewalks; at night, cruisers threw bottles out their car windows. And so it went.

Ruby had rented a little house on the very edge of what most considered the border of the Cooper/Young neighborhood. It was an old bungalow with metal grates on all the windows, grates on the screen door, boarded-up basement windows. The front yard, especially where she chained up her dog, was mostly just barren dirt. She warned the neighbors that the dog was vicious, but he wasn't.

She loved the little house, with its overhanging eaves and flower boxes, a little gingerbread around the windows and doors. Inside, even though she didn't own it, Ruby had painted the walls, torn up the carpet and exposed the hardwood floors, hand-sewn window treatments, and polished up the woodwork. She took her cash from the club and, bit by bit, bought furniture and knick-knacks, antique lamps, a nice TV in a wood cabinet. She wanted to buy a house, badly; but a home loan was out of the question without proof of income, and that she never could provide.

Everything seemed quiet when she walked up the steps. She set the milk and one of the grocery bags down, checked to see if the front door was locked—it wasn't—pushed down on the latch and gently kicked open the door with her foot.

She smelled the pot right away, crinkled her nose. *Damn*, she thought to herself. Then she turned on the light.

Everything was quiet, the boys all pretty much passed out. Wade was laying face down on the area rug, not moving. John E. was on the couch, his arms outstretched, his legs splayed apart, his head back, snoring. Haystack was playing with the Nintendo cords and looked up when he heard the door swing open. Hot Rod was in the kitchen, looking for another beer.

Ruby looked around, looked at her house. She slowly set down the grocery bags on the tile in the entryway.

She didn't say anything, started to cry a little, softly, but just for a few moments. Then her eyes hardened. Ruby shook off the tears, picked up the grocery bags and the milk, and went to the kitchen. Hot Rod was standing there with the refrigerator door open. He looked at her, didn't say anything, hung his head down. She ignored him. Aroused by the sounds, John E. had woken up, and he peeked into the kitchen. Ruby ignored him, too; until he slunk back to the living room.

Hot Rod, expecting some sort of commotion when he saw Ruby, was surprised when she said nothing. He proceeded to grab three beer cans from the fridge, then looked at her, as if he had just been caught stealing. Still, she said nothing. *Guess it's okay*, he thought to himself.

"Hey, you make any money today?" he asked Ruby, trying to act normal.

"A little," Ruby answered, her attitude cold, callous.

"Cool," Hot Rod replied. He staggered a little, grabbed at the wall to steady himself. "That's..." He burped, laughed a little. "Sorry. That's....that's cool. At least you made some money. Now we can all party."

Ruby didn't respond. She put away the groceries—some into the cupboards, some into the refrigerator, a few into the freezer. She listened as the boys were waking up, shuffling about. She heard the front door open, shut again. Then everything was quiet.

Within fifteen minutes of her arrival home, they were gone. All four of them. All four including Wade, who hollered something—rather, mumbled something incoherent in a loud voice—about cleaning up later. She knew better, though.

Ruby made herself a sandwich, took a shower, did her hair. Then she slowly packed her duffel bag with her high heels, little outfits, tiny g-strings, and bras. She left for work, to Tiffany's; left the house as it was, left it as Wade and his friends had done.

It was 2:30 in the morning when she got back home. Nothing in the house had changed. Wade was not there.

The next morning, through most of the day, she cleaned, picked up, threw away. She called her sister, cried, bitched. She called her friends Blake and Stacey, wanted to tell them but couldn't. They would tell her Wade had to leave, like they always did. She couldn't deal with that, didn't want to hear what she already knew.

By late that afternoon, the house was almost back to its usual good order but for some stains in the rug still soaking with chemicals and four full trash bags out back. Ruby sat on the front porch, filling out forms for her fall art classes at the university. She was all dressed up, hoping Wade would come home, thought he would have by then.

A hoopdie drove by, tricked-out rims, loud bass resonating from it, boom boom boom. Two young men slouched in the car, and they slowed down, stared at Ruby as they drove by. She knew better, but couldn't help herself as she swore at them to leave her the fuck alone. Her voice was soft, though, soft enough there was no way they would hear her over the loud music. Shortly after they drove by, she went back in, wrapped herself in a thin blanket and stretched out on the bed for a nap.

When Ruby woke up the next morning, Wade was there, dressed, sober. He acted as if nothing had happened, and she tried to forget it had.

* * * * *

A full year went by but little changed. Wade found a job as a carriage driver, working for the tourists in downtown Memphis. Ruby loved his horse, an old Belgian named Cotton. Ruby thought it was cruel to force Cotton to pull the carriages; Wade laughed at her when she talked about it. The gang came over to the house—Haystack, John E., Hot Rod, and quite a few others—but Ruby wouldn't let them stay for more than a couple minutes. She did what she could, but she couldn't break their peer pressure.

"Where are you going?" Ruby asked, often.

"I don't know. Just goin' out." Wade never said much more than that. If she pushed, sometimes he would fight back a little.

"Look, I'm not doin' nothin', okay? Can't I hang out with my friends? You won't let them over here, so I have to go there, okay?"

Sometimes she tried to argue, sometimes she didn't. Most often it was an exhausting back and forth, not worth the effort.

He found and took her cash, until she started to hide most of it.

"Gotta eat," he said when she caught him one afternoon. "Look, if I could make the dough like you do, I would, you know. You're lucky."

She didn't feel lucky.

"You can," she told him. "Why don't you go take your clothes off and dance. You're good lookin' enough."

He gave her a sheepish grin back, didn't respond further. She stared at him.

"But you wouldn't do that, would you? I guess I'm the only one here with any guts. Or is it desperation?" With that, she walked out.

Sure there were times when they were together, just the two of them, and things were good. She loved him then, loved his sense of humor, his quiet ways, and when they went out and he wore what she asked him to; then she felt proud, talked about how he was going to mechanics school the next year, how nice his parents were. She called him her "Baby Cakes," which he tolerated when no one else was around.

But mechanics school never happened, and the weeks together became fewer. Time passed, nothing changed. He was like an apple from a tree; sweet and tart when first picked, but all too quickly bitter and rotten.

Their romance, if it could be called that, didn't end with a fight or affair. There was painfully little drama. Instead, it died on the vine, a slow death, spring turning to summer, then a dragging fall and a cold winter. He stayed away longer and longer; she stopped caring. Nights turned into weekends, weekends into weeks, until she was more surprised to see him than not. And then he just never came back.

The few belongings he had she put into the basement, put his toiletries into a plastic bag. She went to her parents for Thanksgiving; lied about her life, laughed at the family jokes, and tried not to act bored. When she came home after the holiday, put her bag away, she noticed he must have been there; his things were gone. There was no note, no message on the answering machine.

There was that moment, of course, when she realized it was over. It was the first time in her life that she realized people change, drift, and maybe that's okay. That moment occurred the Saturday after the Thanksgiving holiday, as she was in the kitchen, cleaning out the sink and putting dishes into the old dishwasher. She stared out the kitchen window, out at the backyard and a few barren trees and crinkly, brown, wintery grass. Two or three big leaves from the oak tree fluttered down; it was always the last tree in the yard to lose its leaves. Some brown leaves even lasted through the whole winter.

There was almost no breeze. One of the oak leaves caught a little draft and crashed right into the window, startling her. She paused, stared at her hands for a bit. Finally she shook her head and turned on the little TV that sat on the counter. And that was pretty much it.

The next day she changed the locks, thought that would be a good idea. She called her sister. They talked about it for a while, but not all that long. Her sister said what sisters are supposed to say.

"He was an asshole. You know you didn't love him. He sure didn't treat you right."

"Yep, I know."

"You deserve better, you know. And now you actually might, so, ya know, now you'll find someone, if you'll just let yourself."

"Sure. I suppose."

"I can't believe he didn't at least leave a fucking message. What an ass. Just, I mean... that's just shitty."

"Well, it wasn't ... He probably didn't know what to say."

"Whatever. You're going to be so much better off. I know you thought he was cute and all, but Ruby, believe me, he was really a loser. He just was. A big, fuckin' loser."

"That's... "

Her words trailed off. Ruby didn't know what to say. Enough had been said already.

"I gotta go. Gotta get ready for work."

Her sister was worried.

"Ruby. Really. Listen to me. He's not worth getting upset over. This is for the better. Come on. Talk to me."

"I know, I know. I'm fine. Really." Ruby fought back.

"I am, really. I know it's for the better. Really, though, I gotta get ready for work."

Tanya hesitated. The phone stayed silent for twenty, thirty seconds. Tanya thought about going over to Ruby's, but knew it wouldn't make any difference.

"Okay. You will call me, though, if you need to. Promise?"

"Yeah. I will. Promise."

* * * * *

That night, at the club, her emotions stretched from sad to angry, then to defiant. Who the hell was he to bother me, to make me feel bad. He was a loser, Tanya was right. And she didn't need him, didn't need anyone. She made a vow to herself, a vow that she didn't—wouldn't—care. If she found someone, someday, that might be nice. But if she didn't, if that never happened, it wouldn't matter.

The club was awful, of course, but it was familiar and oddly comfortable at the same time. It was, had been for years, a constant in her life. It brought money, some security, and at times, also offered an escape. That night it was all of those things, and she let it be them. She closed her eyes and soaked it all in, the disco lights, a cocktail or two, and the costumes and the loud, always loud, blaring music. It was winter, 1984. The DJ was playing Run DMC, *Rock Box.*

It was the next day that Ruby discovered her stash of money in the house—about $700—was gone, that Wade must have taken it. She canceled her plans with her friends, realizing she would be working the whole week.

CHAPTER 8

The black BMW M3 sedan sped south on I-5, then took the exit ramp for tiny Charbonneau, Oregon, and pulled into the full service lane at the Citgo station.

"Fill it up," Victor Booth told the attendant. "Premium."

"No problem, sir. Nice car." The attendant seemed impressed.

"It's all right," Victor smiled, walked around and leaned against the hood, soaking up the midday sun. He peered over his sunglasses; the wind caught his paisley tie and flipped it over his shoulder.

"German, right?"

Victor was amused. "Yup. German. BMW; Bavarian Motorenwerk."

"Fast?"

"Yeah, it's pretty fast. Corners well. I like it."

Victor had left the military after his first tour. He went back to grad school, got his broker's license, his CFP, his CFFC. He joined Merrill Lynch, then switched to UBS, United Bank Switzerland. He bought a condo in a high rise in Nashville, favored technology stocks, traveled often to California.

The wind blew around Victor as the attendant washed the sports car's windows. Victor thought about Charlie. Wondered why he had suddenly left the USS Glover. It seemed strange that the executive officer of a fast frigate would transfer off while the ship was still at sea. But Victor's navy days were long past him, and he had forgotten much of his training and the idiosyncrasies of military service. Perhaps it was nothing, just a routine transfer; perhaps they had something else in mind for his shipmate and colleague—the Pentagon, perhaps, or teaching at Annapolis.

"Anything else, sir?" The attendant asked.

"Nope. Thanks." Victor made his way back to the freeway, made his way to the little naval reserve base in Oregon, made his way to the old gymnasium.

"Good morning, Captain." Victor sauntered in wearing civilian clothes, not worried much about formalities or security. *Unlikely to be much trouble here*, he thought, *or much attention to protocol.* He was generally right.

"Good morning. May I help you?" Captain Luedtke looked up at the well-dressed, young man.

"Here to see Commander McGurn. Old friend of mine; classmates together at OCS."

"From the looks of that haircut, you're no longer in service. What's your name?" Luedtke asked him.

"Victor Booth."

"Mr. Booth, I don't know how much you know. You're a friend of Charlie's, yeah?"

"Yes, sir. Good, good friends, Captain. He'll be happy to see me, I promise you that."

"He's not here, Mr. Booth. Most unfortunately..." His voice trailed off a little. "Do you know about his condition?"

Victor grew a bit more serious, didn't understand such a question.

"No."

Capt. Luedtke hesitated, but decided the commander could use an old friend right about then.

"It's his eyes. It's not looking good. Something about some blunt trauma years ago, just now manifesting itself, and suddenly. At least that's what I've heard from the medics.

Probably not supposed to be telling you that, but I guess it's not exactly top secret, either."

Victor's swagger was gone. He looked a little pale. The captain, now convinced from the reaction that Victor was truly an old friend, continued on.

"He's in town, civilian hospital. St. Catherine's I think. Right downtown, you can't miss it. Ask for him at the front desk, tell them you're from the base. They'll get you up there. He could use a friend right now. Glad you're here, actually. I'm having trouble knowing what to say. We don't have much history together. Strong young man, top-notch officer."

Victor shot the captain a glance, murmured a quick thanks, half-saluted out of habit, turned to his car. Twenty minutes later, he was at St. Catherine's. He was out of breath by the time he got to the reception and information desk.

"McGurn. Charles. Commander."

"Visiting hours are over, sir."

"I'm his brother, family," Victor lied.

"Third floor, west wing. Surgical recovery. There should be a nurse at the desk. Tell her you're family. I think you're the first to arrive; I don't think he's had any other visitors."

Typical, Victor thought. Probably no other family because the bastard just hasn't told them. Too stubborn for his own good.

Victor was out of breath again by the time he got to the nurse's station. An older, heavy-set nurse was sitting there, wearing the traditional Flying Nun cap with wings, filling out papers. When Booth asked for McGurn, she pointed him down the hall. He was headed that way before she could give him instructions. As he rushed away, she reminded him in her best nun's voice, "Quiet, please. No loud noises. He needs his rest."

He heard her, but barely.

Room 32A was on the right side of the hallway, with windows facing outside, to the west. As Victor walked toward

32A, glancing through the open doors, he notices that to his left, the windows to the east faced the courtyard; scattered about were religious statues and little park benches which were rarely used. It was 5:30, and the sun was just setting over the horizon. 32A was a two-person hospital room; the bed closer to the hall, was empty, its bed sheets pulled tight. It reminded Victor of their old bunks at Officer Candidate School in Newport.

Charlie was on the other side of the green vinyl privacy curtain. There, things seemed busy; food trays on the side table, IV bottles hanging from metal poles, computer monitors blinking, a big television hanging from the ceiling with the sound turned down. The scene looked ominous to Victor. It smelled like fresh cotton sheets and antiseptic and gauze and liniment. It felt cold and sterile.

Charlie was asleep. He was intubated, his mouth curled around a plastic tube, gurgling air and spittle. His head was heavily bandaged, the white wrapping over his forehead, completely covering his eyes. His arms were at his sides, palms up. An IV line was taped on his right arm. A little clip of plastic was wedged onto his left index finger, hooked up to a big monitor that blipped out a steady pulse.

An overstuffed, flower patterned, quite hideous looking easy chair stood near the foot of the bed, toward the window. Victor sat down on it and put his hand on his friend's leg through the thin sheet. His friend's leg seemed frail, lifeless. Victor closed his eyes for what seemed just a minute, visibly shuddered with emotion, verklempt. When Victor opened his eyes again, he looked right at Charlie, stared at him, tried to regain his composure, then peered out the window. He didn't think he had been there that long, but now, it was pitch black outside. When he had first gotten there the sun was just settling into a comfortable groove on the horizon. Charlie's chest was heaving up and down, steadily and rhythmically. *That's good*, Victor thought. *At least that's good.*

A doctor came in. Victor read his name tag. Dr. Bjork. Swedish, apparently. The tall, blond man in the stiff white coat was holding a pen and chart. He glanced at Victor; didn't ask who he was or why he was there, just said "hi."

"Hi," Victor replied.

"He's doing okay. I don't know, though. We tried." The doctor assumed Victor was a relative, since it was past normal visiting hours. He also assumed Victor knew what had happened, what the surgery had been, the likelihood of success. But he didn't.

"It was pretty late for surgery," he continued. "But maybe, with a little luck, it'll come back. He will see blurs. Probably not much else. The coronas were badly damaged; I'm frankly amazed he never complained before. The headaches must have been pretty intense."

Victor replied, without thinking. "He's always been pretty tough. Not much of a complainer."

"Sometimes it's good to complain. It helps us figure things out earlier," Dr. Bjork went on. "I'm just hoping the nerves reconnect in there. We opened the tendons up, gave the nerves a bigger channel." Again, his assumptions of Victor's knowledge were far off.

"So what are the odds?" Victor asked. He had figured out enough to know his friend was likely to lose his sight.

"Are you his brother?" Dr. Bjork assumed that, without much thought.

"Yes," Victor lied again.

"Look, I don't want to mislead you. It's not likely. Maybe ten percent. Maybe not even that. He's going to be fine otherwise, he's very healthy. It's just that once the corona is damaged the chances of recovery, of those nerves reconnecting, are pretty slender. Statistically. We never know, though.

Miracles do happen; let's pray for one here." Dr. Bjork wrote something on the chart, touched Victor on the shoulder, then walked back out into the hall. Victor and Charlie were alone again.

Ten percent, Victor thought. *Ten percent!* If that. And the doctor was probably being optimistic, trying to keep hope alive. Victor tried to figure it out. How could this happen? How could God let this happen to this man, to this man who sacrificed so much, who worked so hard, who deserved better?

Victor thought back, thought about Dr. Bjork mentioning blunt trauma. He remembered, in flashes, the incident in Thailand, where Charlie had been beaten. He remembered how bad Charlie's face had looked, how the blood had seeped through the bandages in that remote military hospital.

* * * * *

Victor stayed the night. Stayed the next morning. Stayed one extra day, then two. After almost a week, after Charlie wasn't intubated anymore, they started to talk. Most often it was superficial; about the weather, about sports. Several times, not for very long, they talked about the surgery, about how Charlie truly felt.

"I am so sorry, buddy," Victor let out some of his own emotion.

"Hey, no matter what, I can still tell which nurses are pretty," Charlie replied, trying to stay upbeat, but his voice was strained.

"You're going to be fine. Give it time." But Victor didn't really believe it.

Charlie didn't reply, tried to change the subject then. But other times, during the long, dull hours they both sat there, they let the conversation linger, tried to deal with it candidly.

"It's going to be tough for you," Victor said bluntly.

"What, being blind?" Charlie replied, somewhat as a joke, but not really. "Of course it's going to be fucking tough, you asshole. Jesus Christ."

"Sorry. Of course it is. I'll help any way I can, you know."

"You bet your ass you will ..." Charlie paused. "I'm a little scared. Okay, a lot scared. Sometimes I just can't stand it, Vic. Sometimes it just seems—shit, I mean, everything's just dark. It's like my whole life was just snuffed out and I was put into a room with no lights on and....I can't drive, I can't grocery shop, I can't even see to shave or to comb my hair. It's like, it's everything, man. It's just everything. All at once."

The words trailed off. Victor didn't know what to say. Silence engulfed the room. Eventually, there would be interruptions by the nurses or the doctors, or they would both just fall asleep, or something on the television would divert them.

* * * * *

Before Victor drove back to Nashville, he spoke with Dr. Bjork, told him about a rehabilitation hospital near Nashville, told him there he could help "with things." Victor convinced the doctor that Charlie didn't have much other family. Charlie didn't argue with the decision; Nashville was as good a place as any.

Baptist Memorial Hospital's "rehabilitation campus" was ten or twelve sprawling buildings, none more than two stories, spread across twenty acres just east of Nashville. There was a little pond with willow trees, there were walking paths, there were benches and old-fashioned street lights, there were manicured lawns and little memorials with donors' names. There were classrooms and physical therapy units spread around, with a beautiful courtyard and gravel walkways connecting the various buildings.

Charlie had a private room, but things weren't exactly luxurious. A brick outside wall, with a tall, thin window, a handicap-accessible bathroom in the room, toward the hallway. Sparse furniture; a couple of old wooden chairs with leather on the arms, a single bed, a dresser with a small television on top of it. It had a tile floor that felt cold to his bare feet, and there were no area rugs because they would be a trip hazard. The walls were plaster, and felt good to his touch. The wallpaper was fuzzy, with a raised flower pattern he could actually feel and understand.

He told time by the smells and the sounds. Breakfast foods in the morning; bacons and grilled meats and eggs and, of course, coffee. And in the mornings there was a bustle of activity by the staff, and he could hear them walking up and down the halls and doors shutting and closing. By mid-morning, things settled down and the kitchen was closed. There were just the normal smells of the room; the washed linens and sometimes the smell of freshly mowed grass from a partially opened window. At lunchtime, he smelled pizza sauce or fresh bakery or butter.

Victor brought him a nice radio, with a tape player, and some tapes. He plugged it in next to the dresser. Charlie fiddled with it for hours, memorized all the AM stations, then the FM ones. He didn't care for country music, this being Nashville and all, so it didn't take long to narrow down his choices of music stations. Most often he liked 91.3 WKEY, "The Key."

"91.3, the key to the best music in the mid-south."

The Key was playing *Crazy* by Seal. Charlie listened for a while, but before the song ended, he was interrupted. It was Rita, his instructor, there to teach him—as she did for two hours every weekday morning and two hours every weekday afternoon—how to survive in a visual world with no sight. And when she wasn't there, Everett did the same thing. And when

Rita wasn't there, and Everett wasn't there, sometimes it would be Cora or Patty. And so it continued, day after day, week after week, month after month.

The doctors and nurses, the therapists and the staff, they all told him they would be working with him for six months, and that is exactly what they all did. The time went by quickly, too quickly. And then someone took him to an apartment. And then various ones, only some, visited about once a week, for never more than an hour. And then no one came. And he just tried to cope.

* * * * *

He wasn't totally blind. Legally, yes. But he was able to see outlines and shapes, could navigate larger objects as he moved around. But that was it. And it never seemed to get better.

He was on full disability. And he had saved plenty of money. And the apartment was nice, certainly nice enough for a blind man. And set up for a blind man. No counters with sharp edges, no fireplace, nothing fragile. A big kitchen and cupboards with big knobs. First floor. All on one level. No stairs.

Victor helped him at the apartment for the first couple days, but then was away to California for work. It was a full three weeks later that he finally returned. When he dropped in on Charlie unannounced, Victor was surprised that Charlie wasn't there. Everything was in its place; it was obvious the apartment was lived in and things were fine, but Charlie wasn't there. Victor had kept a key, let himself in. He sat on the couch, waited about an hour. Then he heard a key in the lock, heard the door open. He didn't want to scare Charlie, so he spoke up right away.

"Hey there. You're here. I figured you'd be right back."

Charlie stopped in the doorway. He was surprised, a little. He realized, right away, that Victor must have kept a key. A key to his apartment. A key he shouldn't have. But he let it go.

"Hi there. Nice to see you." Charlie chuckled at his own comment.

"Yeah. Nice to see you, too." Victor replied. "And quit fucking laughing. You can probably tell what I look like just by the way I smell. Bastard."

It worked. It broke the ice.

"Sit down," Charlie told him. "What do you want? Scotch or bourbon. I can never tell with you; you suck both like water."

They talked for about an hour. Then they ran out of things to say. Charlie was anxious; he wanted Victor to leave. He wanted to keep working on his life, on learning his new life. He wanted to do it on his own. He felt he was making some progress. He had books to read and errands to run. He wanted to learn to pay his bills; a tutor was coming the next morning to help him with the Braille checkbook.

Victor sensed it, knew his friend was going to be fine. In a way it bothered him. Part of him wanted this man to need him, to be dependent upon him. But that would never happen.

"Gotta go. Sorry," Victor lied. It was becoming a habit around Charlie. "I might be able to stop down again later next week."

"That's cool. Anytime." Charlie walked towards the door, making the exit easier. He felt Victor move by him.

"See ya."

"Yup. Bye, Charlie."

In the past, when Charlie could still see, they had a ritual whenever they parted. They would shake hands, of course, but then they would also give kind of a half hug, then punch each other on the shoulder. It wasn't that way every time, but usually.

Now, though, Charlie just stood there, unable to sense Victor enough for any kind of handshake or embrace; too awkward now. Now Victor put his arm on Charlie's shoulder rested it there. They both unintentionally breathed a little sigh. And then Victor walked away, down the little path to his car.

Charlie shut the door, steadied himself for another long, scary night. He did fine during the day; it was different during the day. There were the blurs. There were noises and smells. The world was awake. At night, when things got quiet, he desperately wanted to see, to see what was out there, to look for things in the night. It was scary at night, even there, in his own secure apartment.

So he had turned on the television and started keeping it on at night. He found a music station on cable, music television. It was unique; he hadn't heard anything like it before. They played songs most all day, apparently with videos, which of course he couldn't see. But it was a good play list, better than the radio stations he had tried. That night, it was soft pop, not totally his style, but it was okay. Mariah Carey, *Emotions*. It helped the night seem like day, and it helped calm his nerves.

RUBY. 1990. 28 YEARS OLD. MEMPHIS, TENNESSEE.

Two green and white plaid overstuffed chairs sat next to each other on the screened-in, wooden porch that wrapped around the front of Ruby's bungalow. The old chairs were worn from use, covered with cotton throws, and not really intended to be outdoors. Between them was a wooden side table, more like a TV tray. On the tray were scattered newspapers, a couple of magazines, coffee cups, packets of real sugar. Ruby, her long legs stretched out, lounged in one of the chairs, her head back and her eyes closed. In the other chair was her new neighbor, Kelly Cunningham. Kelly was sitting straight, her posture perfect, her feet planted firmly on the floor, her arms folded neatly in her lap. Kelly and her husband had moved in less than a week before. The two women were fast becoming close friends.

Both young women were undeniably beautiful. The contrast between them, however, was striking.

Ruby's blue eyes sparkled beneath heavy, long eyelashes. Her skin was as smooth as silk, a light caramel color. Her long, dark hair had subtle auburn highlights and a natural wave, usually untouched by rollers or sprays. She almost never wore makeup but for a little eye shadow, and most often she chose casual clothes and went barefoot. Her clothes were beachy, soft, natural fabrics that draped across her body, with many parts left bare. She always looked comfortable, always looked sexy. She was very thin, small breasts and hips, incredibly long legs.

Ruby most often slept late, never set an alarm, crawled from the bed like a sleepy cat and crept to the kitchen for coffee. She tossed back her hair, ran a brush through it once or twice, and splashed some water on her face. Quietly efficient, within minutes her bed would be made, her soft little pajamas put away, and her cats fed and their water bowl full. Most often, Ruby would then spend at least twenty minutes, maybe half an hour, sitting on her porch, reading the newspaper or just sitting, before she started her day.

Ruby knew she wasn't like Kelly. Ruby certainly hadn't grown up with a silver spoon, Kelly being the Senator's daughter and all. Sometimes that bothered Ruby, sometimes not.

Kelly's alarm clock was always set early, but most often not needed. She awoke before her husband, and was wide awake within moments, sitting straight up in the bed, taking inventory. Her thick, blonde hair was always done up in a bun the night before, and her house slippers were placed perfectly by the edge of the bed. She took hours to get ready; her hair was first straightened then curled, moisturizing cream liberally applied to her entire body, then her face adorned with makeup, eyeliner, mascara. Twice a week she had a manicure, once a week a pedicure. She wore gloves when doing dishes or yard work, leaving her hands soft and supple. She applied sun block and wore hats her pale skin was like fine ceramic.

Kelly wore tailored clothes she bought from Valentina's, and silk scarves around her tiny neck. Her hands and feet were delicate and petite, her features; nose, ears, mouth, just the same. But she was quite tall, and had unusually large breasts and hips, both accentuated by a tiny waist. She commanded attention, easily took control of any room. She was driven, controlling, almost always in charge. Certainly in charge of her husband.

Ruby and Kelly sat together, that morning in early September, 1990. The weather was calm, overcast, a pleasant temperature. They spent hours sitting there, talking comfortably, candidly, both consciously deciding to ignore the demands of their days, instead relaxing and enjoying each other's company.

"You met him at college?" Ruby asked.

"Yes. That was five years ago, almost six now. He was always in the library studying. I guess I was, too, for that matter." Kelly enunciated her words, spoke in complete sentences.

"Huh. The library?" Ruby's words were sparse, but her eyes and body language, the intonation of her voice, Made it clear she was listening and interested.

"Yes, the library. I know, it wasn't exactly romantic. We were both good students. I respected him for that. And he came from a good family. That was obvious."

"College boys. Of course."

"Well, you know what I mean. He carried himself well. He wore nice clothes. He already had a car, an older one but a good sedan, four door. He didn't swear, at least not around me. He didn't smoke. Sure, he drank at parties, but he was, well, a gentleman. He had been brought up a gentleman. It was obvious." Kelly knew who she was, knew she was Old South conservative to a fault. Her Daddy had drilled it into her. She never really had a choice. She laughed at her own answer, at the attributes she found attractive in her husband.

"I know, Ruby. I know it sounds trite. But that's who we were, who—I guess—who we are. We're kind of boring, actually."

Ruby wondered why they lived in her neighborhood. It didn't make sense. They belonged in Germantown or Collierville; one of the more upscale suburbs. Manicured lawns, little statues part of the landscapings. *Maybe they couldn't afford that yet*, she thought. Sure, they came from money, but Kelly had said Kevin was still in graduate school. Kelly said she had a degree in marketing, but apparently didn't have a job. She worked almost constantly; fixing up the house, ironing clothes, doing yard work, shopping—but not a job for money, not one where someone else was her boss.

"Do you want kids?"

"Of course Kevin and I want kids. Of course we do. It's just, not the right time yet. We're both still young. It's our plan to wait five more years. At least five more years. So let's see, by then Kevin will be almost 35, which I think is about right."

Ruby laughed. "Is that his plan or your plan?"

"It's our plan. Really, it is. I know you don't believe me." Kelly smiled, looked over at Ruby.

"Look, I know I'm kind of a perfectionist. And I suppose I can be a little controlling of Kevin."

Ruby sat back a little further in her chair. She glanced back at Kelly.

"Unhuh," she mumbled, more as a question than a "yes" or "no."

"Okay, a lot controlling. But I don't want kids yet, and he seems fine with the plan. How about you? As long as we're on the topic."

"No plans. Either way. Might be good, but I don't know. They're adorable. I love children. But I tend to believe in fate." Ruby paused, debating whether to go further, debating whether she could trust her new friend.

"I....I came close once. He was an artist, tall, great looking actually. We went out just a couple times. I never told him." Ruby stopped talking. Kelly sensed her friend's vulnerability so she waited patiently, looked down at her coffee, took a sip.

Ruby's words were clear, abrupt, businesslike. "You know, I...I had an abortion."

Ruby looked at Kelly. Ruby's lips quivered a little; her eyes told the rest of the story. She wasn't proud of it, didn't like it, had made the decision of necessity and somewhat hastily. Ruby then cast her eyes down, just as Kelly had earlier. She took a small sip of coffee, then glanced back at Kelly, then away again, as if she was begging her newfound friend not to be judgmental.

Kelly looked back, stared at her for a moment, leaned over towards Ruby. She stretched out her hand—it was quite a ways between the two chairs—and let her long, polished nails gently push Ruby's hair back. Ruby let her, didn't move. It was quite a gesture, really.

"I'm sorry," Kelly said. "I'm really sorry."

"Me, too, yeah. I ..." Ruby said nothing further. They sat in silence for a little while. A few cars drove by, some black-birds chirped in the distance.

"I love your dress, Ruby."

"Thanks." Ruby wanted to move on, talk about something else. Kelly's change of subject made that easier. "I made it.

Pretty simple, really. I'm really bad at math. Darts. Subtractive method. But I love to sew."

"It looks perfect. It fits you well. And I love the fabric and the pattern." Ruby could tell Kelly was sincere.

"Do you want more coffee? Anything?" Ruby asked.

"Sure."

Ruby got up, walked barefoot into the house. She came back with more coffee, sat the pot down between them. Just then Kelly stood up, deftly took Ruby's hand in hers. They looked at each other. It was almost noon. It was cloudy, but it was very hot, and the usual muggy. They were both perspiring a little.

"This was...nice. Thanks for coming over." Ruby broke the stare first, shuffled back a little.

"Yes. Absolutely. You're...you're very sweet. To have me over. The porch, it's...it was such a beautiful morning and all." The sentences weren't as complete, the words not as crisply spoken now. Kelly fought her way out of the trance, tried to regain her balance. "Let me grab my shoes." She had taken off her patent leather pumps—an astonishing thing for her—and had been lounging in her stocking feet. She sat back down in her chair, deftly put them back on.

"Yes. That was really marvelous. Thank you so much." She thought about what to say next; wanted it to be just the right thing.

"Will you be home tomorrow?" It was a silly question if taken out of context, out of the moment. But it was the perfect thing to say. Of course Ruby would be there; they both knew that. But the question was intended to convey their mutual desire to be together again, to replay the morning, perhaps to extend it, let it simmer and boil to a finishing point, whatever that might be.

"Sure. I'm here. Anytime." Ruby's words were again short, sparse, but again her eyes and body language told Kelly everything she needed to know. As she spoke, Ruby leaned forward, emphasized the word "any," slurred it out. Aannnyytime. Then, surprising even herself, Ruby continued. "Even later today." At that she laughed a little.

"Great. Ruby, thanks again." Kelly gathered herself, folded up her purse. Ruby stood on the porch, watching as Kelly walked across Ruby's yard—brambly and bare where the dog ran—to Kelly's, with thick grass cut short and pruned shrubs. When Kelly got to her sidewalk, and just before she started up the steps, she turned and looked back; she caught Ruby's eye again, winked. It was too far for Ruby to see the wink, but perhaps.

Kelly laughed to herself, laughed at her silly wink and her lack of proper comport. She stiffened, checked her posture, outlined her plan for the rest of the day. Unconsciously, she started humming to herself; it was a song that had been playing at Ruby's. Tom Petty, *Free Falling.*

CHAPTER 9

CHARLIE. 1993. 38 YEARS OLD. NASHVILLE TO MEMPHIS, TENNESSEE.

L ife is all about habits and routines. Going blind, though, forces changes in those habits and routines—drastic changes. But eventually, over time, they return; different, but habits and routines nonetheless.

Two years after his surgery, less than a year after "finishing" his rehabilitation, Charlie was starting to develop his own routines again. He set a time schedule, he dressed for the day, he made his way to breakfast at the diner next to his apartment.

"Good morning, Charlie."

"Hi. Good morning. Is that coffee I smell?"

He met new people, they met him, they learned each other's names, and they became—if not friends—at least nice acquaintances.

He read the paper, Braille, delivered daily, which he took with him to the diner each morning. Then he spent the rest of his mornings at the apartment, most often sat in the screened in porch, reading, always reading; most often it was investment magazines, all in Braille, all specially delivered. He also had some finance books, economics, the like. He became obsessed with the stock market, with puts and selling short, profit and earnings ratios and long-term forecasts.

Thursdays he shopped for groceries.

"Is that all today, Mr. McGurn?"

"Yes, ma'am. That's it for today."

"Cash or check?"

"Cash. Please." Charlie kept his cash sorted in his wallet, the bank teller helping him with every deposit and withdrawal. He would bend the corners of the bills, like he was taught at rehab, so he could identify the bills; small for ones, a little more for fives and tens, and so on.

"There. Two twenties, a ten, and a one. That should be enough." The teller put them in separate piles, so Charlie could tell.

"Yes, sir. It's perfect. Here's your change, 54 cents."

Being blind wasn't easy, but he managed.

For the first six months, he had tried to work out in his apartment. He did sit-ups, ran in place, jumping jacks. It wasn't enough. Victor helped him find a gym nearby, where he used some free weights, worked out on weight machines and a treadmill. He went religiously, four times a week, in the afternoons. Four sets on the bench, then incline, another four sets. Over to the decline bench for four sets. Barbells, curls, lat pulls. A full half-hour on the rowing machine, as fast and as hard as he could, the whirr of the spinning wheel creating a breeze; sometimes it even felt like he was actually outside, rowing a real boat. Then leg presses, lifts; always working on crunches. The routine varied, as he learned it should. Some days chest, some days legs, always work the core.

He worked the muscles hard, released his frustrations.

There were the sporadic special needs—haircuts and shopping for clothes. Those he usually saved for Saturdays. He had friends who helped willingly, and he often enough let them. Holidays and vacations were pretty much avoided, for the most part. He didn't know what he would do for Christmas, dreaded the thought.

He had also discovered a video store nearby. "Watching" videos didn't make sense, he knew that, but if he listened carefully, the old movies were great. Action films and comedies that were dependent on visuals—not so good. But old, classic movies; Jimmy Stewart in *Rear Window*. Dialogue. Music changes, foretelling the story. Dramas, mysteries—movies where things moved slowly, where he could listen for the click of a shoe or the opening of a door. He watched, listened, and started to enjoy them. It was pleasant. He could relax.

Victor always pushed him to spend time together. He invited Charlie to play specialty board games cards, to go to sports events. Sometimes Charlie did; partly to appease Victor, partly because he knew it was good for him to do it. It always started with a phone call.

"Hey, Charlie. Hey, what's up?"

"Hi, Vic. Not much."

"Look, I've got some business in Memphis. Thought you could go with me. We could check into a nice hotel. Maybe get some dinner. I've got one easy meeting in the morning, nice clients. Great guys. Then Saturday night, we could go to a bar or something. You need to get out, and you know it."

Charlie tried to beg off. He truly didn't know if he was ready for a longer road trip. He felt secure in his new world. Maybe it was too soon, maybe not, but it just didn't sound like a lot of fun.

"Maybe next time."

"No. No next time. Look, we leave Friday late afternoon, maybe get a drink at the hotel bar, crash for the night. You can sleep in a little—you never do that—and then after my meeting, we'll do something fun. I can write the whole thing off, you know. You're on such a roll with your investments. Hell, you're one of my largest clients at this point. And we're still friends, at least I think so."

Charlie hated feeling he owed anyone anything. It bothered him. But he felt he owed Victor, and he caved to the peer pressure. It was something he almost never did.

"Okay."

Victor was surprised at the early acceptance, at the lack of a tougher fight.

"Great. That's good. You're gonna have fun. It will be good for both of us. And it's all on my credit card; of course, I'll have to up your commissions accordingly. No more one percent for you, my friend."

"What time Friday?" Charlie asked.

"Pick you up at 4:30. I'll kick out of the office a little early. You'll like these two guys, Tom and Jeff. Our age, successful businessmen, looking to invest some money. Perfect. I think one just got divorced, the other guy's married, but he's cool. Maybe we'll find some girls."

Girls. It was a most difficult subject for Charlie. He loved women, always had, knew he always would. And things were better, maybe better than he even thought they could ever be, under the circumstances anyway. He was physically stronger than ever before, he was financially independent. He was gradually getting more and more comfortable with his lifestyle and friends and acquaintances.

But he hadn't yet crossed what he considered the final barrier. His flirting with the nurses, then with the waitresses and checkout girls, was a defense mechanism; he knew it. He was the friendly, nice, funny blind guy; the "oh, isn't he sweet" one. He wasn't the leading man, the protector, the warrior, and that was what he felt most women wanted, needed, looked for long term. He hadn't crossed that barrier yet, and sometimes doubted he ever would again. He used to be that man.

"Yeah. Girls. That might be fun." Charlie left it at that.

"Of course, man. They'll love you. Just like those nurses, remember that? God, they were all over you, Romeo."

Sometimes Victor was a little too juvenile for Charlie's taste. He didn't like that.

"Okay, buddy. Let's keep it cool. If we meet someone, that would be nice. If not, I'm fine with that, too."

"Friday. 4:30. I'll pick you up."

"That's fine. I will talk to you later." There was a short pause. "Thanks."

"It's about time you thanked me. You're welcome, by the way. I'll see you soon."

"Bye."

* * * * *

F riday came more quickly than Charlie expected. He had to skip the gym that afternoon, because he hadn't packed his bag yet. He picked out one of his best shirts by feel. He had some special order shirts that had flat beads ironed on in the back to identify the color and style. Suits and sport coats had the same flat beads sewn into the inside lapels. More casual clothes had safety pins with metal tags that helped identify them; an embossed "b" for brown, "bl" for black.

He had already gone to the store and bought some of the little toiletries—a small tube of toothpaste, a little bottle of mouthwash, new deodorant. He was ready by 4:30. Victor was a little late, but that was to be expected.

Victor still had the M3. Charlie loved the leather, the way it smelled and the way it felt. He liked the sound of the engine, the rush of acceleration. He could tell when it hugged a big curve, when it rushed up a freeway ramp. For some reason, Victor never talked much when he was driving; that was fine with Charlie. And he let Charlie handle the radio—fine metal knobs and precise tuning. Charlie liked that, too.

Once they got to Memphis, they checked into the Peabody. Charlie insisted on separate rooms, insisted on paying for his own. They had a couple of drinks together at the lobby bar, but it stayed pretty quiet. Charlie was pleased: pleased Victor wasn't pushing him too hard, pleased he was finding his way around the hotel, pleased with his room, pleased to tip the bellman extra. It was all just fine, and was a nice change. Perhaps Victor had been right.

And Charlie did sleep in the next morning. Instead of 6:00 a.m., he didn't wake up until 7:30. He made his way to the lobby, remembering it was left out the door, roughly ten paces to the elevators, then down to the first floor. The floors were also numbered in Braille. *First class*, he thought to himself. He found the café, ordered breakfast. He felt self-conscious eating alone. At the diner, whenever he ate alone, he would read the paper. Here at the Peabody, there was nothing to read, nothing in Braille nearby.

But Charlie still liked the Peabody hotel, and had been there enough times that he knew the layout, felt comfortable. That morning, Charlie was patient, just waiting for the server and sitting upright, staring forward. Sometimes it seemed like forever, but sometimes he was able to daydream and let his mind wander wherever it wanted to go. Most often, though, there were enough other distractions to keep him amused. He could often hear people in the kitchen, louder than most people would expect if you just tried to listen. Or the servers talking behind people's backs; that was often very amusing.

Victor met him back in his room at noon, just as planned.

"How was your morning?"

"Pretty good. I had a nice breakfast. This is a nice hotel. And you? How was your big meeting?"

"Great. Fantastic, really. These guys are really nice, and I think they're going to drop a lot in. At least 100 Gs. Maybe double that. Enough to make this trip worthwhile anyway. I'm pushing them on tech stocks, too. Forget the NYSE, it's NASDAQ all the way, baby. Aggressive growth. Domestic, small caps. Yes?"

Victor was the expert, but Charlie had shown a better ability to pick the best stocks. Charlie was more thorough and more current on his research. Victor spent a little too much time wining and dining, not quite enough studying and working.

"Yes. Right now, anyway. At least for right now. I wouldn't lock it in for more than three or four years, though." The comments were prescient, as if Charlie had a window view into the future. "Then I would get into bonds. Stay in five years max."

"Yes, sir. That's what I told them." Victor's comment was only partially true; he had told the two men to invest in NASDAQ, in tech stocks, small caps, all that. He left out the part about not locking it in for too long, that the bubble might burst, that at some point they would want to get out. Charlie figured as much; didn't really care, though. Whoever they were, it was their fault if they didn't keep track of their own investments.

"So, they're up for going out. Now, this afternoon. Tom— goes by Tommy—he wants to go to the strip club. Tiffany's. I've been there. Probably more than I should. Hell, I'm practically a regular."

This was news to Charlie. He knew Victor liked to have fun, but he never talked about strip clubs.

"I'm sorry. Gentlemen's club. It's a gentlemen's club. Really nice, actually. You're cool with that, right?"

Charlie didn't really care. What difference did it make to him now, he chuckled to himself. It's not like I can see the skimpy outfits; bare breasts don't mean much to a blind guy. Blurs. Sexy blurs.

"Sure. Whatever you guys want. I'm just along for the ride."

"No, you're not. You're going to have fun, probably more than we are. I know a couple nice ladies there who you'll just love, and they're gonna go for you, too, my friend."

Victor was acting a little too immature again. Charlie got a little short.

"Okay, then, let's go already. Quit just talkin' about it."

Victor's eyes opened a little wider. He cocked his head back, stared at Charlie for a second, surprised at his tone. "Okay." A pause. "Then." Another pause. "We'll go. Get your damn jacket."

"I'm not taking a jacket. I'm wearing this sweater. So there. Fuck you." Charlie cracked a smile. It relieved the tension, they both started to laugh.

"And a beautiful sweater it is, monsieur. Cashmere, I assume?"

"Why, of course. Only the finest." And it was, $260 from Macy's, tight leather buttons, hand sewn. Charlie had started to enjoy nice clothes.

* * * * *

Victor pulled up to the club at about 2:00 p.m. Tom and Jeff, his two clients, were supposed to meet them there. Victor knew better than to lead Charlie; instead, he kept talking to Charlie as they walked to the front door, so Charlie could follow his voice. Charlie seldom used a cane or wore dark glasses, so often people didn't realize he was blind until well after they were introduced, until they caught him staring straight ahead or not looking them in the eye. It helped a little that Charlie could see the blurs—he literally called them the blurs—the odd shapes and movements he could kind of see, fuzzy but there. The blurs had no color, and no detail, but there was something. Enough to avoid a parked car or—usually—a person.

"So, you're going to like this place. Looks nice, purple carpet and all. There's little lion statues."

Victor kept up his patter as they walked toward the entry door.

"Looks like there might be a cover charge. Let's see...."

"I've got it. Whatever it is," Charlie offered.

"Five bucks each. Not bad. Hello, young lady. My friend here's got it. Five bucks each, huh?"

Charlie kept listening for Victor's voice, knew his friend would help him. He found the counter, took a twenty dollar bill out of his wallet, set it on the counter.

"Hi, guys. Yup, ten bucks. Five each. Two drink minimum."

The door girl was obviously young; Charlie liked her voice, though. It was deep, gravelly. She was obviously a smoker. He slid the bill closer to her on the counter.

"Do you need change?"

Charlie knew it was a twenty, not a ten. "No, the extra ten's for you, sweetie. I love your voice."

"Thank you." It sounded most sincere.

"You're welcome," Charlie flirted back.

A strong smell of cigarette smoke came through the interior doors. And the music was loud; very loud, '80s rock music.

"It seems you're doing okay there, buddy. Seems you liked her." Victor tried to keep the conversation going as he walked into the club. He started to talk louder, over all the noise.

"So, let's see...nice place, really. Like I said, I've been here before. It's great, really." Victor kept talking and walking, Charlie behind him. It was very dark, and Victor had trouble avoiding chairs or tables to stumble against. It was way too dark for Charlie to see the blurs. But no one seemed to notice when Charlie also bumped into one of the chairs.

"Here we go. A couple of stairs down." At that point, Victor reached back, helped Charlie a little. Charlie had no choice but to let him.

"This, my friend, is what they call the VIP lounge. And I am a VIP, a very, very important person. And there, of course, are my very important friends, just where they should be."

Victor was practically yelling, trying to be heard above the din of the crowd and the blaring music.

Victor continued. "Tom. Hey. Jeff. I want you to meet my friend, Charlie."

"Hi, Charlie. Thanks for joining us. We've heard a lot about you."

"Yeah, hi, Charlie."

Charlie had to talk loudly, too, so they could hear him. "Hello, gentlemen. Victor tells me you had a good meeting this morning." Victor guided Charlie to one of the chairs. It was round, like a bucket, like something you might see in a casino. And it had little brass wheels so it could spin around. Charlie felt for the table to steady himself, felt for the chair, sat down. He was surprised when the chair rolled around a little on him.

"Victor, go get these gentlemen some drinks. Whatever they want. It's on me." Charlie settled into the chair, listened for the voices to get his bearings.

But by the time Charlie said that, a waitress was already at the table.

"What would you like, boys?" She was wearing nude tights, black pumps, bikini bottoms, and a halter tuxedo top, complete with cummerbund and bow tie.

They all ordered drinks. Each threw money on the table, in spite of Charlie's offer.

They seemed nice enough. Not bad guys, anyway. Charlie tried to relax.

The conversation drifted. They talked about the weather, about the trip from Nashville. Tom was from Olive Branch, Mississippi, about thirty minutes from Memphis. Jeff was from Little Rock, Arkansas. Tom had an office supply business, Jeff had two restaurant franchises, wanted to open a third.

Charlie was starting to get bored. Suddenly, though, that changed.

He first heard her high heels chattering across the floor near him. Then Charlie felt some silk fabric graze his hand as she walked by. He smelled her perfume, even some skin lotion. He heard her whisper softly into Victor's ear, wished it would have been him instead.

"Hello, stranger."

"Ruby, Ruby, Ruby. Oh, I'm sorry—'Sascha.' God, it's my lucky day. I didn't know you were on today. It's Saturday, right? Tommy? It's Saturday, isn't it?"

"Saturday is my regular day, handsome. You know that." Charlie thought she sat down on his friend's lap, but he couldn't be sure.

"Gentlemen, is this a nice place, or what?" Victor asked the group seated around the table.

"Cheers."

"Cheers, Victor."

Charlie said nothing, continued to stare forward, but he was very alert. Captivated, actually, by the little sequence of events, by the girl, the woman—Ruby. He wanted to go over to her, touch her, smell her hair.

Ruby didn't talk much after that. Tom, Jeff, and Victor talked sports for a while. Eventually stocks, of course. They pushed him for his thoughts, he reluctantly told them, still having to shout above the noise. Charlie grew edgy, restless. He knew the girl—Ruby—was close, that she was still right there sitting on Victor's lap. He could still smell her perfume. He even thought he could hear her breathe. He stood up, thought he would splash some water on his face.

Victor tried to help him.

"Whooaaa there, buddy. What the hell do you think you're doing?"

"Going to the bathroom, thank you."

"Well, that's fine, but here. Let me help you out a little."

Charlie recoiled. "I'm fine," he barked.

"Hey. It's okay," Victor tried to settle him down. Charlie wanted to hit him, to push him against the wall, to tell him it wasn't okay, it wasn't. Instead he softened, knew it would be better, didn't want to make a scene, not then, not there, not with her right there.

"Really. I'm fine. I know where it is."

He made sure he stood straight, arms back a little, chest forward. He had been listening intently as people walked by, had figured out where the men's room was, at least he hoped he was right. But he wasn't sure. He reached down for the side table, made his way around it, felt he was facing the right direction. As confidently as he could, he walked over to the far wall, five, maybe ten feet. He smelled men's aftershave, heard the door open and close. The bathroom was there, where he hoped and thought it would be. He used his right hand to guide himself around the corner. Charlie knew he would then be out of the sight of his companions—and Ruby.

As soon as he entered, he paused, exhaled, tried to breathe; in, out, in, out. He stumbled then, reached out with both hands to the walls, made his way into the bathroom, and found the sink, one of three lining the wall.

Several minutes passed. He knew he had to go back, had to somehow find his way to the little table again. This time, though, things didn't go so well. He made his way out of the bathroom and down the little corridor, but as he walked across the aisle, he bumped into a waitress.

"Hey, watch it."

"Sorry." He stopped, let her go by. He prayed no one saw it. He made his way to the table, thought he was getting close. He recognized Tom's voice, then Jeff's. Perfect. He listened for Victor; nothing.

"Charlie. You're back." It was Jeff. "Here." Jeff stood up, touched his shoulder lightly, guided him to the chair. Charlie was grateful; it was a helpful gesture, but not too obvious.

"Thanks. That's great. How are you all doing?"

"We're fine." It was Tom now. "But we lost Victor. Can't blame him. Ruby, wow...I mean, she's gorgeous. Trust me on that one, Charlie."

"Lost him?" Charlie asked. He didn't understand.

"They went back for a private dance. More than one, I imagine. God knows how long they'll be back there," Tom laughed.

The three men talked for another twenty minutes—maybe half an hour. Jeff said he wasn't feeling well, thought he'd go back to the hotel.

"Mind dropping me off at the Peabody on your way?" Charlie asked. He didn't want to listen to Victor, didn't want to hear about his dances with Ruby, couldn't believe they weren't back to the table yet.

"Sure. No problem. Tom, you're going to stay?"

"Oh, yeah. I'm stayin' right here. It doesn't get better than this, gentlemen."

"Well, that's probably true. We may be back, probably soon," Jeff joked.

Just then the music started to fade, and the DJ started calling out the name of a new dancer.

In one of the back rooms, Ruby asked Victor if he wanted another one.

"One more, kitten," he told her.

At that moment Jeff and Charlie were making their way out of Tiffany's. The new song started. It was Deee-Lite, *Groove Is In The Heart.*

RUBY. 1993. 32 YEARS OLD. MEMPHIS, TENNESSEE.

Tiffany's had changed over the years. The bright costumes from ten years earlier were gone; the purple hues were gone; most of the other dancers, bit by bit, were gone, too. Ruby was one of the oldest now, still just two years over thirty. Two or three other girls were well into their mid-thirties as well, out of fifty or more girls total. *Most were incredibly young*, Ruby thought, *too young to be there*. But they were no older than Ruby had been when she started.

The third stage had been taken out and an addition added. All of the private dances were done there now. It was a big, open area—especially dark—with small couches instead of chairs. Another bar area, the VIP Lounge, had been added there, too. It was furnished with more modern furniture, better chairs and tables. During the day, it was mostly businessmen who hung out there.

Ruby got to the club about half an hour late that day. She begged Barb to write her down for starting on time, at 11:00, but Barb just laughed.

"No way. Ruby, you'll make that tip out in about ten minutes. You always do."

Ruby didn't fight her. Barb was probably right, anyway. Within minutes, Ruby saw two of her regulars at the bar, knew the money would come fast and easy. She was still very pretty, perhaps even more so than when she was younger. Her skin was still just as tight, the extra ten pounds had magically gone to her breasts and hips, not to her stomach. But what she worked at, what she excelled at, was the art of conversation.

She knew what the men wanted to hear, what they needed, what they craved. Sure, some were there only to ogle, to look, to grope. But she found that others, usually the older men, were there for something much more: for someone to be nice to them, to treat them well. Or perhaps, more likely, they were just looking for a woman who still found them attractive, even if they were starting to lose their hair or had grown fat. Ruby had learned to feed that desire. She looked them in the eye, listened, paid attention. And all that came quite naturally to her. And her style tended to attract the gentler men, men she came to know and—in a strange way, she made them feel good, and they in turn grew to like her, too.

Victor was one of Ruby's regulars, had been for the last two, three years. He wasn't necessarily Ruby's favorite. He was a little too loud, too brash for her taste. And he always talked, rarely listened. But he was charming in a way, and each time he came in, she was almost guaranteed three dances. Plus he tipped well.

It was Victor she went to first that day. He was sitting in the VIP area with three other men, clean cut, well dressed. Two were in business suits, the third wore soft, gray slacks and a cashmere sweater.

Ruby approached Victor from behind, put her arms around his neck and whispered into his ear. She knew it would only be a matter of time before he bought some private dances.

"Hello, stranger." She just called him stranger for now because he hadn't been there in a while.

"Ruby, Ruby, Ruby. God, it's my lucky day. I didn't know you were on today. It's Saturday, right? Tommy? It's Saturday, isn't it?"

"Saturday is my regular day. You know that, handsome." She fell into his lap, her arms still around his neck.

"Gentlemen, is this a nice place, or what?" Victor raised his glass, in it a poorly made Manhattan.

"Cheers."

"Cheers, Victor."

The gentleman in the cashmere sweater stayed quiet, his eyes staring into space. Ruby noticed him, noticed his nice clothes, his quiet nature. His hair was cut short, peppered with a little gray, but thick and full. He was thirty-five, if that. *Probably a military officer*, she thought. She was drawn to him, didn't know why. He didn't seem to be paying her any attention.

She stayed on Victor's lap, but didn't talk for a while. Instead she listened, let them talk among themselves. They talked sports for a while, at first. Typical.

"Who do we play on Sunday?"

"Dallas Cowboys."

"I can't stand Michael Irvin. If he showboats, I'm gonna kick the TV in. Aikman, though—he's gonna be a good quarterback."

Ruby found their chatter boring, caught some of the names but not most.

"If they stop the run, they'll be okay."

She noticed the man in the cashmere sweater didn't join in the sports talk. The words all started to run together. Finally they quit talking sports. Ruby listened more carefully.

"So, Tommy, how's the single life?"

"Good. Great. I mean, I wish I could spend more time with the kids, but thank God, I'm away from that woman."

"Man, I have to tell ya, she was a bitch. A true bitch." They all laughed.

Women, divorces, family; nothing special about any of that, Ruby thought. The conversation changed again, though.

"What's the latest pick, Jeffrey? I got a little I want to invest." The stock market—Ruby liked that subject.

"Tech. It's all tech stocks right now. I think they're gonna take off. The Silicon Valley stuff, some new IPOs. Microsoft is high right now, but they've got the market. I don't think the antitrust suits are gonna stick."

"Yeah, probably right. Anything Internet. Charlie. Hey, Charlie. Victor said you've hit on a couple."

Until then Charlie, the gentleman in the sweater, the gentleman who intrigued Ruby more than she had been intrigued in a long time, hadn't said anything. He didn't look at the other men when he spoke; it was odd.

"Did all right."

That's all he said. The others pushed him.

"All right? Victor says you turned ten-fold in six months. Says you've got some kind of magic going on there. All right... ha. All right, my ass."

"I'd stick with the tech stocks for a while," Charlie continued to stare straight ahead.

"Yeah, but which ones? Come on, buddy. Since you've got the magic going, give us some of it."

"The price to earnings ratio is out of line. But I'd go with America Online out of Virginia. I'm riding a lot on that."

"America Online, huh? I think they just launched DOS. And some chat room-type stuff? Are you into that?"

"Doesn't matter if I'm into it," Charlie replied. "What matters is if everybody else is into it, and if the advertising revenue goes up."

Ruby had heard of AOL. She had heard of chat rooms, although she hadn't tried it. A lot of her friends had talked about it. She stared at Charlie. He was quite handsome; sharp features, bright teeth, a dimpled chin. And she found him mysterious; he seemed to command the others' respect.

Just then, Charlie lifted himself out of the chair. He used both hands, firmly grasped the chair arms, stood straight up, took one step forward. Ruby noticed how tall he was, how he carried himself.

"Whooaaa there, buddy." Victor got up at the same time. "What the hell do you think you're doing?"

"Going to the bathroom, thank you."

"Well, that's fine, but here. Let me help you out a little."

Charlie recoiled. "I'm fine," he barked.

"Hey. It's okay." Victor went over to him. Charlie softened.

"Really. I'm fine. I know where it is."

Victor backed away. Charlie reached out his arm to the side table, guided himself around it. He continued to stare ahead, his head always up. He waited a minute as someone passed in front of him, then he walked slowly towards the bathroom. When he got closer, he reached out, touched the wall, kept his hand on it as he went around the corner and into the men's room.

Victor sat down again, and Ruby eased herself down onto his lap.

"Incredible. Fucking incredible." Tommy looked at his friends. "I don't know how that fucker does it."

"I'd be lost. Just worthless." Jeff said.

"He's one tough son-of-a-bitch. I'll tell you that. Wouldn't want to take him on in a fight, blind or not."

Victor jumped in. "He's not blind yet. Right now, maybe, yeah....but I know this next surgery is gonna work. It's....hell, I just think it's gonna work."

The others joined in quickly. "Yup." "Gonna work."

Ruby released her grip on Victor's neck, got off his lap. She stood up, adjusted her outfit. She looked over to the men's room door; Charlie was still in there. She wanted him to come back, she wanted to look at him more closely, look at his eyes, try to see what was wrong with them. It tore at her. She choked up.

"Hey, Ruby. Come on, let's take a break." Victor was staring at her. She was reluctant. She wanted to wait for Charlie, then thought better of it.

"Sure. Of course." Ruby answered She glanced toward the men's room again.

* * * * *

She was with Victor for over half an hour. She danced for a
while, sat with him for a while, then danced again; a
typical routine for him. He loved to hear himself talk; she was
more than happy to let him. By the time they got back to the
VIP area, Jeff and Charlie were both gone.

"Hey, Tommy, what's the deal?"

"Jeff said he had to go. Charlie said he was ready, too."

"Well? Where did they go?" Victor asked.

"Dunno. Didn't say."

Ruby was visibly upset. "Is he okay?" she blurted.

"What do you mean is he okay? Is who okay?" Victor
replied.

"Your friend. The one who can't see."

"Charlie? Sure. Of course he's okay. He's always okay.
Trust me, he can take better care of himself than anybody. He's
fine. Worried about my buddy, kitten?"

Ruby fought to get back into character. "Oh, just wondered. He seemed like your friend, wanted to make sure he was
okay. Just like I want to make sure you're okay, Victor." She
tugged on his tie.

Victor smiled. "Aw, Ruby, you're sweet." Ruby didn't like
it when he called her Ruby instead of Sascha. But she had made
the mistake of telling him her real name once, when she was
trying to get him to buy yet another dance. And he didn't
forget, and she didn't have the energy to push it, didn't want to
risk making him mad.

Victor seemed restless. "Tommy, we might as well go,
huh?" He slipped Ruby another $20 bill.

"Thanks, Vic. You're a doll. Remember, Wednesdays and
Thursdays daytime, Friday and Monday nights. Got it?"

Victor nodded his head. He grabbed his overcoat. Ruby
watched the two men leave.

* * * * *

The next morning, when Ruby slipped out of bed, she thought about Charlie. Thought about the man in the cashmere sweater. Hoped he was okay. Hoped he would come back to the club. Realized he probably wouldn't, so she tried to forget.

When Ruby walked out to her porch, coffee in hand, Kelly was already there.

"Mornin,' sweetie."

"Hey. How ya' doin'?"

"Good. Great, actually. Kevin got the promotion. Finally." Ruby nodded. "He got what?"

"A promotion. He's going to be vice president of finance. The M.B.A. is paying off, we think. It means substantially more money."

"That's good." Ruby let her friend talk.

"I'm still not sure about that house. It's beautiful, and the yard; my God, the yard is perfect. There are three big elm trees in the back, and a stone patio. It's hard to describe."

"Sounds pretty."

"I don't know if we're going to get it, though. What would I do without you next door?"

The Cooper/Young neighborhood where the two young women lived had done well. Crime was down, more young couples and families were moving in. It was quickly becoming the chic neighborhood, with newer restaurants and clothing stores, nightclubs and bars. On Ruby and Kelly's street, practically every house on the block was being fixed up, painted, or subjected to some improvement of one kind or another.

"I love it here, I really do. And the neighborhood association—he is president of that, you know—and it is growing.

Kevin thinks he might get even more involved if we stay. That would be good."

"Then stay." Ruby wanted her to stay.

"Yeah, there will be other places, right? I just worry if we have kids; it would mean a private school." Kelly was a worrier. Sometimes it bugged Ruby.

"Not necessarily. And you're not exactly pregnant yet."

Kelly paused. "I'm sorry. I don't want to talk about this. We're not moving, I love it here. And I can't live without my best friend next to me."

Ruby wanted to change the subject. Ruby wanted to tell her about Charlie.

"Hey. Last night, at the club. I was taken a little, by a guy." Ruby had long ago confided to Kelly that she danced at Tiffany's. Kelly found it fascinating.

"You know your rule. Don't violate that, Ruby." Kelly was reminding her of Ruby's own rule: never see a customer outside the club.

"Yeah, but this is different. And he's not a customer. He was a friend of a customer. There was just ... something about him. Trust me, I'm not falling for him or anything. I hardly know him. I mean, I really don't know him at all. I just, kind of found him interesting." She laughed. "Well, very interesting. He was blind. I mean, well, at least pretty much blind. The other guys said he was having another surgery or something, and he didn't wear sunglasses or whatever it is the blind guys wear so we all know they're blind. But he was blind."

"Really?" Kelly seemed surprised. "You're taken with a blind guy?"

Ruby laughed. "Well ... You never know, right?"

"Right. Can you put on some of your music? I love your music."

"Sure." Ruby went inside, opened up the window to the screen porch so they could hear the stereo. She found an old album, The Cure, *Upstairs Room*, put it on the turntable, let the needle drop.

"Perfect." Kelly sat back a little in her chair.

Ruby went over to Kelly, picked up her feet, put them on a little stool, pushed her back further into the chair. "I've told you, you need to learn to relax, girl. Now let it go. You're not movin', you're stayin' right here. You can't live without me and you know it."

Kelly put her hands to her face, rubbed her eyes. Ruby crawled into her own chair, curled up. They rested together, happy, content.

That afternoon, Ruby went to her bank. She talked to the bank manager—she knew him from the club. He never asked much, knew better. She withdrew all of her savings, over $30,000. She got a cashier's check. She took the cashier's check and went to A.G. Edwards.

"Buy America Online," she told the broker.

"Good choice." He gave her back paperwork. She took the papers home, and put them with all the other papers, all similar, all in a nice, neat little stack. And she never told anyone about them, not even Kelly. She hid them in the secret drawer in the built-in china cabinet.

CHAPTER 10

I f there was anything that Charlie was in a good position to do, it was to disappear for a while.

His military discharge was complete. The disability checks, both the government one and the one from AIG, were all deposited directly into his account. Victor paid all his bills, took care of his various investments. Although he had thought about it—many times, actually—he had yet to buy a pet. And the few plants he had were quite hardy, and hardly worth losing sleep over anyway should they go without watering for some time.

He had finally told his mother about his sight. She was hysterical at first, of course, but hardly dwelled on him. He was no longer—never was, not since she met Peter, anyway—an integral part of her life. She had visited, twice, actually. But she didn't really know what to do, disturbed his routines, and made him crabby. They both knew it. She left earlier than planned, and it just seemed right that she did.

"I'm going to visit my mom," Charlie told Victor.

"Really. I didn't know you would ever want to do that," Victor was a little incredulous, but let it go. A man's relationship with his mother was his own business. "How long will you be gone?"

"Don't know. I'll call you. Not that long."

"All right, man. Be careful, though. Do you need a ride to the airport or anything?"

"No, thanks. I can just call a cab. Remember, don't let either WorldCom or Global Crossing fall below $20 a share. If it does, I expect it to be sold and the funds put into my cash account. Promise?" Charlie didn't always trust Victor to be thorough.

"Yeah, yeah. Quit complaining already. You've made more money than you know what to do with. Relax. I've got it covered."

So that was that. One white lie to Victor, one call for a cab. He was free to disappear.

* * * * *

The lobby of the Peabody Hotel seemed the same. The gurgling of the fountain in the lobby bar, the bustle of people in the inner hallways, the high ceilings reverberating the sounds from below, the smells of perfume and leather luggage and starched bellman's suits.

It was $360 for the cab ride from Nashville, but he couldn't imagine trying to take a bus. And it wasn't far enough to fly. Besides, airports were difficult to navigate alone.

"Here. Let me get your bags. Let me find a bellman for you." The cab driver was overly friendly; worried about the blind man traveling alone, not sure what to do next. The bellman quickly took over.

"This way, sir. Follow me." Charlie liked the fact he assumed he wouldn't need help.

Once at the smooth, cool reception desk, the clerk chirped, "You're back again, Mr. McGurn? I see you were here just three weeks ago or so. Nice to have you back, sir." The receptionist had a high, squeaky voice. Charlie didn't like it.

"Would you like the same room? It's available. 502, near the elevators."

"That would be fine. Thank you," Charlie told her. He hadn't thought about it, but it would be easier. He was already familiar with the layout. "Thank you," he said again.

It was a little after noon; still four hours before his planned arrival. He found the barbershop; asked them to nicely "trim everything up." He spent an inordinate amount of time in the bathtub. Splashed on too much cologne, washed it all off and tried again. He worried about wrinkles in his slacks; his fingers couldn't detect if things were wrinkly or not. It was 3:30 p.m. when he left the room, a little earlier than he had planned, but his schedule was arbitrary anyway.

"Hello again, sir. May I get you a cab?" The bellman remembered him, remembered the generous tip.

"Thank you. Yes. Please."

"Where to, sir?" the bellman asked. Charlie didn't want to tell him.

"Germantown area."

"Good enough."

The next cab in line pulled up. The bellman leaned in and spoke with the driver, came back around to help with the door. Charlie felt around for the door opening, had to duck to get in. The cabbie didn't say a word until after they were out into the street.

The cab driver's English was colored with a foreign accent, probably Pakistani or Indian.

"Germantown. Where in Germantown." It was phrased as a question, but not stated as one, more just stated as a kind of fact.

"Tiffany's." Charlie said the words softly, half embarrassed.

"Aaahhh, yes. Very good, sir. Very good."

The cab driver was playing something Charlie thought was from India. It was Kula Shakur, *Hush*. It was soothing in an odd way. Charlie spread both of his arms out wide, adjusted his feet for balance, and laid his head back. He felt the cab accelerate onto the freeway and towards Germantown. To Tiffany's. To her. To Ruby.

CHAPTER 11

CHARLIE. 1993. 38 YEARS OLD. MEMPHIS, TENNESSEE.

C harlie sat at the table by himself, with his back straight, his arms stiff at his sides, and both feet planted firmly on the floor. He ordered a 7-Up; they gave him a Sprite. The Sprite wasn't quite right; somehow, the syrup and carbonation mix was off. Or the ice was bad. And they had put a cherry in it, skewered on a plastic sword.

His senses were on high alert, but she found him before he could sense her.

Ruby spoke loudly, out of habit; the music at Tiffany's was always loud.

"You're Victor's friend, aren't you?" she asked.

A shiver went up Charlie's back. It was her. He was sure it was her. His pulse was racing. Goose bumps pricked through the hair on his arms.

He regained his composure quickly, his anxiety imperceptible.

"Victor Booth? He is an acquaintance, yes. And you are?"

He knew full well who she was.

She leaned in closer to him so she wouldn't have to speak so loudly. Her breath smelled oddly of cocktail peanuts. "Sascha. No, really it's Ruby." At that she chuckled a little, at herself. "They both sound like stage names, so...anyway...I'd rather you called me Ruby."

He waited for her to say something more, but she didn't. Charlie tried to think of something to break the silence, but couldn't—not just then, anyway. She asked his name; he told her.

She sat down next to him. It was a quiet night, sprinkles of customers here and there and most of the girls in the dressing room smoking and talking.

They sat in silence for a while. Charlie remained stiff, his arms and legs still straight and his back now arched almost backward. But Ruby cuddled right up to him, like a little Siamese cat.

"I liked that you weren't into the sports so much," Ruby whispered softly.

It seemed an odd comment. Did she remember that much from three weeks ago? It hardly seemed possible.

"No, not really. Not really into sports." He left it at that, consciously stopped talking. It's never good to say too much, especially at first. There was another period of silence. Charlie didn't try to fill it.

"Where are your buddies?" She had moved so close to Charlie her words were now just a sultry hush. When she spoke, he felt her breath; it shivered his neck.

Charlie hesitated. Thought about lying. Thought about telling her he was meeting some people who would be there shortly. Thought about how his leg was shaking; he consciously stopped it. Finally he answered her, and as he did, his face turned ever so slightly toward her.

"I'm alone."

It was contrary to his nature and not as he had planned. But he couldn't help himself. He had to be honest with her. And he wanted to tell her.

"I couldn't stop thinking about you. I've been thinking of you for three weeks, every day since I was last here. I came back to see you. That's the only reason I'm here. You're Sascha. I guess Ruby, really. I know the perfume. I know your voice."

His own voice cracked during the last sentence, and she caught it. She sensed, for the first time, vulnerability. It was tremendously endearing to her.

Ruby didn't respond right away. Charlie let the silence build, let the gaping hole in his heart sit there wide open. He prayed for her to grasp it, and for her to gently put his heart back into his chest. But he was afraid—and he closed his eyes in a long blink just at the thought of it—that instead, she would sneer, chortle; callously squeeze the blood out. Leave him there, shredded, rejected.

She noticed a tear in his eye. A tear he didn't even know was there.

She moved closer to him, so close he could feel her breath. So close his leg started to tremble again.

Finally she spoke. Slowly, succinctly, as if she knew he would be hanging on to every precious word.

"I remembered you. I thought about you, too. When you left, when you left the last time you were here, I was so scared I wouldn't see you again. And when I came back to the table, you were, you know, you were already gone, and I thought 'That's it,' I'll never see him again. But I didn't know. Didn't know for sure. And to be honest, I've been working all the time. I've been working every day just…just hoping that maybe you would come back."

Her voice grew thin and the words started to tremble. There was another pause, but this time it was a short one, and she was able to continue.

"And, you know, and you did. Incredibly, you're here. And I don't know what it is, and I know this sounds crazy, but I feel I know you already. I feel I've known you for a long time. I feel you were supposed to come back here. Come back here to me. And…and you did. You came back."

He didn't respond out loud. He wasn't elated, he wasn't thrilled. He was moved by her words and by the moment and by the intensity of it, and by her honesty. He certainly didn't expect it there, at a place like this. And he was incredulous. Absolutely and thoroughly incredulous. Fascinated, stunned—at what she said, and at the thought that she may—actually did—remember him, and had thought of him, and was glad he was there. Ruby was glad he was there.

She knew he wasn't there to buy dances. She knew she needed to get up and work the room, to make some money. It had been a slow night, and she didn't even have her tip out yet. But still, she sat with him. She couldn't leave him.

He nodded his head, just a subtle gesture.

They sat there, in the dark of the club, on the hard chairs, under the loud speakers. But the room, to them, had turned quiet.

"I can't explain it," he whispered.

"We hardly even met," she said, and her head dropped and her eyes scanned the floor, as if to search for answers there.

"I know," he replied. "But we did meet. Thanks for remembering me."

She nudged him. "I certainly didn't forget you. You are hard to forget—a blind man in a strip club." She smiled at her own joke.

"Blind? I'm not blind...Strip club? This is a strip club?"

She laughed. He smiled.

They sat together quietly for a minute, maybe two, and then she reached over and held his hand under the table. He made no move towards her, just sat quietly, absorbing the moment.

Charlie was the one who broke the silence.

"Either/or," he said.

"What?" She didn't know what he meant.

"Either/or. It's a game. I give you an either/or, and you have to pick which one you like best. Gut feel. Just pick one or the other."

"Okay," she hesitated, but was willing to give it a shot. "Sure."

"City or country."

"What, I pick one or the other?" she asked.

"Yes. Pick the one you like best. Right away, no hesitating," he told her.

"Okay then, I guess… I like both."

"No," he said. "You have to pick one. And don't wait so long. Quick. Right away." He wasn't demanding; he was just playing.

"Okay, city."

"Mountains or ocean."

That was one was easy for her, and she responded right away.

"Ocean."

"French provincial or art deco."

"Art deco." She loved art deco.

"*Casablanca* or *The Godfather*."

"*Casablanca*. Definitely. Not into gangstas." She slurred out the word "gangstas."

"Green or blue."

"Oh, blue." She loved the color blue.

"Wait a minute," she said. She wanted to pause, to look at him. The game was fun, and she wanted to keep playing. But she just, at that moment, wanted to look at him.

Finally Charlie asked her. "Ready?" He sensed her staring at him, and it made him nervous.

"Okay," she said. "But now your turn." It was more a question than a request. He nodded his head.

"Sure. Go ahead."

"Okay." Ruby hesitated, then asked her either/or question.

"A splinter or a paper cut."

Charlie hadn't heard either/or bad things before. It was always something good, or something better.

"That sounds like "what's worse, not what's better."

"Answer the question," she chided. "Not fast enough, Mister."

"Okay, okay. I guess I'll say splinter. I guess it's better than a paper cut. But you should try nice things, not bad things."

She didn't care. "Shut up, it's my turn." She laughed again.

"If you're going to die, would you rather be hit by a train or drive off a cliff?"

"Cliff."

"Long hair or short hair." It was a setup; her hair was quite long.

"Oh, long, I guess."

She tried to set him up again. "Classical or jazz."

"Disco," he joked.

"Come on. Classical or jazz."

"Classical." He didn't like jazz; classical was only okay.

"Interesting," she said. "I much prefer jazz."

They continued for another twenty, thirty minutes; until Ruby's name was called to go on her stage rotation. He didn't hear it; he was too mesmerized by her. But she was subconsciously attuned to listen for her name.

"I have to go," she suddenly said.

Charlie was crushed. He didn't understand. She saw it on his face

"Don't leave. I have to go on stage. I'm not leaving. I will come back. Six songs."

Charlie tried to recover. "Oh, of course. Of course. I understand. You...you go ahead."

She suddenly felt very insecure. Even though he couldn't see her, he would know what she was doing. He would know she was taking her clothes off for strangers. She didn't want the crowd to roar, or the frat boys lined up on the front row of the main stage to whistle or call out her name. She didn't want him to think of her that way. But she had no choice.

She got through the dancing, watched him from the corner of her eye. He didn't seem to notice and more importantly, didn't seem to be upset by it.

And after her six songs and after organizing her dollar bills and tucking them into her purse, she went right back to him.

"Hey. I'm back. Sorry about that." She didn't know what else to say.

"So, tell me," he asked her "What does your costume look like?"

She smiled to herself. He was sweet and kind, but he was still a man.

"Sure. I made it myself. It's a little Indian girl outfit. It's my favorite. It's white and it's got tribal patterns of beads that are, you know, bright colors like red and blue and yellow and green. And I like the noise it makes," and with that she shook her shoulders, and her bikini top went swish, swish, swish. "But my favorite part," and she sounded excited about it, "is that this outfit has a rabbit pelt that snaps on." And she reached out for his hand, and placed it on the rabbit pelt covering her butt. "And I have one little, blue feather pinned in my hair." And she took his hand from her butt up to her hair, just above her ear, and had him feel the feather.

"A little Pocahontas," he chuckled.

"Yes. A little Pocahontas."

They started to touch each other, very gently. Just little caresses. Ten, fifteen minutes went by, and they both became disoriented, conscious of neither time nor place. Then they became aware of the music again, blaring through the big speakers. And the haze lifted, and the dark room seemed a little lighter, even to Charlie. As if they started to wake from a dream.

"This is crazy," he said. "I don't even know you." But even as he said it he reached for her hand again, held it in his, lifted it up to his face. And the words were gentle, and loving, in spite of their substance.

She backed away a little, wanted to talk. Smiled. She needed a little reality again. She realized she had questions—lots of questions.

"Well, let's see what I know. How good my memory is. You're from Nashville. You're into the stock market. You have some buddies, at least a couple. You wear very nice clothes—cashmere sweaters, expensive shoes, soft slacks, amazing cologne. You have great hair ... I just love your hair."

Charlie smiled. He was content to let her continue. He, too, felt he was just waking from a dream.

"What else? I can assume some things. My guess is you used to be in the military. Seems like a military-type haircut, and you always seem to be at attention. Even when you're sitting. And you've never been married. At least I don't think so."

"So? Pretty close?"

"Pretty close," he said slowly. "Navy. Twelve years active duty. Never married. No kids. Oh, and I've got a little issue with my eyes."

"Yeah, I noticed that. Doesn't seem you can see anything at all now, does it?" Ruby wasn't about to ignore it. "But you found me, didn't you, handsome? And...well, I'm... "

She started to cry, choked it back. He didn't catch it. She tried to continue her thought.

"I'm glad you did. I'm..." His voice had cracked before, but this time, it was hers. She spit it out. "I'm glad you did."

He waited just a few seconds before responding.

"You're right. I, I can't see much. Blurs. Can't see anything in here. It...it's tough sometimes." He wasn't going to hold back about it, either.

There was another pause, until Charlie started up again.

"My turn. Stop me when I'm wrong. If I'm close that doesn't count. Only stop me if I'm really wrong. Let's see... you're about 25. Single. You have a boyfriend, though."

At that, she interrupted him.

"Nope. Wrong on that one. Used to have a boyfriend. That's a long story. You're going to have to come back and stay a while for that one."

Charlie smiled. "Okay. Former boyfriend. I was hoping I was wrong about that one."

He continued.

"And you're brunette, blue eyes."

It was a total guess, but an incredibly good one. A twist of fate; Godlike intervention.

"Yes. Brunette. Blue eyes. Yes. How did you know that?"

He didn't respond, rather just continued.

"Soft, luxurious hair," he told her. He wanted to keep complimenting her; genuinely, sincerely, as he truly felt. It was easy.

"Long, feminine hands. Long, long legs that go on forever."

She didn't interrupt, didn't want to.

"Tan. I can smell that. Really."

At that she laughed. Probably tanning oil, or the smell of the sun. She had noticed it herself; when she had been in the sun her skin smelled different. Coconut.

"Okay, blind man. Pretty good."

He continued. "Sweet. You're sweet. I can sense it. No hard edges. And such a beautiful voice." He paused a second, truly thought about her voice, truly wanted to hear it.

He wanted to ask her out to dinner, just as if he had met her at a regular bar. But he didn't know whether she would go out with a customer. He didn't like the thought of being her customer, didn't feel like one, but he was a customer.

But he asked anyway.

"Could I … could I take you to dinner sometime?"

She looked at him, really looked at him. It was her long-standing rule: don't date customers. A lot, but not all, of the other dancers had the same rule. And there were good reasons for it. She thought of Vanilla.

But Charlie was a total exception to pretty much every rule.

"Well, handsome. I suppose we could do something like that." And she took his hand in hers and brought it up to her face, and he caressed her cheeks and ran his fingers through her hair.

And a soft, slow song came over the speakers; a rare ballad. It was Oasis, *Bittersweet Symphony*.

CHAPTER 12

CHARLIE. 41 YEARS OLD. RUBY. 35 YEARS OLD. 1996.
TODOS SANTOS, MEXICO.

Pods of wind, intermittent and light, crept over Charlie as he lay with his bare back towards the midday sun. His baggy swim trunks fell between the strands of white vinyl coiled around the lounge chair. Ocean water dripped and formed a little puddle. A few dried up leaves, curly and with their stems still on, skittered across the weathered wooden decking of the old dock. Puffy clouds, wet air, the smell of salt water and the depths of the ocean—fish and seaweed and mud and clams and shellfish—all of it wafted up and around and into the day.

And she lay next to him, Ruby Clarisse, in her tight, bright yellow, one-piece Spandex suit, and he could smell her hair, feel strands of it brushing his face when the trade winds blew it towards him. Her hair was as thick as strands of twine but tousled soft, and it was coated with lotions and crèmes so the water beaded up on it, and the lotions and crèmes were infused with chemicals to fake the smell of honey and of apricot.

Behind and all around them, for the dock they were lounging on was long, the ocean swells first started to build up from the depths, then gradually crested in long swaths, until finally, violently, they crashed upon the gravelly rocks to the south. There the sea-green water foamed and frothed, eventually simmering down to a gentle ripple until the waves, one by one, curled behind the rocky point and faded out of view.

Seagulls flew overhead searching for small fish, cawing incessantly over the beat of the surf.

Ruby stretched out her legs, then her arms. She wiggled her fingers and her toes, shook her head, and pushed her hair back away from her face. Then she stretched out as far as she could reach, her legs taut and her feet pointed, her arms above her head and angled inward, as if she were about to dive into the ocean—but she was just lying on a towel on the dock.

Charlie heard her stirring, stretching. He felt her breath on his back, then felt her pulling away from him. But Charlie was too tired, too relaxed to move or respond. All of his defenses had long since vanished. The city was now thousands of miles away. And their hotel, a decadent, overstaffed hideaway with fine linens in thatched bungalows, was just around the beach-head. Everything was prepaid and reserved for another two full weeks. Food and drink awaited them, in whatever quantities they wanted, whenever they wanted.

Little mopeds stood lined up to explore the island at their leisure; surfboards and scuba gear and diving masks and paddleboards were available on a whim. The weather was, and was expected to be, as constant and boring as possible; highs in the low 80s, lows in the upper 60s, partly cloudy with a slim chance of warm showers in the afternoons. It was hard to imagine what, if anything, could go wrong.

The wedding, just three days' earlier, had been blissfully simple, yet sophisticated, elegant, and fun. There were moments, of course, when Charlie longed for his sight; to actually see his bride, to see her eyes sparkle and fade, to see for himself the smiling faces of his—and her—friends and family. But the silk wedding dress was soft to his touch, the fresh-cut flowers smelled wonderful, and the guests' laughter was a melody.

And at practically every moment—as they drove to the little church, while they stood together at the altar, when he was told he could kiss the bride—Ruby was always there, always whispering to him at just the right time, her voice loving and her gestures intimate. She never, not once, embarrassed him in any way. She made sure that he maintained his masculinity, his sense of power and control that for years had been second nature. And though she guided him to his friends, once he was with them, she slipped away quietly, letting him enjoy their congratulations and banter. And he loved her more than ever.

When the time came to say his portion of the vows, he choked up, ever so slightly, imperceptible to all but her. And she loved him all the more for it, and she longed to be with him forever, to cherish him just as her vows said she would. And his mother cried, just then, just as they kissed, putting her face into her hands and weeping tears of joy. She knew nothing of Ruby's past—how she and Charlie had met, how Ruby had survived all those years—all Charlie's mom knew was that Ruby took care of him, treated him gently and kindly, supported him and loved him.

The rice was thrown, the flash bulbs popped, and the champagne flowed. The various and abundant toasts were dramatic, campy, short and long. Victor, the best man, spoke of perseverance and strength, offering more of a solemn tribute to his friend than a toast.

"He is a man's man, the type of man you would trust in the foxhole next to you, the type of man whom others admire and trust, who was born to lead. And in Ruby, he has found true love, and that is to be cherished."

The words were rehearsed, classic, spoken with conviction and in a deep, throaty voice that added drama and effect. Victor would become obnoxiously drunk later, and his words would then slur and his demeanor would turn sour. But that hadn't happened yet. It was a good, well-delivered toast.

"He deserves the best life has to offer, and I am sure all his friends and family, and all who are congregated here at this special time, join me in this toast to a great man and a great woman who are now together, to venture forth as one."

In another context, with different people, it would have been too much hyperbole, too sweeping and verbose. But it wasn't, not then, not there. Charlie was the tall, strong, handsome blind man sitting straight and proud at the head table in a striking black tuxedo. And next to him was Ruby, her youthful beauty incredibly intact and striking, her skin flawless and her eyes smoldering, a stunning strand of pearls around her neck and her hair tousled away from her face, accentuating her sharp Indian heritage features and tight jaw line. And in her hair was a little blue feather, from the night they met, from the little Indian girl outfit that only Charlie knew about And when she smiled, it lit up the room. And when she moved, graceful and silky, the world moved with her, longing to be in her presence. They were a powerful, real, stunning couple.

* * * * *

It was very late that night—early the next morning actually—when Ruby whispered to Charlie.

"Let's go. I want to go."

Charlie had been caught up in the ceremony, in the event, and had lost track of time. For days, weeks, he had been anxiously awaiting the wedding and dreading it as well. He was social and terribly diplomatic, but deep down, he did not particularly like gatherings. He was content alone, happiest with just Ruby and no one else. But in the right circumstances—and the wedding was sure to have some of those moments—the camaraderie of a group of people could be wonderful. When Ruby whispered to him just then, and told him she wanted to go, he let the thought sink in. And after a moment's pause, he whispered back to her. Ever the diplomat, always concerned about appearances and propriety, his sudden longing to be alone with her, remained tempered.

"Yes. It went well. Very well. Do you believe we can slip out? Quietly?"

By then, most of the guests had left. Ruby glanced around. There were still about two dozen couples on the ballroom dance floor, moving in dreamy circles to a slow song. About the same number of people sitting at the tables, sipping drinks and talking quietly. No one was at the bar and the bartenders were starting to tidy up for the night. The band was to play another half hour—until 2:00 a.m.—no later. Then the lights would come on.

And in the harsh fluorescent light, the floor would be linoleum, and the dirty plates and glasses would be stacked on the tables, and the tablecloths would be stained, and the fabric wouldn't quite cover the platform for the head table anymore, and the platform would show its gnarled, nailed-together plywood. And the earlier magic would disappear.

That had not happened yet, but it soon would.

"Yes," she said even quieter this time, pushing her body next to his and whispering even closer into his ear. He felt her breasts against his chest, her hair across his face. She was impatient, more narcissistic and less social, almost childlike in her desires. And her desire then was to leave.

"I want to go. I don't want to be here any longer. I want to be with you. Just you."

Charlie asked one more time.

"There's no one else we need to say goodbye to?" Military decorum, protocol; proper respects, and goodbyes needed to be said. But she would have nothing more of it, and was on the verge of a little tantrum.

"Noooo. I don't…. Go. I want to go. Now."

Charlie said nothing further. He put his arm around Ruby's waist, pulled her from his side so that she was facing him. He lifted his hand from her waist, slowly up her back, and then cupped her neck. She willingly moved even closer as he pulled her in, and they kissed yet again. This time the kiss was not at the urging of the crowd or to quiet the tinkling of glasses. This time, it was a kiss of desire; an intimate, soft, short kiss, a kiss for no one but them. And after the kiss, she moved back from his embrace, took his hand in hers, and led him to the back door. She had an overcoat in the closet, and in it was her clutch purse. The car keys were there, as she hoped they would be, and she gently pulled him out the door.

The stairs out to the back alley were awkward, and the alleyway itself was difficult to negotiate with potholes and an uneven surface, but Ruby pulled Charlie along and—although he stumbled once or twice—they got to the car and Ruby clicked the doors open. She helped Charlie into the passenger's side, a dance they had perfected many times as she guided him part way and he instinctively crouched down and settled into the soft leather. She shut his door, and looked into the passenger's side window from the outside.

The overhead light of the parking lot was just to their side, and it shone in, framing Charlie's face. He did not know Ruby was looking at him, as he pulled and buckled the seat belt around him and then stared straight ahead, patiently waiting for his bride. She looked at him, sitting there, his bow tie skewed to the side and his hair all messy, and her heart started to swell and tiny tears crept into the corners of her eyes.

She made her way around the back of the car, and got into the drivers' side. She slid the key into the ignition, and started the car.

"Are you all right?" Charlie asked her softly. The routine of getting into the car had taken longer than usual.

"Yeah. God, yeah." Ruby paused and looked at him again. His head had swiveled her direction, and he was looking at her, but not directly. She noticed his pretty blue eyes looked tired, and a little bloodshot. It had been a long—absolutely wonder-ful—night.

"Yeah. I'm … I'm good. Really good," she said. Charlie turned his back to stare straight ahead, and he grinned.

She drove them back to the hotel. The doorman was still at his post, even at that early-morning hour. They nodded as he held the door for them, and then they cuddled as they walked, and they kissed in the elevator as it took them up to the 25th floor on the club level, to their elegant suite. They made love, of course, and it was exquisite and passionate, to be cherished and remembered. But their intimacy was also uniquely calm, and unhurried; their bodies confident and their minds unclut-tered with fears or worries, knowing they would be intimate the next day and the day after that.

Time would creep by, of course, eventually would seek its subtle, inevitable revenge. But not then, not that night, and not for a long time.

* * * * *

E arly the next morning, they casually gathered their bags, enjoyed a small breakfast in the lobby, left the car keys at the front desk for Ruby's sister to retrieve, and took a cab to the airport.

They slept on the plane, both of them, their heads uncon-sciously tilted towards each other.

The shuttle to the resort was old and smelly, the roads rutted wide. But the trip was not too long, and as the shuttle passed the hewn rock pillars and iron gates, and as it started down the winding entry road, the dust settled and the vegetation thickened and the air freshened. By the time they got to the resort itself, they could feel the ocean breeze. And beyond the *palapa*'s lobby, Ruby saw the luxurious and expansive grounds spreading before them, a beautiful, park-like oasis in the middle of the jungle, with the glittering Caribbean lapping at all of its edges. She described it all to him, excitedly, in vivid detail. She hardly stopped talking.

Their cabana room was ready upon their arrival: chocolates on the table and cut flowers on the bed, and a fancy bottle of tequila with a little note providing congratulations for the newlyweds. The bellboy was tipped, the curtains opened, and the breeze allowed in.

"Swimsuits. Get the swimsuits." Charlie was sitting on the edge of the bed.

"Sure. Right…right away?" Ruby thought they might make love first, but the ocean was inviting.

"Yes. Let's. Let's put on our swimsuits and go to the ocean right away."

Ruby chuckled. He always spoke so formally. She decided to do the same, as she sometimes jokingly did.

"Well, yes, sir, then. We shall put on our swimsuits and go to the ocean right away. Yes, sir."

Ruby had intentionally packed the swimsuits toward the top of the suitcases, so it was only a matter of minutes before they were walking hand in hand, barefoot, their path taking them across the warm sand, the ocean periodically stretching out in little tentacles tickling their toes. After a bit they were far enough down the beach that they had escaped the myriad hotel staff and were on their own. They stumbled upon a long, old wooden dock that reached far out into the ocean, a long, narrow gangplank, a bit rickety and almost unsafe.

They claimed it as their own, and took some old, beat up vinyl lounge chairs from the beach out to the end of it. And they sat together, not talking; soaking up the sun and the salt water spray and the moment. Minutes passed, then an hour, before the breeze eased and the sun rose further and their skin heated.

"Gotta go in. Time to go into the water. We can dive." Ruby had stood up and was looking over the edge of the dock down at the sparkling water.

"It's deep, calm, clear." She was describing it for Charlie. "I can see bottom...sandy bottom...but it's deep. Wow, talk about clear."

"Go then. Dive in," Charlie was still lying in the lounge chair, but he was gradually starting to sit up, his legs and feet finding the decking.

"Here," Ruby turned towards him. "We'll both go. Here."

He sat up straight, then stood up. She led him to the end of the dock

"Here. Sit here, on the edge. Then when you're ready, just stand up and dive straight ahead. It's fine. It's perfect."

Ruby put her hand on his shoulder.

"I'm going in. It's okay, if you want. If not, I will swim right back."

She said nothing further, hesitated for a moment, and then dove into the ocean. Had anyone been watching, they would have seen a slender young woman in a bright yellow swimsuit make a beautiful, graceful dive into the water. Charlie barely heard her splash, heard her bob back up and gasp in air.

"It's...," She spit out some water. "It's fantastic. Charlie. It's just wonderful. Warm."

He laughed softly. He did want to join her. He wanted to dive in, to be with her in the water.

He felt around, reaching out to each side. He leaned far to his right, and felt the heavy timber pier. Then he leaned far to his left, and felt the other timber pier. He estimated the dock was about six feet wide. *Plenty*, he thought. He positioned himself in the middle, then stood up, his feet on the very edge.

He listened for Ruby. He heard her swimming off to the side.

Charlie took a deep breath, crouched, and dove. It was much further from the dock to the water than he had anticipated; he felt he was in the air for a long, long time. But he hit the water just about right, and his hands were positioned in front of him to push the water away. His head and his body followed his outstretched hands and arms in perfect alignment. There was hardly a splash; a textbook dive. Because it was farther from the dock to the water than he thought, though, he went in straight, and thus dove deep.

The water was warm on top, but cooler the further he went down. He had to rely on his own equilibrium to separate up from down, and as he kicked his way to the surface, he had a moment of panic that his senses were wrong. It was just then, though, that he broke the surface, bobbed up and took a deep breath. He was relieved, but tried to remain calm, cool. He trusted Ruby, loved her with all his heart, and was totally comfortable with their entire relationship. She was his best friend. But he still wanted to impress her.

"Nice," he said in as normal, nonchalant a voice as he could, trying to act as if blind men routinely dove off a dock into the open ocean. He tried to control his breathing while he treaded water.

"Nice dive," she answered. "And yes, the water is nice, isn't it?"

"Very nice." His breathing was now more under control. "Beautiful."

Ruby knew it must not have been easy for him and she had been terribly nervous as she watched him dive in. She knew he was nervous, too, just as she knew he would try not to show it. She also knew him well enough not to talk about it, and not to have offered to jump with him in tandem or to tell him he shouldn't.

"Swim over here. Over here. To your left." She felt he was drifting out to sea, and the thought of it scared her practically to death. But then she looked to the shore, and realized they were hardly 100 yards out, if that. She took the edge off her voice.

"Come see me," she said. And with that he started a slow, easy sidestroke towards her. When he got close, she reached out for him, and they awkwardly embraced while both trying to tread water.

"Come on. Come on." Ruby started to make her way to the shore, and Charlie followed her. Ruby swam gracefully, long strokes moving her quickly and easily. Her rhythm was smooth, and she did not stop for breath. As Charlie swam, he periodically stopped, let himself sink, and reached for the bottom. It took three attempts before he finally felt the soft sand on his feet, but even then, the water was still over his head. From there, though, it shallowed quickly, and Ruby took his hand as they splashed to the shore and stumbled back to the dock.

Charlie and Ruby stretched out again on the lounge chairs. The sun started to evaporate the water, and their skin tightened. Wet rolled off their bodies and salt kissed their lips. The sun burned them and the wind cooled them. Their muscles relaxed, their limbs fell limp. Time stood still and then became irrelevant. Worries and tasks faded away, their thoughts turned to nothing. They fell asleep, slowly, marvelously, alone but together.

It was a slightly cooler breeze that woke them, about an hour later, the breeze a precursor to a slight afternoon rain shower. They could see it building on the horizon, dark but rather innocent-looking clouds flicking gray wisps of visible rain out across the open ocean.

"Thirsty," Ruby whispered.

"Yeah, we'll head back," Charlie acknowledged. They dragged the lounge chairs back to the beach, pushed their feet through the soft, hot sand, and ambled back.

Closest to the beach was the Barracuda Bar—an open-air hut with a bar in the middle, perhaps a dozen cane bar stools around it, old life preservers and conch shells and beachcomber finds nailed and roped to lacquered posts. Modern-looking stereo speakers were also strapped up, dangling precipitously. Classic Bob Marley, *No Woman, No Cry*. They stumbled up to the bar and ordered margaritas.

"Thanks," Charlie said to the bartender.

"It's good," Ruby slurred her words—not from the drink, which she had yet to finish—but from the sun and the nap and the beach and the sand.

"I like it. I like it."

And day turned to night and back to day, and the days stretched out marvelously, one into the next, until, finally, it was enough. Charlie and Ruby then trudged out to the big plane on the big asphalt strip and the big plane yawned open, and swallowed them up, and flew them back home; tired, relaxed, happy, together.

CHAPTER 13

CHARLIE. 1996. 41 YEARS OLD. MEMPHIS, TENNESSEE.

I t was a work day.

Charlie woke up before the alarm clock, as he most often did. He reached over to the bedside table, pushed the button, confident he would not fall back asleep. He rolled over and lay on his back, wiggling his toes. There were soft noises from the little gray cat snuggled up against Ruby, curled with its paws covering its eyes and its tail wrapped around itself and contorted into a tight ball of fur within Ruby's outstretched arm.

Charlie felt the urge to pee, got out of the bed, and made his way down the stairs to the bathroom. He lifted the toilet lid, sat down, reached between his legs pushed his penis down and away from the edge of the porcelain, and let out a long stream.

When they had first been together, when they first felt comfortable enough to share the bathroom, Ruby had laughed at him when he sat down to pee.

"I thought you said you had to pee."

"I do. I am," Charlie had said sleepily.

That was when she had laughed. "Then why are you sitting?"

Charlie was still sleepy and didn't take offense. "Uh...I'm blind, remember? Unless you want it all over the place, this is probably a good idea...."

"Oh, sweetie, of course..." It was the first time Ruby had called him sweetie. She went over to him and wrapped her lovely arms around his head while he was still sitting on the toilet. "I am so sorry..."

"It's fine. Really." And incredibly, it was at that very moment, very shortly after they had met, that Ruby had first told him that she loved him. And without any hesitation, Charlie had told her he loved her back.

That memory came back to him that morning, years later. He remembered Ruby's faux pas, remembered how sorry she felt and how she had cradled his head in her arms while he sat there on the toilet. How they told each other they were in love. It was an odd memory, but a good one. And it made him laugh; not out loud, of course, sitting there in the bathroom all alone that morning, but it was enough for a hint of a smile to cross his face.

He shaved carefully, by feel, letting hot water slowly fill the tub for his bath. Charlie managed his morning routine just fine. It was a quick routine, most often with no problems and always—as much as possible—exactly the same. He had counted the steps, knew the heights, the locations of the faucets—hot on the left cold on the right. The toilet, the shave, the bath, the aftershave, an old flimsy robe. Then breakfast: sugary cereal, skim milk, dishes into the sink; underwear drawer, sock drawer, t-shirt drawer. Pre-arranged outfit from the night before, neatly laid out on a valet and on top of the dresser: a pressed shirt, tie, dark slacks and dark blazer. It was the business professional's uniform, slight variations but inevitably quite the same.

After he was dressed and ready, he always went back to check on Ruby. Most often, as she was this particular day, she lay stretched on her side in the king bed, the cat still next to her, her hands together as if in prayer, and her face resting upon them. Charlie made his way to the side of the bed, and sat on the edge of it. He felt for her, traced the bulge in the down comforter up to her face and then caressed her hair.

"Goodbye, baby," he whispered to her. "Sleep in." On days she worked early—for Ruby that wasn't until 11:00 a.m.

—she would sleep at least another hour or two past that point. On days after she had worked late or when she had the day off, it would often be two or three hours after Charlie left for work that she would sleepily get out of the bed, struggle to the kitchen and make her coffee. At night, no matter their schedules, they always went to bed together.

The overstuffed, green plaid couch in the living room was where Charlie sat and waited in the morning. Sometimes it was only five to ten minutes, sometimes it was fifteen or twenty. Regardless of how long the wait, Charlie always sat patiently, quietly, his back straight and his arms rigidly at his sides to keep his shirt from wrinkling. Charlie most often heard footsteps before the doorbell, but not always. And when the doorbell rang, Charlie would get up slowly, reach for his briefcase, and go to the front door where Stanley Cunningham would be waiting for him.

"Hey, Charlie."

"Good morning, Stan. How are we doing for time?" Charlie would routinely ask if they were on time.

"We're fine." Stan never gave a specific answer. It was always "pretty good," or "we're fine," or on those rare occasions when it was a little later than usual, he would say something like "Traffic is bad, but we'll be okay."

Stan knew better than to help Charlie to the car; he just made sure to walk ahead and let Charlie listen for his footsteps. And Stan always tried to park the car in the same spot in the driveway .

It was about a twenty-minute drive from Central Gardens, the inner suburb where Charlie and Ruby lived, to FedEx in Millington. Sometimes the two men said nothing, sometimes they talked a little. They never turned on the radio, never stopped along the way. This day they talked, Stan more than Charlie.

"Election's coming up pretty soon. Could be interesting this year, huh?" Stan asked.

They had been commuting to work together for over three years, and never once had they discussed religion or politics.

"Sure," Charlie answered, intentionally vague. "Not much to it this year, not all that interesting. Can't imagine Clinton won't be re-elected."

And then, much to Stan's surprise, Charlie added. "Fine with me."

Stan couldn't tell exactly what that meant, but it alluded to a preference, although that was quickly dispelled.

"It'll be fine either way, though." In the end, Charlie remained noncommittal.

And that was that. For the next fifteen minutes, neither man spoke. It wasn't that they didn't like each other, or that they didn't get along. In fact, it was quite the opposite. They got along and liked each other very well. They were just the type of men who didn't feel the need to talk for no reason, so they didn't. They were the type of men who stayed quiet in meetings and listened to others talk themselves hoarse, and only when the banter died down and, almost always only after asked, would they provide their input to the discourse. When they did speak, though, it was noteworthy, succinct, and often enough, quite brilliant.

Stan was the Chief Financial Officer of Federal Express, having steadily risen through the ranks over the last twenty years, quite easily and without any tumult. Hardly anyone was surprised by his success; each promotion met with knowing nods of approval. He commanded a large salary, significant perquisites, a corner office, and insipient but quiet power that he rarely used—but when he did, he wielded it with the utmost authority and very swiftly.

But Stan Cunningham hardly functioned alone, and some argued it wasn't Stan who was ultimately responsible for

FedEx's almost meteoric rise. Although they rarely spoke during their short commute, at the office, Stan and Charlie formed a most compatible team. Stan had more seniority—and the obvious advantage of eyesight—those close to the two men knew how valuable Charlie was to Stan and the huge company's great success.

At first, Stan had taught Charlie the ropes, but over time, Charlie had brought innovative ideas, powerful insights, and never-ending enthusiasm to the table. And Stan made sure Charlie was appropriately rewarded, not with titles or accolades, but rather with loyalty, security, and respect.

Charlie started work at 8:30 a.m. Unlike Stan and the rest of his colleagues in the finance department though, Charlie left work relatively early; promptly at 2:30 p.m. He took no lunch break. No breaks at all, really. And meetings were routinely scheduled early, deferentially for Charlie's schedule.

At 2:45 p.m. every day, Charlie had a driver pick him up in a limousine and take him home. The driver's name was Luke. Luke was only 22 years old and still in college. He worked for the limousine company part-time, and his primary duty was driving Charles McGurn. Luke had quickly grown to respect the man: his wit, his intelligence, and his generosity. At the end of the year, for each of the last three years that Luke had been chauffeuring Charlie home from work, Charlie had handed him an envelope. And each year there had been exactly enough money in that envelope to pay Luke's tuition for the upcoming academic year.

And unlike the morning ride with Stan, the limousine ride with Luke, Charlie sat in the passenger side and the huge, empty back of the limo was filled with conversation. Politics, religion, economics, women, movies, art, and life. Luke was a young man on the cusp of true adulthood, cognizant and fully aware of the amazing opportunity somehow bestowed upon him by one Charles McGurn.

Charlie didn't like the radio. The announcers were too silly, and he hated commercials. But sometimes, towards the end of the commute, Charlie would ask Luke to play some music on the limousine's CD player; something "of the day," Charlie would say, or something "hip." Luke would laugh a little, say "Sure."

This particular day, Luke decided to play Skee-lo, *I Wish*. Charlie liked it, and asked Luke to "play it again," even though by the time the song ended, they were already parked in Charlie's driveway. So there they sat on that cool September day in 1996, quietly listening, bopping their heads to the beat, as the limousine purred in idle.

CHAPTER 14

C harlie's deodorant had a light scent, but it was quite distinctive, and Ruby remembered it always. And although she was very tired that morning, Ruby still sensed him and smelled him when he kissed her goodbye, his stiff dress shirt wrinkling for the first time that morning as he leaned over and caressed her hair. She wanted to waken, to reach up to him and hug him and kiss his cheek. But she was too tired, just then, and sleep still enveloped her. It was too early, the need not strong enough. He would be back that afternoon, as he always was, and they would have their time together then.

So he crept back down the stairs. And she fell back asleep. And as she did her arm curled a little tighter around her small, gray cat. She was hugging the cat like a child would hug a teddy bear, petting it and cradling it and loving it. And the docile creature—his domesticity having fully taken over—lay limp, one little paw stretched out to pat her face.

The old, metal, Big Ben alarm clock on the nightstand said it was 11:15 when Ruby first lifted her head from the pillow and squinted to look at it. But as hard and as long as she might have slept, when she woke up, it was never subtle or slow. Rather, after that first glance at the clock, she opened her eyes wide and bolted up in the bed. The cat was thrown inadvertently across the down comforter, eventually skittering to its feet and bounding to the floor. Ruby swung her legs off the side of the bed and wiggled her feet until they found the maple floor underneath. One quick rub of her eyes, a shake of her head— thick, long hair twirling—and she was standing up. She still needed coffee, still needed to totally gather her senses, but once she was awake, she didn't linger in the bed.

She never set the alarm; never fiddled with the tiny grooved knobs or pulled the shiny little button on the clock. And even though she slept late, her internal clock still knew when she should get up for the day. On this particular day, 11:15 was about as late as she could have slept without having to rush to be at what she always told Charlie was her new, "real" job by 1:00, her morning rituals a languorous, almost theatrical routine, with soft music on the stereo, steaming coffee, bubble baths and skin lotions, soft whispers to the cat.

Her bath often took twenty minutes to half an hour. The big, deep, porcelain tub had wide sides where she put her coffee cup between sips while she lay in the tepid water. She had long, slender arms, legs, feet and hands that searched for places to go. So quite often, her legs and arms stretched out over the edges of the tub, painted toes and painted fingernails draping over the sides.

Depending on the day, after her bath, she would pluck her eyebrows or shave her legs, manicure her fingernails or curl her lashes. She knew she was beautiful before the adornments: her skin still rosy, her eyes bright and wide, her lips soft and inviting. When Charlie thought of her he envisioned her as the alluring girl next door, standing on the lawn on a spring day, wearing nothing but jeans and a t-shirt, chatty and fun, sporty and laughing. But he knew she was also feminine, sophisticated, aloof; friendly but demure.

Ruby liked to get to work early, abhorred being late—this was a real job, not the club; so she left the house at least half an hour before she needed to be there, even though the commute was only fifteen minutes. She loved her little BMW Z3 convertible, a pretty blue with a white top. She wore big sunglasses on her face, pulled her hair back, and liked the top down even when it was a little cold. Charlie had bought the sports car for her 34th birthday—sparkling new and smelling of plastic and leather and glue and things that new cars smell of that nobody knows why. And she loved it and she kept it washed and polished and maintained, and she kept a little, handwritten service notebook in the glove box.

She liked to park away from the store, on a side street where the traffic was light and the limbs of the big oak trees stretched way out over the roadway, their very ends of their branches touching the very ends of the branches on the other side, creating a sun-filtered canopy. And she liked to look at the houses on the block, big brick colonial houses with tidy lawns and curvy sidewalks leading to front doors with heavy brass knockers. And she liked turning the corner and seeing the flower beds and ornamental trees the commercial landscaper had placed perfectly around the perimeter of the upscale mall.

The convertible top went up automatically with the push of a button, and then it bumped up against the windshield. There were metal levers—one on the driver's side and one on the passenger's side—which Ruby manually cranked until the top was pulled down tight onto the frame. The remote door lock button on the key was a thrilling novelty, and Ruby sometimes waited until she was quite a ways from the car before she pushed the button and heard the beep that meant the locks were engaged. She smiled when that happened, loving the cool, sophisticated feeling it brought her. She felt proud, lucky. A bystander might just as likely have found it all haughty and arrogant.

The jewelry store was pristine, its big glass cases constantly cleared of fingerprints and smudges, and each morning, its displays were filled with thousands of exquisite rings and watches and necklaces and bracelets and earrings and even cufflinks and tie stops. And each night, everything was gently removed and stored in the safe. At the very center of the store, with the counters all around it, was a gigantic safe, as big or bigger than one in a bank. It was at least eight feet high and eight feet square, and the big metal wheels that turned the gears for the locking mechanism were massive, and required two people to operate when the heavy metal door was opened or closed. And it was functional, of course, for it held and protected the jewelry, but the massive safe was a shrewd marketing tool as well: only the finest, most expensive jewelry would need a safe that big and that fancy to safeguard the baubles from the hordes who craved them.

Ruby was one of a dozen or so salespeople who rotated shifts throughout the week and weekends. Only two of those salespeople were full time, both middle-aged women, the rest part time. Ruby was technically classified by the franchise store as a "limited, part-time employee," which meant she worked somewhere between 15 and 25 hours per week on average, but her hours would vary based upon the sales cycle, with the Christmas season and Valentine's Day being busier times where she would work more. She rarely worked weekends, and never at night.

The owner, Lee Hutcherson—a very thin, serious-looking man with thick glasses who liked to work in the back, at his own jewelry bench, doing repairs and constantly evaluating the gemstones with his loupe—accommodated Ruby always, not because she was pretty, about which he didn't truly care, but because her sales numbers were literally off the charts. At the corporate meetings in Atlanta, the comments were almost funny, often ribald. "Look at those numbers. $15,000 sold in a 6-hour shift. What the hell is that woman doing—giving her phone number away with every purchase?" The men would laugh, pat each other on the back. "Lee, you'd better keep that girl happy."

Whether it was a young man mesmerized by her figure or an older man taken with her eyes, the men were routinely an easy sale for Ruby. But what was surprising was that Ruby—almost in spite of her rather intimidating good looks—charmed the women, too. Perhaps they wished to emulate her or maybe they simply trusted her obvious good taste and hoped it would rub off on them with an expensive purchase. Or perhaps it was all simply because she was so genuine and sincere, and truly loved much of the jewelry she sold. When Ruby told someone about the sparkle of a diamond's cut or the design quality of a necklace, the depth and truth behind her comments were obvious. And if she didn't like the look of something, or if it didn't suit the customer, she would express her feelings, sometimes quite coldly and bluntly—but then quickly move them to another piece that she somehow knew would be the right one.

So people bought from her and came back to her and paid lots and lots of money to her and thus to the store and Lee Hutcherson, who in turn gave a little of it back to Ruby. And the relatively little he gave back to Ruby was quite enough, as to her it seemed almost a gift, the work hardly difficult or laborious. And to Lee Hutcherson's great delight, Ruby never seemed to bother with the simple math to compare her sales with her pay, which was, of course, greatly distorted in the store's favor.

Working for Lee Hutcherson wasn't fun, exactly—it was a job—and Ruby treated it as such and could easily have left it. But it was an easy job. And after leaving Tiffany's cabaret and struggling for years—Charlie being totally supportive—she was so pleasantly surprised that a "regular" job could be so easy and pay her so well. Lee had, of course, paid for her to become certified as a gemologist, which was wonderful for Ruby's confidence.

The money wasn't as much as the club, but actually quite close. The tax withholding took her by surprise; her declared pay at the club had been laughable compared with the actual take—but with Charlie in her life, it didn't matter anyway. She felt she had luckily stumbled upon the one thing she could do that did not involve taking off her clothes.

Ruby never worked past 6:00 p.m. except on those rare occasions during the busy season or when she was working on a big sale. After leaving work, she rushed directly home, knowing Charlie would already be there. Sometimes when she got home, he would still be working out in the gym downstairs, in the big room in the basement where he had everything set up, iron barbells clanking and hard rock music piped in. But other times, he would be in the living room, intensely concentrating on some work project or reading the New York Times—often frustrated that the Braille edition came out a day late and wasn't current.

If it was a work day for Ruby, dinner was either ordered in or they went out. Charlie usually gave her the choice. It was a typical early evening routine.

"Hey, have you thought about dinner?" Charlie would ask.

Then Ruby would think for a minute, about the weather or whether she was tired, and then she would finally respond.

"Can we go to Coquette?" she would ask him back. The Coquette Café was one of her favorite restaurants, a stylish French bistro with good drinks and pomme frites with garlic aioli sauce. She always asked Charlie, never demanded. They shared their salaries, put everything into a joint account. His salary more than Ruby's, but hers substantial enough. There was never a doubt that Charlie was the provider, and she liked that. It helped him with his independence, his self-worth.

"So you would like to go out to dinner again? You would like to sip your red wine for a while and order your fancy meal, would you now?" Charlie's question was stated teasingly, knowingly.

"Why, yes, I would," she would formally reply.

"Then we shall, my dear. Are you dressed appropriately?" Often, after asking such a question, Charlie would go over to his wife and touch her clothes, her jewelry, her hair, letting his hands roam over her lovely curves.

"Of course I am,' Ruby would tell him and gently push him away, laughing softly. And of course she would be, most often anyway, still dressed from work in an outfit more than appropriate for a nice restaurant.

And at the restaurant, the maitre d' would call them by name, and escort them to a nice table. And the waiters and waitresses would provide more personal, faster service—for Ruby and Charlie were easy to remember. They were known as nice, undemanding, and most generous. And for years, they had talked and held hands and softly touched each other.

* * * * *

Five years passed, then ten. The dinners continued, but the talk between them started to become less animated, less engaged. And their hands, which had once been almost constantly intertwined or caressing the other, started to drop to their sides or their laps. And the gestures and subtleties of new romance faded, and gradually became less intimate. And Charlie would think about the stock market, and Ruby would think about her daytime TV shows. For time, eventually, grindingly erodes everything in its path.

But despite the inevitable growing together that includes growing apart, it was okay. Because even though their new romance had eroded, in its place was a fine, mellow romance.

Charlie knew it was all like a beautiful view from a window; it is at first stunning. But over time you forget about it, and don't bother looking out. It is only later, when you happen to look out the window again, that you realize the beautiful view is still there. There will be subtle, perhaps imperceptible, nuances. But inevitably the view will still, as it did before, mesmerize. Charlie felt that he and Ruby had, as a couple, grown quiet. But he also knew they had also grown deep. And although they often forgot, the patterns and routines of the day having taken over, at those moments when they did look at each other, Charlie felt the view was still beautiful and he thought they were still mesmerized.

And sometimes there was music playing. And sometimes there was not.

CHAPTER 15

I t was a little before 6:30 p.m. on September 24, 2003, in Memphis, Tennessee. Rain showers had been predicted, but didn't happen. The sun was parked low on the horizon, behind some light clouds to the west of the city. The clouds stretched in a line, mirroring the contours of the Mississippi River, some light and airy and others darker, more ominous. Ribbons of bright light poked through a few of the cloud breaks, balanced with shots of darkness where the clouds were thick.

The Mississippi River was its classic, muddy brown color, almost black-brown in places, and it boiled and churned from the heavy currents and sandbars and wing dams. It rolled on by, its width and breadth dramatic, living up to its legendary status. A tugboat pushing a particularly impressive string of barges, two abreast, five long, struggled upstream in the middle of the channel and was just passing under the bridges as Victor crossed.

Victor was heading east, and he wasn't paying attention to the sky behind him or the river below. He was speeding, about 20 miles over the 55 mph limit, to the dinner party. And as he flew along, he pulled the vanity mirror down. He was trying to adjust the part in his hair to hide the thin spots. He was already about half an hour late, even though it was only a short drive from his condo on Mud Island to Charlie and Ruby's house in Central Gardens. Part of the delay had been intentional (he never liked to get to a party early), and part of it was due to his last-minute decision to watch the end of the Cardinals game.

So it was about 6:45 when Victor pulled up in front of the house.

Central Gardens was within the Memphis city limits, and it was surrounded by pockets of ghetto and blight. Some felt it was dangerous to live there. They preferred the far suburbs, which in recent years had exploded with "white flight." Huge subdivisions and entire little towns—once considered the country—were being swallowed up and transformed into tidy enclaves for middle-class families. Farther out, stretching into the state of Mississippi, the upper middle classes built their "country estates" on two to three acres, but the Wal-Marts and Costcos were never far away. It didn't seem like the country and they didn't seem like estates.

But even if Central Gardens' crime rate was a little higher, for many, the tradeoff was worth it. Dating back to the 1920s and 1930s, the homes in Central Gardens were stately, plantation-style edifices of real brick and stone, not facades. There were windows with etched and leaded glass, patios with pillars, stone gazebos and greenhouses with cupolas. And most all of them had big, fancy, wrap-around front porches. The grounds around these houses were lush, mature, on the verge of overgrown. And inside the homes in Central Gardens, there was thick woodwork and tall ceilings, cut-glass doorknobs and polished wood floors that showed traffic patterns, and Oriental rug runners and hanging chandeliers—real chandeliers, with draping filigree, sparkling crystals, and tarnished metal.

The biggest and most elaborate homes in Central Gardens faced Overton Park. And although children played there and people picnicked, Overton wasn't like the parks in the suburbs or next to the neighborhood schools. Instead, Overton Park was like an English garden, but an English garden of gargantuan proportions. Here visitors found huge, mature willow trees with draping limbs; magnolia trees with giant white flowers; leafy bushes, ponds with lily pads, rolling grassy slopes, tidy hedges and stone walkways. There were no jungle gyms or tennis courts, no band shells or soccer fields. It was nature's showcase, tended carefully by the arborists and laborers hired by the city, still successfully fighting off dwindling budgets and resources, a last bastion of a decaying park system. It was quite magnificent.

Charlie and Ruby's house was relatively small compared to most in Central Gardens, but everything about it was exquisite. It was two blocks in from Overton Park, in the heart of the quietest few blocks, and stood on a slight rise to elevate it slightly over its neighbors. Its exterior was primarily stone, thick slabs about two feet across, solid gray and weathered. Indented into the stone were numerous nooks and crannies, subtly patterned, and in the nooks were recessed windows, narrow and tall, many of which did not open.

It was two stories tall, with the second story set back from the first. The house was fairly long and narrow, and at each end there was a chimney, brick juxtaposed with the stone, and the chimneys seemed extraordinarily wide and tall. Ornate hedges and two big trees stood in the front yard, symmetrically offsetting the chimneys. To one side of the lot was a long, curving driveway, brick with stone edging, leading to the garage, which was tucked around the back of the house.

When he finally got there, Victor pulled his long, black Mercedes right into the driveway, and drove right up to the garage doors. Instead of using the front walkway, he opened the iron gate and walked directly into the private back yard, which housed a pretty little pool. He expected the guests would all be outside, on the back patio next to the pool. But he was surprised they weren't. Instead of going all the way back to the front door, he pulled on the French doors in the back to see if they were open, and when he found they were, he let himself in.

"Hello," Victor called out quite loudly. He could hear voices in the kitchen, and went in that direction.

He called out again. "Hello there."

This time Ruby responded. "Well, there you are." Ruby went up to him and gave him a compulsory hug.

"What, did you get lost?" she chided him. "Come on, most everyone is still in the kitchen. Dinner's almost ready."

"You're the boss." The tone was condescending. Ruby ignored it, didn't respond. Victor followed her into the kitchen.

Steam was rising from a pot on the stove; two couples were sitting next to each other on barstools at the island, and a young man was standing holding a drink off to the side. The young man was Luke, Charlie's chauffeur, and next to him was a pretty young woman. Charlie was in the other room, talking with Stan and Stan's wife.

"Tom, Jennifer, this is Victor Booth." Ruby started the introductions.

Victor went over to them, politely shook hands. "Nice to meet you."

"And this is Bob and Sheryl, our next door neighbors."

Bob spoke up, put out his hand. "Nice to meet you, Victor."

"Likewise," Victor replied, and shook Bob's hand first, then his wife Sheryl's.

Victor looked over at Luke. They had met before.

"Well, sport. Who's this next to you?" Victor was eyeing Luke's girlfriend, to the point that Luke noticed.

"This is Stephanie," Luke said.

"Stephanie. My, you're a beautiful young woman," Victor said as he looked at her, his eyes travelling up and down rudely. Ruby stared at Victor, subtly showing her displeasure. Victor turned and looked back at her, grinned.

"And Ruby, you look marvelous as always."

"Why, thank you, Victor." She said it curtly, but kept her temper. "What would you like to drink?"

"Can you make me one of your great martinis? Vodka, Ketel One if you've got it."

"Sure." Ruby went to the liquor cabinet to find the vodka. Victor settled into one of the low chairs next to the breakfast table, and kicked his feet up onto an empty chair. He looked around, surveying things.

"Is that a new painting?" he asked. Hanging on one of the kitchen walls was a 3x5-foot impressionist oil of children playing in a park.

"I love it. I noticed that, too," Sheryl chimed in. "You both have such good taste. Now Ruby, which of you picked that one, you or Charlie?" The group laughed at the idea of Charlie picking a painting.

"I would actually have to say Charlie," she surprised them. "I describe art for him, and he tells me if he likes it." The statement was true, and Charlie took pleasure thinking about his surroundings, even if he couldn't see them.

"Good for him," Bob said. "That's pretty cool, and I should have guessed."

"I don't know how he does it," Sheryl added, realizing as she spoke that it was a little awkward with Charlie right there.

The conversation drifted, mundane things like the weather and sports, then the new airport security rules, the war on terror. Victor sat in the corner, fairly quiet for a time.

Luke and Stephanie had joined the conversation, but also stayed busy passing flirty glances at each other. It was their third date and Luke relished the thought of dinner at Charlie and Ruby's with her at his side. He was convinced Charlie would like her, which was important to him. And he thought Stephanie would be favorably impressed with Charlie, Ruby, the house; which she was, almost immediately. Luke and Stephanie had been the first to arrive, and while Ruby gave her a little tour of the house, Stephanie kept telling Ruby how wonderful she found everything.

Earlier, Stephanie had searched for the perfect dress, and was pleased to have found a patterned, close-fitting sundress, off the shoulders with ruffles, fairly tight. She was just twenty-three, Scandinavian and looked it, lithe, most would say skinny. She was a year older than Luke, and in the vintage little dress, she looked both younger and older at the same time. Stephanie kept fairly quiet, tried to speak formally when she did.

The dining room was spacious, with large, elegant windows looking out onto the back yard, the pool, the lush landscape, and the big cottonwood trees rimming the lot line. A plate rail went around the rectangular room, and on it were framed photos. Built-in china cabinets held delicate glass and exquisite silver that Ruby had found at antique and consignment stores over the years.

The gray cat stalked the room. Another calico sat on one of the chairs. The table was set with wooden chargers, mirrored trivets, silk napkins, and a large floral piece in the center. The floral piece, though, was a bit too large. As everyone sat down, it became quite obvious people could not see around it.

"No good," Ruby said with a southern drawl, and took it off the table and set it on the sideboard instead.

It was about 8:00 before dinner was ready, although hors d'oeuvres and snacks had been varied and plentiful—soda crackers and brie, Cajun shrimp dip, deviled eggs. Stephanie helped Ruby in the kitchen, practically insisting. Ruby found her pretty, nice. Later, she told Charlie that Stephanie was perfect for Luke and she hoped they stayed together.

There was a simple garden salad with cucumbers and cherry tomatoes, crumbled cheese. That was followed by chicken cacciatore with chopped onion, minced garlic, thyme, oregano, basil, sugar, bay leaves. And with the chicken were balsamic glazed carrots and fresh asparagus. Chocolate pie for dessert, and to Ruby's surprise, her guests didn't want to wait for dessert later, but voted for it right away instead.

The meal wasn't perfect; the asparagus was a little under cooked, the pie crust perhaps a little hard. But it was nonetheless quite impressive.

"Wow. Ruby. You outdid yourself. This is—everything is awesome," Bob stated bluntly.

"Yeah," Luke said between heaping bites, his youthful metabolism eliminating any concerns about waistlines or high blood pressure. "It's really great. Stephanie? Do you like it?"

"Oh, yes," Stephanie said, trying not to talk with food in her mouth but wanting to express her approval without hesitation. "It's really wonderful. Ruby, you must give me this chicken recipe." The request for the recipe was a gesture only; Stephanie lived in a tiny studio apartment and had never learned to cook.

Even Victor seemed to like it. He spent most of the dinner talking to Bob about investments, somewhat to Ruby's chagrin, but when the pie arrived, he did comment about the dessert. "Wow, great, your chocolate pie. I like your chocolate pie." And he did, not hesitating to ask if there was another piece after devouring his first.

They polished off nine bottles of wine between the ten of them: three Chardonnays, two Merlots, two Zinfandels, a spicy Cabernet, and a very nice Pinot Noir. No one in the group was a wine expert, but the man at the store helped with some good choices after Charlie had told him his price point was a generous $30 to $40 per bottle, prompting the salesman to start calling Charlie "sir," an idiosyncrasy Charlie found quite comical.

At one point, as the night wore on, Ruby suggested they "retire to the living room," but there was too much conversation, too much laughter. The guests pretty much ignored her, and just stayed at the dining table instead. Eventually, though, as people got up to use the bathroom and stretch their legs, the dining room emptied. When Bob went outside to "catch some air," people seemed to gradually join him there. Ruby didn't fight it, just turned on the outside light and brought out drinks and coffee.

The night was marvelous, the sky having cleared after a light shower that no one had noticed during dinner. The moon was bright and the air humid, but not too warm. Charlie had Stan help him gather some wood and they started a fire in the pit next to the pool. When they pulled some beach chairs over to the blaze, the others stood or sat soaking it all in. Conversations turned more private, quieter. There was sporadic laughter, but things turned melancholy, weighted by the rich food and the wine.

Ruby struggled to stay awake. It was almost midnight, and she routinely went to bed no later than 10:00 or 10:30. She had gotten up early primarily to prepare the chicken cacciatore, but also to make sure everything was clean and ready. It had been a long day. Charlie, too, was starting to show signs of tiring out; he was slumping a little in the lounge chair, a rare event as his posture was usually so perfect. Although Stan and his wife had left by then, the remaining guests—Luke, Stephanie, Bob, Sheryl, and Victor—just lingered there, seemingly content and quite oblivious of their tiring hosts.

About a half an hour later, when Bob got up and yawned, they seemed to realize it was time to go home. And they hugged and said their thank yous, and vowed to "do this again soon," and that "next it's our turn." A few minutes later, all was quiet. Ruby looked around the kitchen, debating whether she should try to at least rinse the dishes. Charlie was at her side, and instinctively knew what she was thinking.

"Not tonight, honey. I can try to help you tomorrow. Let's go to bed."

And they did.

Charlie fell sound asleep, sprawled across the big, king-size bed. But Ruby struggled, her mind racing, thinking too much. She thought about the dinner party. Thought about how she had changed. She was no longer naïve, no longer from the wrong side of the tracks. Not anymore. She thought about Victor, about how rude he had been. She had once been afraid of him, awed by the fact that he had money, a higher education. She thought that put him at a higher level than she could ever be; that because of those things he was somehow a better person. But he wasn't. He is just kind of an ass, she thought to herself. He is kind of an ass. But still she couldn't stop thinking about him.

* * * * *

It was about 9:00 a.m. the next morning Ruby finally woke up and got out of bed. She crept downstairs, and saw Charlie sitting on the couch. He was listening to music, keeping it quiet so it didn't wake her. He was always kind that way. The stereo was playing Natalie Merchant, *Carnival*. *Ironic*, Ruby thought to herself. *Carnival*. Life is like a carnival. Crazy, bewildering, always changing, and full of games.

CHAPTER 16

Ruby sat down at the kitchen table, and looked at all the dirty dishes, the piled-up garbage, the spent bottles of wine. It was a mess, and she hated a messy kitchen. She was tired, but she couldn't go back to bed. Instead, she slowly got up from the table and gradually started in on the clean-up, her head throbbing and her stomach upset.

She reached into the medicine drawer and dropped two Alka-Seltzer into a glass. Arms bent on the counter, Ruby put her head between her hands, holding her temples. She watched up close as the Alka-Seltzer fizzed. She had yet to even say good morning to Charlie, who was in the living room, the stereo still on too loud.

"Honey," she yelled out at him. "Honey." He didn't hear her. She drank down the Alka-Seltzer drink and stumbled towards the living room, still calling out.

"Charlie. Honey."

"Hey. You're up. It's fairly early." He laughed a little. "For you, anyway." Charlie had enjoyed the dinner party, had only a little wine.

"Yeah. Anyway. Can you...could ya turn down the stereo? Please?" She sounded like she was begging, obviously irritated.

"Sure. Sure. Of course." Charlie immediately got up and turned the knob down part way.

"Are you okay?"

"Yeah. I'm fine," she told him. "Just…tired. The kitchen's a mess."

Charlie didn't seem to be listening.

"I had fun last night. You? Did you have fun?"

"Yeah. It was a blast." Ruby's tone was sarcastic.

"Hey. What's wrong? It seemed like you had a good time." Charlie didn't like her tone and thought she had been a little cool to some of the guests at the party.

But her stomach hurt and her head throbbed. She felt ornery, angry, and a little out of control.

"What's with Victor? He's such an ass," she blurted out.

Charlie had heard Ruby complain about Victor before. He sensed that wasn't the real problem and snapped back a little.

"Hey, enough already. We've had this discussion before."

Charlie should have let it go, at least that morning.

"He's an ass. Trust me. I saw the way he looked at Stephanie. He's an arrogant ass, Charlie, and you know it. And he looks at me the same way. Bastard. I remember when he used to come into the club. He was the same way then, and he hasn't changed."

"Look. You can bitch about Victor all day long, if you want. But I'm still going fishing next weekend."

Victor had been pushing Charlie to go fishing in the Ozarks for months. Victor's business partner had a cabin on one of the lakes, and even though Charlie didn't particularly care to hang out with the guys, he also had trouble saying no. At times it was fun, and he sometimes needed to get away. Often, he would escape from the guys anyway—let them go fishing while he stayed behind in the cabin and enjoyed some time alone. He assumed Ruby's complaints about Victor were about the fishing trip instead.

"You don't get it," Ruby replied, too tired to explain. Her eyes narrowed, her brow furrowed, and she glared at him. He didn't see it, but he sensed it. Charlie had a long fuse, but he did have a temper. Just then, it got the best of him.

"Why do you have to act like such a bitch?"

"What did you call me? What the hell did you call me?" Ruby's headache was gone, her adrenaline kicked in. She went into a tirade.

"Did you just call me a bitch? You bastard. After all I do for you. You fucking bastard. Go on your fucking fishing trip. I don't give a shit. And someday you will realize it for yourself. Your fucking 'friend' Victor... he's an asshole, Charlie. He really is. And you should quit defending the son of a bitch. And clean up the fucking kitchen yourself. I'm not your maid."

Charlie wheeled around in the easy chair, almost knocked over the lamp with his arm, tried to look at her, but was badly mistaken about where she stood. He started yelling at the front window while Ruby was ninety degrees the other way, back towards the kitchen.

"Yeah, you controlling witch. You bet I am going on that fishing trip. And I can't wait."

Ruby was half smiling, half crying, as she watched Charlie yell at what he thought was her but wasn't. She couldn't help herself, but her response was vitriolic, cruel.

"You're fucking yelling at the window, you idiot. I'm over here."

Charlie's face grew red and his fists clenched. He set his jaw, but didn't move. He didn't say anything else, just waited and listened.

Ruby was beside herself. She knew she had crossed the line, and suddenly, she didn't even know what they were fighting about. But she also knew she was still horribly angry, frustrated. She tried so hard to always do the right thing, to say the right things. They rarely fought, as they both always struggled to avoid any conflict between them. They wanted so desperately for their lives, for their relationship, to be perfect.

They thought their love was stronger than anyone else's, and that it would never fade.

But it was an arrogant ideal, not based in reality. Periodic, little fights would have been better, less severe, easier to overcome. But that wasn't how it turned out, and years of built up tensions over inconsequential things were being unleashed with fury that morning.

For an instant, it seemed that the fight would end there. Ruby almost started walking back to the kitchen. Charlie almost kept quiet. But instead, she stood there a while longer, staring at him. And instead, he turned towards her, having gotten a better bead on where she was standing.

"I'm the idiot? I'm the idiot? Tell me what continent France is on, smart ass."

Ruby was miserable at geography. They had talked about a trip to Paris once, and during the course of the discussion, Ruby had to admit she didn't really know where it was. She was self-conscious about it, her inner city, public school education failing her too often. Charlie had known what button to push, and he had pushed it.

She spun back into the kitchen and picked up one of the china dinner plates. She threw it against the tile above the stove. It shattered. She paused, seething, pounded her fists on the countertop, then grabbed another china plate and threw it at the same place. It hit directly on its rim. Remarkably didn't break on impact, but then ricocheted down to the stove, split cleanly into three pieces, and then smashed into little bits after falling to the floor.

The tantrum was such a sharp contrast to the night before, when she had been charming, sophisticated, preternaturally calm and in control; aloof, even.

Charlie was beside himself in the living room. He paced the floor as she was throwing the china. Finally he went to her.

"Ruby. Ruby. Stop. I'm sorry." Charlie stood in the doorway to the kitchen, pleading, racked with guilt, consternation. "We're better than this. This isn't us."

She turned and looked at him, tears running down her face. She stared at him, her stomach in knots.

Charlie tried to break the ice.

"I didn't like that china anyway," he said. The joke had little effect. They both stood silent, drained of emotion. Ruby stared at him as he stood in the doorway, and Charlie stared into space, again unsure of exactly where she was. He hoped she would come over to him, tell him she was sorry, fall into his arms and hug him.

Instead, she spoke softly. "I'm over here."

He went to her, reached out, felt the countertop, then her arm on it. He slowly enveloped her, put his arms around her waist. He turned her around, so he was holding her from behind. And he rested his head on her shoulders. She slumped, her elbows now resting on the counter. She buried her head into her palms. He kept hold of her from behind, tightly, and slumped down with her, his face now buried into her neck. She was sobbing so hard it affected her breathing. He remained stalwart, as best he could, his own emotions a boiling cauldron but still well hidden.

It had been a wicked morning.

The stereo played on in the living room, a compact disc twirling softly around and around in the plastic. Cracker, *Gentlemen's Blues*.

CHAPTER 17

There is no direct freeway route from Central Gardens to Olive Branch, from the inner city of Memphis to its outer suburbs. The freeways arc around the city, not through it. So the old city streets and boulevards became diagonal thoroughfares: Lamar, Poplar, Park, Union, Winchester.

The most direct route for Ruby to get from Central Gardens out past the old village of Olive Branch, Mississippi— out to the newest of the luxury subdivisions—was to take Winchester. Winchester; the road she knew all too well.

The first ten miles of Winchester Road, and everything on, around, and near it, was decaying. The wood of the electrical poles was weathered gray, pitted, rotting, tilting. The wires criss-crossing the intersections were frayed, dangerous, and drooping. When the road widened to the former spread of boulevards, which had once been overflowing with flowers and greenery, it was now tarred over and filled with trash.

Winchester Road stretched north to south for a full twenty miles. There used to be verdant pockets of open spaces even near the city and farm fields further out. There used to be new subdivisions and new stores in the strip malls. Now the subdivisions were fenced up, graffiti covered the fences, and gangs roamed the cul de sacs. The little stores in the strip malls were mostly boarded up and closed. The gas stations on the corners bustled with nefarious activity: Cadillacs with low suspensions and bulging wheels, deep bass thumping from their after-market stereos.

The outlots of the Piggly Wiggly stores were overgrown, littered with nasty trash: used condoms, greasy Krystal burger wrappers, whole plastic garbage bags tied up and smelly, sitting just yards from the overflowing Waste Management dumpsters.

Ruby remembered how it used to be, when you looked down Winchester Road, when it shone with the twinkling lights of middle-class America in the mid-South. The people who lived there were comfortable enough, basking in a false sense of civilized security. But like everything else, it seemed to Ruby, even the road had changed.

Ruby was traveling south. Traffic crept along, constantly interrupted by congested intersections: first Getwell Road, then Airport Road, then Hack's Crossing. Eventually Winchester Road became Highway 101, and this far out, Ruby saw a little less graffiti, a little less trash. The houses in the subdivisions had a little bit more land around them, the dogwoods bloomed, and the windows didn't have bars on them. There were some dirty, unused parks. Mature trees lined the streets, the lawns were better tended. But for each tended lawn there was another that was crowded with weeds, a rusty car in the driveway, and tarp on the roof, the contractors' quotes for repair too high, the budgets too tight.

As Ruby drove down Winchester, she passed the rent-by-the-hour motels—more for the drugs than the sex—and the pawn shops, the title loan stores. Then came the rental furniture stores, auto repair shops, and sleazy lounges.

Even further south on Winchester—Highway 101—where Ruby remembered there being an actual horizon stretching over open meadows and cotton fields. The meadows had since been replaced by Costcos and WalMarts, the cotton fields with Best Buys and Linens 'N Things, big box stores and Super Marts, tens of thousands of square feet of franchised retail. And beyond these, Ruby knew, were gated subdivisions, houses on acres, Audis and Saabs tucked into three-car garages, huge metal mailboxes on brick posts at the end of long, polished concrete driveways.

She felt a sense of déjà vu. She had driven along Winchester many times before, her mind usually occupied on something current, not the past. But she remembered her own past that day, she remembered when she had driven south on Winchester when she was just eighteen, when her car broke down and she had walked to Tiffany's Cabaret.

Even though it was more than twenty years past, it felt like yesterday to her. Life passes so fast, she thought. Time disappears, and you are left wondering where your time went, and then you are scared that just as fast as it passed—that fast—life will be over. It is a desperate, scary feeling.

And as she drove her BMW convertible past Tiffany's Cabaret, the strip club on Winchester, she saw that it was closed. The cabaret sign was still standing, but it was dust-covered, its paint faded, the words barely visible. The oversized columns were still there, but they were not as big as she remembered they were. The limousines in the loop around driveway were long gone, but the heavy, double wooden doors still stood resolutely.

It all seemed so far away, so long ago. But it also felt just a heartbeat away. She knew any wicked twist of fate could put her right back at Tiffany's, that hard, difficult place she had somehow managed to survive. The thought of living like that again hurt to her core and made her sick to her stomach. For Ruby knew that in an instant, things can happen. She was not so naïve as to think she was invincible, and knew she was not, no one was.

She thought about her life, about Charlie. How they had gotten past the wicked morning, how they had grown close again. How she loved him, how he loved her, how beautiful her

199

life was with him, how the house in Central Gardens was so pretty and grand. And how tenuous it all was, how tenuous everything was, their lives hanging in the balance by little threads, sometimes within one's control and sometimes not. How quickly feelings change, fade, crust over. How friends and family and lovers and husbands and wives drift and wander, forward and back, bend and break, survive and, sometimes, wither and die; stay and yet move on.

Ruby was in a bad place that day. That day in September, 2004. And there was no music playing, and there were no songs in her head.

CHAPTER 18

CHARLIE. 49 YEARS OLD. RUBY. 44 YEARS OLD. 2004.
MEMPHIS, TENNESSEE.

C harlie sat on the middle cushion of the sofa. His knees were together in front of him, his arms close to his sides. Periodically he covered his face with his hands, and when he did, he rocked his body forward and back, forward and back. The rest of the time he sat staring straight ahead, his body rigid, his face catatonic.

The big house was empty and silent. Charlie watched as the cats paced, their claws occasionally ticking on the wooden floor. The air conditioner hummed from below but its new, engineered mechanics ran smooth and quiet. Any outside noise was muffled by the heavy double-paned windows and the thick, hundred-year-old lath-and-plaster walls of the majestic house.

On the coffee table in front of him was the TV remote. The TV was on, turned to a sports channel, but the sound was muted and Charlie was staring right past it. Next to the remote was Charlie's cell phone. And next to the cell phone was the cordless home phone.

Charlie reached for the cell phone. He felt for the buttons, called his own number, and entered the code.

"You have no new messages."

He pushed the button to turn it off, and put it back on the coffee table.

Then he picked up the home phone. He felt for the buttons, called his own number, and waited for it to connect. He didn't need to enter a code. The soft, automated, female voice clicked in.

"There are no new messages. You have eight saved messages. If you want to listen to your saved messages ..."

He interrupted her and pressed the button to hang up. He moved his arm and the hand cradling the phone, ever so slowly, back to the coffee table, where he put the phone back down exactly where it had been.

The cats roamed about, in and out of the room. Charlie was able to tell them apart by their voices and the feel of their fur. Ruby had once described them to Charlie—in his mind's eye, he knew there was a black cat with a white tuxedo stripe, and a gray one, a Russian blue, with very soft fur. One of the cats rubbed against his bare leg. Charlie ignored it. It meowed, the food bowl empty. It meowed again and again. Charlie still ignored it.

"No. Not now," he finally said to the Russian blue. He went back to staring past the television, past the thick wall, past everything and into nothing.

It came in waves. It started in his stomach, a knot in his stomach. Actually up a little further, between his stomach and his chest. Just below the rib cage. Like an ocean swell, it moved up and out to his extremities, to his hands, and then it concentrated in his fingers, and they became numb and started to shake. When the swell got to his face, his face started to contort. First his mouth turned down into a frown. Then his upper lip started to quiver. Next his breathing was interrupted, regular breaths turning to short, heavy, noticeable bursts, first through his nose and then, his body searching for air, ragged gasps through his mouth.

Charlie's eyes were shut tight. He cupped his hands, palms in, and covered his face again. He rocked himself back and forth and back and forth. Tears didn't flow, but his eyes moistened at the sides. He wanted to cry, but couldn't.

Suddenly, he stood up. Avoiding the coffee table, he started to pace the living room, reaching out with both hands and steadying himself in the doorway leading to the hall. The thick, original woodwork was cool to the touch. He rested his face, his cheek against it. He breathed in, and could smell the wood and the stain and the varnish and the age of it. He turned, and put his other cheek on it. It didn't seem as cool this time, didn't have the same calming effect.

He turned back to the living room and started to pace a little again. The waves of the panic attack kept coming and going. He jumped up and down, from one foot to the other.

He continued to gasp for air, but with each exhale, he spit out a single word.

"Shit. Shit. Oh. My. God. My. God. I...I...Shit." The words were hushed, soft, but spoken out loud as if there were someone there to hear them. But no one was there. No one at all. No friends, no relatives, and no her. No Ruby. Ruby was gone.

He picked up the cell phone again. Pushed the button to speed dial her number. Pushed the button to hang up before it could connect. Set it down on the coffee table. In the exact same place.

"Shit. Shit." He pushed out the words again. One at a time. Always one at a time. Sentences were impossible. Too difficult a task.

It had been ten days. He had lost twelve pounds. It seemed like an eternity.

At first, when it first happened, he went into total shock. He was probably still in shock, but now, ten days later, it was different. It was worse. It was never ending. And it kept sinking deeper and stronger, sucking every corpuscle and every sinewy tendon of his body into its vortex, a little tornado inside his mind wreaking havoc.

When it happened—when IT happened—it was the morning of September 22nd. 09/22/2004. 92204. 922. Nine

Two Two. nine. two. two. Those three numbers took on epic proportions for Charlie. Nine. two. two.

922. It had been like a dream, an out-of-body experience.

Charlie was lying in the bed. It was a Sunday. He woke up, still hazy. The first thing he remembered was something from the middle of the night before. Something from about 2:00 a.m. His Braille alarm clock had showed 2:00 a.m.

2:00 a.m. So it is still nine two two, he thought to himself It was 2:00 a.m. so the next day, the next day being nine two two. That day had already started, had already started at midnight. So all of it had happened on nine two two. It was not the night before, it was the same day, really. It all happened the same day.

And Ruby was lying next to him. She was lying flat on her stomach, propped up on her elbows. She was using her laptop computer. There was a pillow between them.

Charlie awoke for some reason, for some ungodly unknown reason at 2:00 a.m. on September twenty-second he woke up from a sound sleep. He lay there awake, but had not yet moved. He heard Ruby typing. Not bursts of typing, but consistent typing. Words. Sentences. Paragraphs. Punctuated by periods of silence, and then bursts of typing again. It was a conversation. A conversation over the computer. Two people typing words to each other. Two people talking. There was no doubt. At two in the morning. On nine two two. Nine two two.

Charlie had reached out for her, stretching his sleep-warm arm over the big pillow, touched her bare shoulder. She recoiled, out of character. She immediately stopped typing. He heard the screen click. It made a little noise. His hearing was acute; he knew it was a click to a different computer screen. To a different place. To something else.

"What are you doing?" Charlie asked.

"Nothing. Shopping."

"It's the middle of the night. What are you shopping for?"
She didn't answer him. There was an awkward silence.
"Go back to sleep, honey."
He was still half asleep. He had not processed it all. It didn't make sense, but he was too tired to make sense of it. He did as he was told. He went back to sleep.
But what had happened at 2:00 a.m. was the first thing he remembered later that morning. The actual morning of nine two two. Later the morning of nine two two. It was in his mind the minute he awoke. It throbbed. He felt sick. He knew. He knew something.
He sensed Ruby next to him in the bed. He pushed the big, white, down stuffed comforter away from him, just a little, so he could get his arms out. He reached out for her. She was sitting up with her back against the headboard. She was wide awake.
"Hey," Charlie said, his tone surprisingly normal.
"Hey," she replied, her voice soft.
"You okay?" he asked her.
There was the odd silence again. Something was wrong.
She finally answered.
"Yes. Fine."
He said nothing. Some time passed. It was hard to tell exactly how long. But soon the silence became overwhelming.
And then it happened.
"I have to go," she said.
. On nine two two. At about 8:30 a.m. Lying in bed together. That was when she fired the shot. It didn't miss. It didn't ricochet. It hit him in the middle of the chest. Right below the rib cage. A spot about an inch in diameter that knotted up and throbbed and ached. Ached. Creaked. Radiated.
A full minute passed.
One. Two. Three. Four. Five. Six. Seven. Eight. Nine. Ten. Eleven. Twelve. Thirteen. Fourteen. Fifteen. Sixteen. Seven-

teen. Eighteen. Nineteen. Twenty. Twenty-one. Twenty-two. Twenty-three. Twenty-four. Twenty-five. Twenty-six. Twenty-seven. Twenty-eight. Twenty-nine. Thirty. Thirty-one. Thirty-two. Thirty-three. Thirty-four. Thirty-five. Thirty-six. Thirty-seven. Thirty-eight. Thirty-nine. Forty. Forty-one. Forty-two. Forty-three. Forty-four. Forty-five. Forty-six. Forty-seven. Forty-eight. Forty-nine. Fifty. Fifty-one. Fifty-two. Fifty-three. Fifty-four. Fifty-five. Fifty-six. Fifty-seven. Fifty-eight. Fifty-nine. Sixty. Sixty-one. Sixty-two. Sixty-three. Sixty-four.

Technically a minute and four seconds.

And then she said it again.

"I have to go."

He managed a moment of clarity, was able to respond.

"Go where? What do you mean?"

She didn't answer him. She got out of the bed, turned away, looked at herself in the mirror. She was wearing cotton pajamas; they were loose, tied with a drawstring. She was especially thin, to the point she wanted to gain weight. Her hair was longer than usual, falling just past her shoulders, at the moment all pushed to the right side and away from her face.

She looked away from the mirror, hung her head. Stood for a while. Turned to him. Looked away again. He heard her footsteps, heard her turn as her feet shifted. He could tell she had turned towards him, but it was just for a moment. But he also heard her feet shift back, toward the stairs. Away from him.

As she went down the stairs, Charlie bolted out of the bed. He was wearing only his underwear. At the foot of the bed were his own cotton pajama bottoms, but he just left them there. He hustled down the stairs, to the kitchen, still wearing only his boxer briefs.

"Hey," she said again, still in the softest audible voice.

"What…what…," Charlie was stammering. He lost his voice. He started to wobble, reached to steady himself on the counter.

By themselves, the words "I have to go" could mean a lot of things. But somehow, Charlie knew exactly what she meant. She didn't mean she had to go to the store, or to visit a sick relative, or for a walk. She meant she had to go. To go away. To leave. To leave the house. To leave him. And this knowledge was quickly confirmed that morning, in the kitchen, as they both stood there barefoot and half naked.

"I don't know how long I will be gone."

Her voice was still soft, but certainly loud enough to hear. The words were spoken with deliberation, carefully, but with no hesitation.

"I don't want to fight. There is no reason to fight. It just is." She continued, still deliberate, still with almost total conviction.

There had been more, of course, on nine two two. There was the packing after he left the house, after he told her it was too much for him to bear to hear her pack while he was there. There was crying. There was consternation. It was staggering. He stood like a prize fighter in the last round, wobbly, beaten, bloodied, but somehow still standing. Bewildered by the unexpected onslaught of his opponent. Unable to fight back.

At 3:30 that afternoon, Ruby's little BMW had pulled out of the driveway. And she was gone.

And one nightmarish day turned into the next, and the next, and the next. One. Two. Three. Four. Five. Six. Seven. Eight. Nine. Ten. And nine two two became nine two three. And nine two three became nine two four. And the nine became a ten. September became October.

Charlie's mind raced. It never stopped. Faster and faster, analyzing and thinking, trying to solve the puzzle.

He tried distractions. Work. Friends. Projects. Reading. Television. Sometimes it helped. Most often it didn't. Most often he sat alone in the big house and his mind raced.

Of course, there was a therapist. Of course. There's always a therapist. Sometimes therapy helped. Most often it didn't.

"I don't understand," he told his therapist. He had seen her before, for what he didn't even remember now. Trivial in comparison. Silly. Not like now.

"Simple lust. God, that would be...Just...," He winced, put his head down, felt the pain of it. "Or love. New love. Not real love, right? Of course new love is intoxicating. But it's not real. Or maybe that is just me rationalizing."

There was another pause while Charlie let his thoughts build. "Boredom. Loneliness. I don't know. I don't even know if it's an affair. I don't know if there is someone else. But what else could it possibly be? It's delusional of me to think it's anything but someone else, right? What other possible reason could there be?"

The therapist, doctor of psychology, trained, educated, experienced.

"Do you think it's someone else?" she asked.

Brilliant, Charlie thought. *Brilliant. Do I think there is someone else? That's what I'm fucking here for. For her to ask me what I think. If I knew, I wouldn't be here.*

And the thoughts kept racing. And he spit out some of them.

"Well...I doubt she's out buying a new sports car." His tone was sarcastic.

"No, probably not." The therapist's tone was calm, patient.

"But maybe. I mean, what the hell. I don't know." Charlie response was calmer, then tinged with sadness "I really don't know."

"And if it is, if she is having an affair...," The therapist was asking Charlie a question, but let the words trail. He understood. He understood she was asking him what his reaction would be.

"I don't know that either," he said sullenly. "I can't imagine."

* * * * *

A nd nine days turned into ten, and ten into eleven. And the thoughts kept racing. God created the earth in seven days, right? Not that he believed in that craziness. But seven fucking days. The world could have been created by now. It's over. After this long it must be, has to be.

What a shitty way to do it. No explanation. No discussion. No fight. A fight would have been better. A blow-by-blow, nasty, spill-it-all out screamer would have been better, right? But no, she had to be calm, deliberate. "I have to go." What the hell did that mean? Bitch. No, she's not a bitch. She's incredible. She's sweet. She's so damned beautiful. If she weren't so damned beautiful. I just want her back. I want to turn back time. To where we were before.

And eleven days turned into twelve. And he kept taking the sleep meds. And he started to take the anti-anxiety pills. And they helped, a little, maybe. No. Are they helping? Maybe.

And then, on the twelfth day, there he was again, still sitting on the sofa, staring straight ahead, the house totally, horribly quiet.

And then the phone rang.

And it was her. It was Ruby.

And she wanted to talk.

And he told her he wanted to listen.

CHAPTER 19

CHARLIE. 49 YEARS OLD. RUBY 44 YEARS OLD. 2004.
MEMPHIS, TENNESSEE.

I t was early spring.

Victor was staring out the window. A robin was already out foraging, pecking at a patch of winter-kill grass in the expansive front lawn of Victor Booth's brand-new, huge suburban house. It was new construction with fiberglass Roman pillars and plastic plantation shutters. The bird's iconic mauve-red breast puffed out of proportion, as if the little bird were posing for a strong man competition.

It flitted about, constantly on alert, innately anxious. Little hops from place to place, its body quiet and still but its neck and head bobbing and weaving, eyes darting to and fro. Everything around it was noticed, questioned, determined—before, finally, the bird felt safe enough to quickly push its head into the new, moist ground and try to pull up an earthworm. The attempt was unsuccessful, nothing but dirt.

When it popped its head back up, the robin immediately flicked its head and eyes again, turning this way and that. Nature was wakening everywhere: sprigs of new grass, young buds on the trees, squirrels scurrying about. But it was still relatively cold and people pretty much remained indoors.

Because its sight was so acute, the robin saw the little BMW coupe when it was still at least several hundred yards down the road. At first, it was just a blur of pale blue movement, but it was slowly approaching. The bird watched the sports car as it drove past another sprawling estate, approached

Victor's house, and then pulled into the driveway and came to a stop. Its silky smooth engine revved for a moment before settling into a soft idle.

Ruby didn't get out of the car right away. She sat in the soft leather bucket seat for a bit first, staring straight ahead, as if in a trance. Thirty seconds, then almost a full minute passed, before she shook her head a little, disrupting the inner cobwebs of her thoughts. She looked around her, as the robin did. Her movements were slower, but there was the same sense of being anxious. Her eyes, just like the little bird's, flitted to and fro, looking for signs of danger before addressing the task at hand.

The robins and the squirrels were of no concern to Ruby. No one else was in the yard. No cars drove by. It was very quiet. Ruby finally turned off the ignition. She rested on the steering wheel for a moment, then took a deep breath, lifted her head up, pulled the key out slowly, and opened the car door.

Ruby walked deliberately, unwaveringly, to the front door, past the still dormant, delicate bushes and ornamental shrubs placed so deliberately by the professional landscapers. She did not hesitate when she got to the heavy wooden door, which had been painted a bright glossy red. She did not knock or ring the bell. She just opened the unlocked door and walked in.

The robin stood still, watching her, as Ruby shut the door behind her. The squirrels and the rest of the birds also stood still, just then, or at least so it seemed. But it wasn't long before nature reverted back to its cacophony of chirping and clawing and blossoming.

Under the long front hood of the BMW, the 3.0 liter engine started to cool down. As it did, any one of the nearby robins could hear the little pings of metal contractions, and soft hisses of liquid settling back into chambers. The metal turned from hot to warm, warm to cold. The oils and fluids quit gushing and found their way back into the bowels of the machine.

Mid-morning turned into mid-afternoon, and mid-afternoon to early evening, before the glossy red front door opened again and Ruby walked back out to the car.

Her walk back down the sidewalk was just as deliberate as it had been when she walked up it. Her posture was just as straight, her eyes still focused straight ahead. She made no effort now to check her surroundings, didn't seem nervous anymore. What was done was done, the reason for the earlier panic either gone or unstoppable, obliterated or inevitable.

And Ruby's long hesitation to shut the car down when she had first arrived stood in stark contrast to her almost ferocious turn of the ignition to start it up again the moment she got in the car to leave. She grabbed the shifter knob harshly, tried to push it over and up into reverse. She failed the first time, the clutch not fully engaged, but forcibly slammed it into reverse gear on the second attempt. The extra-wide Yokohama performance tires screeched and left rubber on the smooth cement driveway as Ruby accelerated backwards, and the car spun a perfect ninety as it bounced a little over the transition between the driveway and the road.

Then Ruby hesitated. She glanced over at Victor's house and noticed him staring out the living room window, the curtain pulled to the side, his eyes penetrating the dusk to reach hers, some fifty yards away at the end of the long drive. But Ruby didn't hesitate long and turned her eyes away from the man staring at her through the window, turned her eyes ahead. She pushed her left foot hard into the clutch and shifted into first, let up on the clutch quickly, felt the gears engage.

When she came to the stop sign at the first intersection, there was no traffic at all from either direction. It was eerily quiet for that time of the evening. She let the car idle again, let her shoulders droop, let her muscles loosen, and she let out a solid, big breath of air. Her eyes first moistened at the edges, then welled with tears, until she began to sob uncontrollably, taking her breath away. She spoke to herself, very softly, in between the sobs and the gulps for air.

"It's not fair. It's not fair."

Ruby was still crying when something pierced the twilight in the rear-view mirror. Headlights. Her adrenaline started to pump as she saw the car approach, stopping the tears. Ruby was still dazed. Her left turn signal was still on, had been the whole time she was crying. The car pulled up behind her, but did not honk. Ruby turned left, toward the freeway. She turned on the radio. Amy Winehouse, *Rehab*.

CHAPTER 20

2004. MEMPHIS, TENNESSEE.

The headline on the front page of the Memphis Commercial Appeal was blunt, straightforward, unequivocal:

FINANCIAL ADVISOR EMBEZELS $7 MILLION

The article was crisp, short:

> October 12, 2004. Byline: Robert J. Mitchell.
> MEMPHIS, TN—Financial Advisor Victor Booth of Olive Branch pled guilty to criminal embezzlement of over $7 million in district court yesterday.
> Booth, 48, maintained offices as a financial advisor in Olive Branch. Criminal investigation internally at Merrill Lynch and through the Shelby County Prosecutor's office uncovered the extensive fraud. Charges were brought by the Shelby County district attorney in March.
> According to court records Booth persuaded over a dozen of his clients to withdraw funds from various retirement accounts and reinvest in speculative and often nonexistent investments.
> The press release from the Prosecutor's office was more detailed, having been written up by one of the assistant district attorneys.
> Our investigation revealed that Booth's investment fraud began as early as September, 2002, when Booth solicited a number of his Merrill Lynch clients to invest in an arbitrage

investment offering in India. In the solicitation, Booth represented that this arbitrage investment would yield substantial returns as high as twenty to thirty percent. Fifteen of Booth's clients gave funds which were to be placed in the claimed overseas arbitrage investment offering. Many of the fifteen individuals had been clients of Booth's for many years, and included several prominent members of the Memphis community. Several of the victims claim they lost their entire life savings.

A forensic audit revealed over $7 million in funds had been stolen using this scheme, with significantly more money unaccounted for. It was determined through the criminal investigation that Booth had taken the investors checks and cashed them at a local check cashing store. None of the funds solicited by Booth were ever invested in any arbitrage or other investment opportunities. Instead, Booth diverted all of the funds into cash and spent the money himself.

Booth pled guilty to second-degree theft by deception and second-degree commercial bribery. Both crimes were charged in an indictment. The theft count in the indictment pertains to twelve specific individuals who were identified in the documentation. The commercial bribery count relates to Booth's victimization of Merrill Lynch. Booth also pled guilty to a second charge of second-degree theft by deception. The second charge was contained in an accusation. The second theft charge relates to a group of seven additional victims who were not identified.

Under Tennessee law, a defendant who is being prosecuted as an adult cannot ordinarily be prosecuted for a crime unless and until a Grand Jury has determined that there is probable cause for the charges. Upon a finding that probable cause exists, the Grand Jury returns an indictment. An accusation, which is issued by the Prosecutor's office, is the functional equivalent of an indictment. Before a defendant can enter a plea to an accusation, a Superior Court Judge must first make a finding that the defendant is voluntarily and intelligently waiving his right to have a Grand Jury consider the case, and that the defendant is agreeable to a way of being prosecuted by accusation. The Judge makes this finding by questioning the defendant and his attorney on the record in open court.

Booth entered his plea pursuant to a negotiated plea agreement with the Shelby County Prosecutor's Office. Booth entered his guilty plea before Shelby County Superior Court Judge Victor O. Manian, who is scheduled to sentence Booth on February 23, 2005. In accordance with the negotiated plea agreement, the Shelby County Prosecutor's office will recommend that Judge Manian sentence Booth to a seven-year sentence in the Tennessee State prison system. The negotiated plea agreement also provides that Booth will sign a stipulated money judgment in favor of the victims in the sum of $7,342,222 in restitution.

The case is assigned to Shelby County Assistant District Attorney Paul M. Griffin.. Booth is represented by the law firm of Baker & Torhorst, S.C., and Attorney Sean D. Christian of Memphis.

EPILOGUE

Driving from rural Arkansas to the city of Memphis, Tennessee, you have to cross the Mississippi River. There are two bridges, and you have your choice as you approach: the old bridge or the new bridge. The new bridge is eight lanes, wide, and easy. The old bridge is two lanes, narrow, and quite scary. You can see one bridge from the other. They are very close together. Most people choose the new bridge. Some don't.

Below both of these bridges is the brown, muddy river.

The new bridge is built with concrete.

The old bridge is built with steel. And bolts. Hundreds of thousands of bolts. Big bolts. Four-inch-wide bolts. There is a whole regiment of dirty, failing, four-inch-wide bolts.

One particular four-inch-wide bolt sits near the middle of the old bridge, about four hundred and fifty feet above the river. It is pockmarked with rust. The steel girder this bolt helps suspend above the brown, murky river is also pockmarked with rust. Three or four threads protrude from the underside of the girder; the nut to this bolt is missing.

This particular bolt is suspended about three feet below the bridge deck. It faces out, to the south, a single octagonal eye staring straight down the river, the river flowing with tenacious grit all the way to New Orleans.

For sixty-three years, this four-inch-wide bolt saw nothing but the river and its boats and barges, logs and flotsam, perhaps an occasional bird flying by. Nothing ever directly in front of it but air.

For sixty-three years, this four-inch-wide bolt never moved more than a quarter inch, and only then when the westerly wind of a fierce winter storm deflected the bridge ever so slightly.

If the four-inch-wide bolt could see out its corners, which of course it could not, to its left, to the east, it would see downtown Memphis. To its west, it would see swamps and mud flats, and low-lying, often flooded cheap motels and gas stations, and it would see the sprawling, decrepit little town of West Memphis, Arkansas.

Above it, if the four-inch-wide bolt could look up, which of course it could not, it would see the girder it helped hold up, stretching skyward in a wide arch.

Below the four-inch-wide bolt is, of course, the river. Staring straight ahead, the bolt can see down river, a panoramic view. But if the four-inch-wide bolt could look down, it would see the river up close, see the current and the eddies and the waves lapping up against the buttresses.

As the four-inch-wide bolt stared out that day, in the only direction that it could stare, straight out down the river, that day in November, that day in 2004, it saw the river, and there were no birds, and there was nothing else, really. Certainly nothing unusual.

Until 2:33 that afternoon.

At 2:33 p.m.—and a few seconds, actually—the four-inch-wide, rusty, pockmarked, failing bolt stared its stare down the river. And at that very moment, for exactly the second time since that four-inch-wide bolt had been wrenched into place sixty-three years earlier, an object passed its view. Not a bird. Not the river stretched out before it and way below.

An object.

It was the front headlight of a Lexus ES300. The headlight had dislodged itself upon the car's first impact with the girder. The headlight flew in front of the four-inch-wide bolt first, a forewarning. Its glass was still intact, and it spun around slowly as it passed right in front of that particular four-inch-wide bolt.

Then, after the headlight, then came an orange cone. A traffic cone. A construction cone.

After the construction cone, then came the left front quarter panel of the Lexus, silvery gray, and it flew by right in front of the bolt.

Then the driver's side door, then the rear quarter panel, both also metallic gray, passed right in front of the four-inch-bolt, just inches from it.

The car was spinning clockwise, left to right, as it flew off and away from the bridge. Its front end spun away, and the rear end was oddly spinning back. And as it spun itself clockwise on its horizontal axis, it was also spinning clockwise on its vertical axis, down to up. And at the same time its front end was lifting up, the rear end was going down, as if it had been catapulted out. It seemed staged, the spinning so perfect, the catapulting upward and all of the speed, as if a talented stunt driver had hit his mark and the movie scene would be shot in one perfect take.

It was the left rear tire that smashed into the bolt. The rubber left a mark, the metal rim actually scraping the bolt, a gash opening up across the face of the bolt, the sound a brief nail screech on a chalkboard.

The four-inch-wide bolt continued to stare straight ahead, its eye now gouged and the underlying steel exposed, the metal hot. And as the wheel slid free, the bolt saw the trunk of the car, metallic gray, and the Tennessee license plate, and the right rear quarter panel—then nothing. For the four-inch-wide bolt could only stare straight ahead, and the car fell toward the murky water, out of its myopic line of sight.

But if the bolt could have looked down, tilted its eye downward, it could have watched the car. And then it would have had time to notice more about it. It could have seen the car now spin even more wildly on practically every axis. Like a gymnast or a snowboarder doing a trick. And it would have seen, as the car spun so that you could see inside, it would have seen a woman in the driver's seat and a man in the passenger's seat. And the woman would have been pretty, with long, curly brown hair, and long, thick eyelashes. And the man would have been handsome, with blue eyes and strong features.

But if the four-inch-wide bolt were to see all of that, it would have had to assimilate information quickly, for the car was falling down to the river very fast, its earlier movie scene grace in slow motion but now turned to fast-forward.

And if the bolt could have looked down even further, tilted its eye almost straight down, it could have watched the car hit the water, the passenger side almost perfectly parallel to the river itself, the driver's side aligned with the sky. The impact would shatter the glass in the passenger's side door. The man's head would whip violently back and forth, as if he were already unconscious, which he probably was. The black water would pour in and envelop him, creep into his cavities and slither its way into his socks and between his toes.

And if the bolt could have continued to look down, it would have seen the pretty woman's right arm stretched out towards the man, holding his hand in hers. And it would have seen her grip tighten, the adrenaline rushing through her so strongly that her hand would crush the little bones in his as they neared the water, and as she saw how dark it really was.

And if the four-inch-bolt saw all that, which of course it could not, for it could only stare straight ahead, but if it had seen all that, at that moment, it would have all been too much. It would have had to consciously turn away. For it would be too much, too overwhelming, to watch the man's head slump down to his chest and to watch his mouth breath in the black water. And it would be too much to watch the woman take a desperate gasp of air from the bubble clinging to the driver's side of the car; to watch her then close her eyes, and reach out for him, and claw at his head and his hair. And her eyes, her eyes would then grow big and she would realize the air bubble was gone and the car was now twenty feet under, the current sliding it south towards New Orleans.

But of course the car would not make it all the way to New Orleans. It was too heavy, and the current, although strong, would only take it thirty to forty yards downstream to the south before the car would start to scrape along the muddy bottom. There it would bounce and jerk and eventually settle to a stop on all fours, surprisingly gently. And New Orleans was still be hundreds of miles away.

The car, of course, would never move any further. It would never extricate itself from the black mud. And the police and the EMTs and the divers would not find it, so little of it remained above the sludge of the river's bed. Divers would never find the car, or the pretty girl, or the handsome man. The pretty girl who, in those last moments, managed to spoon herself around the handsome man, her hand around his waist, her hair flowing over his face, tendrils over the teeth in his gaping mouth. Together forever, they once said, and so they would be. Intertwined but entombed.

And the engineers would come to the old bridge. And they would look for skid marks. And they would look at the girder and they would see the scrape on the particular four-inch-bolt that had watched the car. The bolt that had suffered its own injury, its own scrape with mortality, a tiny part of its cold metal turned scorching hot for that horrifying moment when the car brushed past it.

"Here. Look at this bolt. It's been scraped," the engineer would say. "This is where it went in. It's a fresh scrape. The metal is still shiny. It's a pretty long scrape." "Yup. So from this height...No chance, really," the engineer's colleague would observe.

"Doesn't make sense," one would say, not referring to the numbers, for the numbers added up, logically told the engineers the car had gone off the bridge, and where, and how fast. What didn't make sense to the logical, science minds of the engineers was why.

"Nope," the other would say. Then he would say it again. "Nope. It just doesn't make sense to me."

And the bolts, each of the thousands, would watch the engineers. Watch them scratch their heads and note their little notes in their graph-paper notebooks.

Individually, for the bolts could only see straight out, each bolt would have only a snippet of knowledge about what happened that day, that day in November 2004. What happened to the Lexus ES300, and what happened to the couple inside. How they went off the bridge. Why they went off the bridge.

But collectively, if all of the bolts could combine their snippets of knowledge, and if they would have had the eyes of hawks, and if they could have listened with ears as big as elephants, then perhaps they would know what happened. Know how it happened. Why it happened.

What did he say, right before? What did she say, right before? Did they say anything at all? What did she do, while driving the car? Did she suddenly turn the wheel? Was she distracted? Did she scream? Did he pull the wheel, reach over and pull it? Did one of them, or both of them, want to drive the car off the bridge? Or was it an accident, just a wicked, horrible twist of fate. Or pure negligence, mistake, inadvertence; a lapse in concentration, the narrow old bridge waiting, lurking for it, its narrow lanes and construction pylons and rusty girders an attractive, deadly nuisance.

But of course, these were too many questions for inanimate bolts. And of course bolts can't see, and can't hear, anything at all. And therefore—straight logic—there was no possible way to ever figure what or how. And even more tragically, no possible way to tell why.

But, perhaps, the answer to these questions was not to be found from the bolts on the bridge. Perhaps the answer was not to be found by engineers, or from their mathematical calculations, or even from inanimate bolts come to life to tell a story.

The answer could instead come from the history. Answers often lie in history. The entire history, all of it, from the moment they were born until the moment they died. That moment on that day, that day in November, that moment on that day that Charlie and Ruby died.

ABOUT THE AUTHOR

Douglas W. Rose graduated from Marquette University Law School in 1986. He joined the military in 1983, just before starting law school, and was on active duty as a Lieutenant with the U.S. Navy Judge Advocate General's (JAG) Corps until 1991. During his tour of duty, he was primarily stationed in Seattle, Washington, but travelled throughout the United States (including trying cases in Adak, Alaska and LeMoore, California). He was also stationed aboard the *U.S.S. Nimitz* on a "Westpac" tour primarily off the Gulf of Oman, and traveled throughout Asia, including the Philippines, Singapore, Thailand, Hong Kong, and China.

Rose was the senior defense counsel for a petty officer accused of starting a flight deck fire onboard the *U.S.S. Nimitz*, which fire caused the deaths of two seamen and the loss of millions of dollars of aircraft. After his active duty, Rose returned to Milwaukee, Wisconsin, where he entered the private practice of law as a trial attorney. He and his business partner started Rose & deJong, S.C., in 1983, and the firm has grown to ten full-time attorneys. Rose has tried well over 100 jury trials, including a bad faith insurance case in 2010 that resulted in a jury verdict in his clients' favor in excess of $8,000,000.

Rose is listed on IMdB for his acting role in the movie, *The Recovered*, where he played the businessman killer. He started work on *Bolt* in 2006. He has been married—and divorced—three times. Rose has one daughter, Meghan, who is a successful musician and lives and works in Madison, Wisconsin. Rose enjoys art, design, downhill skiing, and travel. He lives in the Bay View neighborhood of Milwaukee, Wisconsin, and owns a co-op apartment in downtown Chicago.

Made in the USA
Monee, IL
04 December 2024